2, 4, 8...

DESTINY OF THE

HUMAN

SPECIES

DON HANSLER

Hansler, Don.
    2, 4, 8-- : (the destiny of the human species)/Don Hansler.
    p. cm.
    LCCN: 95-90811
    ISBN: 1-886839-10-7

    1. Overpopulation--Fiction.   I. Title.   II. Title: Two, four,
eight.

PS3558.A6754T96   1996   813'.54
                                          QBI95-20744

Author's previously published books:
    Purls of Wisdom; Social and political commentaries
    Integrating Thinking Skills Through Inquiry; a textbook

Published by:
    Fun Ed. Productions   Production by:
    22711 - 66th Ave. Ct. E.   Frontier Publishing
    Spanaway, WA 98387   Seaside, OR 97138

    Printed in the United States Of America

Acknowledgments

I would like to express my sincere appreciation for the contributions of the following people, who critiqued my original manuscript, and who offered invaluable suggestions that led to this final version.

Carolyn Blount
Dick Blount
Marge Hansler
Rose Marie McClung
Don Mickey

About the Author

By all standards, the author, Don Hansler, is a "Senior Citizen." Born in 1929, just before the stockmarket crash that shook the world, he grew up in the Great Depression.

A major part of his graduate work involved applied genetics. He taught biological sciences during a 32-year career in education. He is author of a college textbook on methods of teaching thinking skills.

Throughout his life, he has been an avid people-watcher, taking note of the many manifestations of human nature

The lifetime of experiences that led to his current Senior Citizen status gradually developed within him a feeling that overpopulation is the factor most likely to cause the eventual demise of the human race. He envisioned the possibility of numerous different scenarios that could lead to that demise.

This book presents just one of those scenarios. He feels many others are plausible. Furthermore, he feels many of those others possess a relatively high degree of probability.

Read what he has written herein. Consider it to be a warning about the fragility of the human species, and its vulnerability to a variety of potential threats.

2, 4, 8...(Destiny of the Human Species)

Facts of Life!

Part 1   Primium

Part 2   Dissipatium

Part 3   Declinium

Part 1

PRIMIUM

FACTS OF LIFE!

WORLD POPULATION

Year	Population	Year	Population
1 A.D.	170,000,000	1200 A.D.	360,000,000
200 A.D.	190,000,000	1400 A.D.	350,000,000
400 A.D.	190,000,000	1600 A.D.	545,000,000
600 A.D.	200,000,000	1800 A.D.	900,000,000
800 A.D.	220,000,000	1900 A.D.	1,625,000,000
1000 A.D.	265,000,000	1930 A.D.	2,000,000,000

UNITED STATES POPULATION

Year	Population	Year	Population
1800	5,300,000	1920	105,700,000
1900	76,000,000	1930	122,800,000
1910	92,000,000	1940	131,700,000

Chapter 1

Sunday, December 7, 1941

Robert Welton was visibly disturbed, unusually so for a seventh-grader who usually exhibited a positive attitude toward life. He pedaled his bicycle lickety-split over to Tom's house. Tom and Johnny were sitting on the porch, waiting for him to arrive, so that they could go to the Boy's Club gym and shoot some baskets, and maybe play a few games of "21."

Robert yelled excitedly, "Hey, did you guys hear about the Japs bombing the Navy ships at Pearl Harbor in Hawaii this morning?"

"Yeah, I heard about it," Tom replied dispassionately. "Let's get goin', so we can get a few games in before the gym closes."

"I'm going back home and listen to the news reports on the radio. My dad says that President Roosevelt is probably going to declare war on Japan. Don't you guys know that our dads might have to fight if there's a war?"

"Welton, you worry too much. Besides, if we don't get to the gym pretty soon, we won't get very many games in. We'll see you at school tomorrow."

As Robert rode home, he thought to himself, "*Those guys are like everyone else in my class at school. None of them is interested in what's going on in the world!*"

2, 4, 8...(Destiny of the Human Species)

Throughout Robert's life, this tendency to be highly concerned about world problems would prove to be a characteristic that distinguished him from the egocentric masses!

Chapter 2

With his customary precision, Mr. Norman carefully set the three terrariums side-by-side on his desk at the front of the Biology classroom.

"Can anyone see any difference in the conditions of the plant and animal life in these three terrariums?"

Several hands went up.

"Charlotte, what differences do you see?"

"Well, Mr. Norman, the terrarium in the middle looks a lot better than the ones on either side."

Mr. Norman gave a look of acceptance. "How many of you students agree with Charlotte?" About three-fourths of the students raised their hands.

Mr. Norman looked questioningly around the room. "What, specifically makes the middle terrarium look better, Dave?"

In a voice that obviously hadn't matured fully, Dave said, "The plants in the middle one look healthier than in the one on the left, but the two frogs in the middle one definitely look *better* than the two frogs in the one on the right!"

Several students chuckle.

2, 4, 8...(Destiny of the Human Species)

"I mean, Mr. Norman, the frogs in the one on the right look awful *dead* to me."

Another chuckle from the group.

"Class, I set up these three terrariums exactly one week ago. In each one, I placed a shallow dish of water (which you can see), and an inch of soil. In the one on the left, I placed three fern plants. In the middle one I placed three fern plants and two frogs. In the one on the right, I placed only two frogs. Then I sealed all three terrariums, so that no gases could get either in or out. As you can see, and as Dave described, the ferns and the frogs in the middle terrarium look healthy. And, yes, the frogs in the one on the right *are* dead. Now, what about the terrarium on the left? What, specifically looks wrong with it?"

Sally raised her hand hesitatingly.

"Sally, what do you notice about the terrarium on the left, as compared with the one in the middle?"

"The ferns aren't as healthy looking in the one on the left. They aren't as bright green, and they look a little droopy."

"Class, this experiment that I set up demonstrates one of the most basic principles that we'll study in Biology this year. That is that animals use oxygen and give off carbon dioxide. Plants use carbon dioxide and give off oxygen. If a sealed terrarium has too many plants, it runs out of carbon dioxide. If it has too many animals, it runs out of oxygen. If the animals and plants are balanced, they benefit each other by producing the product that the other needs."

Robert Welton's hand shot up! "Mr. Norman, do you think that there could ever be so much animal life on the earth that we would run out of oxygen to breathe?" His concern was obvious.

The snickers from the members of the class embar-

2, 4, 8...(Destiny of the Human Species)

rassed him. Then his distress was increased by Mr. Norman's response.

"Not a chance, Robert", said Mr. Norman, in a highly sarcastic tone. "The earth is just simply too big for that to ever happen!"

9

Chapter 3

(5 years later)
Monday, January 10, 1949

The University's Bacteriology lab was bustling with students trying to complete the lab activity before the end of the period. This was an especially stressful activity, because the students were going to have to drop-in to the lab about noon every day this week to make a determination of the concentration of the bacteria in their cultures. As the bell rang at the end of the period, several students were scurrying to put their equipment away before the lab assistant, Ted Gross, locked the door.

(1 week later)
Tuesday, January 18, 1949

Dr. Frasch placed a transparency of five columns of blanks on the overhead projector. He was a transplant from the University of Georgia, where he had taught Bacteriology for three years, before moving on to the University of Washington.

In his pleasant southern drawl, he said, "Stu-dents, I'm goin' ta ask each of you five groups ta tell me the results of the bacterial-concentration measurements that

2, 4, 8...(Destiny of the Human Species)

y'all took in that lab activity last week. The group leader may report the figures. In chronological order, give me the bacterial concentrations per milliliter for each day of the week."

Joyce, Group 1: " 7, 21, 372, 0."
Darrin, Group 2: "4, 19, 356, 0."
Jerry, Group 3: "6, 20, 368, 0."
Don, Group 4: "3, 24, 352, 0."
Alice, Group 5: "5, 22, 364, 0."

Dr. Frasch recorded the figures on the transparency. Then he said, "The averages for each of the four days are....." He did some quick addition and division on a sheet of paper. "Tuesday, 5; Wednesday, 21; Thursday, 362; and Friday, 0"

Dr. Frasch could see that several students had puzzled looks on their faces. "Y'all kin probably see that there was a tremendous increase in bacterial growth until Friday. What d'you think happened between the time of your observations on Thursday and Friday?"

Carol, the class know-it-all, fired back, "They probably ran out of food from the nutrient medium."

Dr. Frasch nodded in apparent agreement. "How many of you stu-dents think that Carol is right?"

Most of the students raised their hands.

"We-e-ll", said Dr. Frasch, "How could we modify this experiment ta find out whether the decline in bacterial population was due to a diminishin' food supply?"

Carol blurted, again, "We could add a little food each day."

"Good suggestion, Carol. We'll have y'all repeat this experiment next week. You'll do everythin' exactly the same as the last time, but you'll add an additional 5 milliliters of nutrient medium ta the culture each day."

The class groaned in unison (all except Carol, of course).

(2 weeks later)
Tuesday, February 1, 1949

"All right, class. Let's have the group leaders give me the reports on their bacterial concentrations for Tuesday through Friday of last week."

Joyce, Group 1: "6, 21, 348, 0."
Darrin, Group 2: "4, 22, 352, 0."
Jerry, Group 3: "7, 20, 364, 0."
Don, Group 4: "5, 21, 360, 0."
Alice, Group 5: "4, 24, 368, 0."

Dr. Frasch recorded the figures on his transparency as they were reported. After a few seconds of calculating, he said, "Here are the averages for the four days: Tuesday, 5; Wednesday, 22; Thursday, 358; Friday, 0. Who kin summarize how these averages compare with the averages that were observed when no *additional nutrients* were added, during the initial experiment?"

Diane Martin raised her hand.

"Miss Mar-tin," said Dr. Frasch.

"I don't think that the addition of the food during the second experiment made any difference."

"Class, how many of y'all agree with Miss Mar-tin's conclusion?"

The majority of the students raised their hands.

"We-ell," said Dr. Frasch, "if the addition of the nutrient material didn't prevent the drop in the bacterial population, what could've caused the population ta decline so rapidly?"

Phil Seaver's hand shot up. "Could they have killed themselves with their own waste products?"

"Very li-akly, Mr. Seaver," said Dr. Frasch. "Ya see, students, each bacterial colony usually starts with a single bacterium. That bacterium divides ta form two, those two divide ta form four, those four divide ta form eight, and the doublin' continues infinitely, theoretically. However, the bacterial concentration becomes so dense that the waste products of the bacteria rapidly cause the death of most members of the colony."

Robert Welton slowly raised his hand. "Dr. Frasch, could the human population of the earth ever get so dense that our own waste products could kill us?"

"Highly improbable, Mr. Welton," Dr. Frasch said, in a somewhat derisive manner. "The earth is such an extensive environment, that the human population could never pose such a threat ta itself!"

Several students chuckled at Dr. Frasch's comment, and that led Robert to blush noticeably, as he and the other students prepared to leave the classroom.

Chapter 4

(2 months later)
Spring Quarter, 1949

Genetics class at the University proved to be very stimulating for Robert. Words like *chromosome, gene, zygote,* and *meiosis* had been introduced in high school biology, but the social significance of genetics principles hadn't been clear to him until this point.

Friday, April 8, 1949

His excitement was evident. The studies in Genetics class the previous four days had centered around an amazing concept: the effects of gene selection. If organisms died because they were unable to cope with the natural environment, 'natural selection' occurred. If they were selected for further propagation by humans because of desirable genetic characteristics that they possessed, 'artificial selection' was the result. How could anyone who knew what he now knew doubt the slow but inexorable process of evolution? But, there was a question that gnawed at him, one that he could barely wait to ask in today's class.

Professor Abbott glanced over the top of his reading

glasses. "Class, before I summarize the week's studies, are there any questions about the material that I have presen...?"

Robert couldn't restrain himself any longer. "Professor, I have a question. This week you've told us about some of the biological mechanisms by which the genetic makeup of a species can be changed. You've shown how defective genes can be eliminated from the gene pool of a species through natural selection....."

"Yes, Mr. Welton, what is your *question* ?"

"Well, when you were talking about defective genes, you mentioned those that cause conditions like diabetes, sickle-cell anemia, and many other harmful or disadvantageous conditions."

"Your *question*, Welton!" Professor Abbott's irritation from the frequent questions asked in class by Robert was obvious.

"All of the conditions that you mentioned are being counteracted by various kinds of medical treatment! Doesn't that make it likely that the abundance of the genes that cause those conditions is eventually going to be increased in the human population, and doesn't that mean that the whole process might make the human race a *weaker* species?"

"Mr. Welton, you're obviously envisioning a highly unlikely and extremely hypothetical situation! After all, what do you suggest that we do? Refuse medical treatment to those suffering from all of these conditions? Or, maybe even sterilize the people carrying those genes?"

Robert melted down into the seat of his chair, ears burning from the guffaws that came from several of his fellow students.

Chapter 5

(1 month later)
Tuesday, May 17, 1949

At home, during his earlier years, economics seemed pretty simple to Robert. Dad worked forty hours a week; Mom wrote the checks for the bills, and she bought the food and cooked all of their meals. Mom made sure that she didn't spend any more than Dad brought home, and they got along quite well, thank you!

Now, in Economics class, he was being pelted with all kinds of gobble-dee-gook about investing for maximum yield, refinancing, and Gross National Product. That last one was especially bothersome!

When question-time came, near the end of the period, Robert wasn't sure whether his question would irritate Dr. Mulligan.

"Dr. Mulligan, you stated that growth in the Gross National Product is needed to insure a healthy economy. And, you pointed out that the GNP is a measure of our ability to produce goods and services. But, it seems to me that the Gross National Product is also, indirectly, an indication of how fast the population is growing, as well as an indication of how fast we're using up a lot of scarce raw materials. Isn't it conceivable that someday we might

2, 4, 8...(Destiny of the Human Species)

run out of some of those materials? If so, what would happen to our economy then?"

Dr. Mulligan glared at Robert for several seconds before responding. *"Mr. Welton*, the earth is *so large*, and the raw materials are *so abundant*, that growth could *never* have the negative effect that you are suggesting!"

Chapter 6

(1 week later)
Tuesday, May 25, 1949

As usual, the "Current" section of the bulletin board in Johnson Hall was filled with a potpourri of activities that a serious-minded college student could attend. Lectures, movies, discussion groups, debates; the list went on and on. As Robert scanned the collection, one item caused him to turn his attention to it:

FRIENDS OF THE ENVIRONMENT
Campus Discussion Group
Friday, May 28th; 7 p.m.
Room 223, Smith Hall
Topic: "Chemical Changes in Lake Washington"
Guest Speaker: Dr. J.W. Foster

"You going?"
"The voice behind Robert startled him. "Oh, I didn't realize anyone was standing behind me."
"Sorry," the petite girl replied. "Are you thinking

2, 4, 8...(The Destiny of the Human Species)

about attending the group? They're fairly new, you know."

"What is this 'environment' slant that they have?" Robert asked quizzically.

"By the way, I'm Susan — Susan Ferguson. Environment — you know, our earthly surroundings. They're just a bunch of students that are concerned about the way people's activities are harming some of our recreational spots and threatening some of our resources, like water supply." Her enthusiasm for the group's purpose was evident.

Robert had always been so busy with his studies and part-time jobs that he hadn't had time to get to know any girls on campus, but the first, quick assessment of Susan told him that she had curves in all of the right places. He thought to himself, *"Pretty grave topic for such an attractive girl to be concerning herself with."* "Have you ever attended any of their meetings? Are they *really serious* ?"

"Oh, sure," Susan affirmed. "They're a fairly new group on campus. Why don't you go just once to see if it's a group that you'd like to join?"

"Are you going?" Robert's interest was piqued mainly by the chance that it would be an opportunity to see some more of Susan.

"Yes. I've been to *all* of the meetings so far. The members are a little different from your average campus crowd — not much into sports fanaticism and beer busts."

Robert yearned for some companionship of people who thought once in a while about something other than just having what he considered to be mindless fun! Not only that, but Susan's smile was very inviting, indeed! "I'll think it over," he said.

2, 4, 8...(The Destiny of the Human Species)

(3 days later)
Friday, May 28, 1949

Robert made an inconspicuous survey of the group in Room 223. *"Not too radical,"* he thought. All of the guys looked clean-shaven and fairly well-dressed. He half-expected to see some of the campus characters in tennis shoes and jeans. There was about an equal number of girls, all attired appropriately in skirts or dresses. *"No Susan,"* he thought disappointedly. His interest in this meeting was primarily based on the desire to see Susan again. He could tolerate an evening of boring discussion just for the opportunity to get to know her better.

"Hi," a slightly familiar voice said behind him.

He turned around. It was Susan, long hair done up in a ponytail this time. He especially like ponytails on girls.

"I was just looking for a place to sit down."

"Why don't we sit over here?" she invited, gesturing toward a couple of empty seats near the front of the room.

The *we* was reassuring to Robert, who didn't feel at all comfortable around most girls. But Susan's friendly demeanor helped him feel at ease.

Dr. Foster's lecture was filled with technical details about the alkalinity of Lake Washington, the changes in the Daphnia population over the past nine years, and the life cycle of the sockeye salmon that inhabited the lake. Robert wasn't very excited about that information. After all, who cared much about water-fleas and fish? It was pretty boring stuff, not the kind of thing that your average college sports nut could handle. Even to Robert it seemed to be a bit too pessimistic a topic to waste an evening on. Except, of course, that he got to spend a little

20

2, 4, 8...(The Destiny of the Human Species)

time next to a delightful new acquaintance.

"It's O.K. if you buy me a cup of coffee," she confided.

Robert was pleasantly surprised by her forwardness. He had been trying to decide whether to invite her out for a snack after the meeting, but he hadn't wanted to offend her by seeming too aggressive at this early stage in their acquaintanceship.

"Dr. Foster has a valid point, you know," she offered after sipping her coffee a couple of times."

"What point? Some of the characteristics of Lake Washington are changing. But it's no big deal!"

"Of course it's a big deal," Susan responded emphatically. "All of the pollution from the sewers of Seattle, Bellevue, Kirkland, and other places around the lake is damaging it."

On the walk back to the dorm, Susan's arm brushed against his now and then. It was a new experience to have an attractive girl at his side. The ever-so-slight contact might have been intentional. At any rate, it left him with an increased awareness of the existence of the opposite sex.

"Thanks for the coffee, Robert," she said. "Maybe we can go to the next meeting together." Then she disappeared through the front door of the dorm.

FACTS OF LIFE!

1950 A.D.

World Population:
2,500,000,000 (up 500,000,000 since 1930)

U.S. Population:
152,300,000 (up 20,600,000 since 1940)

Chapter 7

(6 months later)
Friday, January 13, 1950

The usual crowd was at the meeting. Friends Of The Environment meetings had been presenting Robert with a dual opportunity: the lectures and discussions had turned out to be surprisingly interesting, and he had now attended five meetings with Susan, whose companionship he enjoyed more and more. Robert's interest in this topic 'environment' had grown over the past few months as he heard one guest lecturer after another discuss ways in which the activities of the human population were causing subtle but disturbing changes in the lakes, streams, and forested areas around western Washington. He had told Susan, "So far, none of the speakers has even given the slightest hint that all of these changes are a result of population density. They keep talking about how we need to improve the sewage systems, the garbage disposal methods, and the water supply systems. But, no one has said a thing about the necessity of reducing the population that's the basic cause of all of these problems, if anything more than a small dent is going to be made in the overall situation."

2, 4, 8...(Destiny of the Human Species)

Tonight's agenda was a little different from the typical one's. Instead of a guest lecture, the chairman was opening discussion on the direction that the organization should take, and what kinds of topics should be discussed in future meetings. With the usual formalities of introductions and organizational reports out of the way, Tod McKenzie, the chairman, invited participants to comment on the past meeting topics, and to suggest new ones for later meetings. Susan had urged Robert to speak up about his idea for a meeting on population control. When the opportune time arrived, he arose to speak.

"Mr. Chairman, I'd like to propose that we invite a population expert to present a future lecture. It might be interesting to hear about trends in world population and ways to cut down on the birth rate. After all, the many environmental changes that we've been hearing about over the past few months can all be traced to human activities."

"Robert," said Tod, obviously angered, "we've formed this group for the purpose of trying to identify some of the ways in which we're harming the environment. Our goal is to promote changes in human activities in such a way that the harmful effects of those activities can be avoided. To suggest that this group should pursue the topic of *population control* is very inappropriate!"

Robert blushed, and slid down slightly in his chair.

On the way back to the dorm, Susan detected Robert's frustration over being criticized by Tod McKenzie. As her lips brushed his cheek in a fleeting kiss before she went into the dorm, she said encouragingly, "Don't give up on this. You've got an idea that I think is worth pursuing! In fact, I think that you should run for president at the next Friends of the Environment election. From conversations that I've had with many of the members, it appears that most of them share your feelings about the dangers of overpopulation."

Chapter 8

(10 months later)
Friday, October 20, 1950

President Robert Welton brought the meeting to order. Friends Of The Environment had become a well-knit organization under his leadership of the past few months. Never mind the fact that it had only a minor following on campus. In the minds of the active members it was promoting principles that were crucial to the survival of the human race.

After the routine business matters were out of the way, Robert asked for a report from the Sign Committee. Committee chairman Polly Perkins arose and came to the front of the room. Her frail appearance belied her forceful personality and dogged determination to put the problems of overpopulation in the forefront of campus politics. Polly reported, "Our committee has, as you all know, placed signs in conspicuous locations all over campus. The new signs have been the center of considerable debate throughout the student body. Some students like our theme of equating population growth with a wide variety of social ills that we see in our society today. I think that we're winning a few converts to our way of thinking about the population problem. That's reflected in the 12

2, 4, 8...(Destiny of the Human Species)

per cent increase in our membership over the past two months. Unfortunately, the vast majority of students cling to conventional ways of thinking, and feel that we're just a bunch of pessimists who are trying to create unnecessary feelings of alarm."

Next, Robert called on Dale Olson, chairman of the Demonstration Committee.

"Our committee's planning a single-file march to snake between the buildings on campus, all the way from Smith Hall to the football stadium next Saturday. We hope that all of you will make signs of your own design to carry in the march. Bob Harmon will pass out sheets of suggestions for slogans and drawings to promote our central theme. You'll receive the sheets on your way out of the meeting in a few minutes."

"Thank you for your reports, Polly and Dale," said Robert. He had hand-picked Polly and Dale for these positions because he knew that they shared his deep concern about the problems that would be inherited by future generations if something wasn't done now to slow down population growth. He realized that they were feeling frustrated by the constant negative comments in the *Daily*, the campus newspaper. He shared their frustration, particularly because his name had been mentioned in association with adjectives like *weird* and *kooky* and phrases like *off the deep end* and *way out*.

Susan took hold of Robert's hand as they left the meeting room. "Let's celebrate, Robert."

"Celebrate what?" he said.

"Celebrate the 100 mark in club membership. That's quite a remarkable level for a club that's less than two years old and supposedly appealing only to 'weirdos'!"

"Well, I have ninety-five cents that we can celebrate

29

on," he said. "We can't even both get into a movie for that."

"We could get a quart of ice cream and a bottle of root beer and make root beer floats at my apartment. And we can watch the Jack Benny Show." Her parents had given her a television set for her birthday. It was one of the newer deluxe models with a 12-inch screen.

Robert hadn't been inside Susan's apartment before. Since she had moved out of the dorm at the end of the last school year, he had only walked her to her door after the club meetings. She had even kissed him on the lips the last time they parted. He hadn't yet gotten up enough courage to ask her out on a date.

It was almost beyond belief that here he was *in a girl's apartment, alone with a girl, for the first time in his life*! While Robert adjusted the controls on the television set, Susan put together the root beer floats in the kitchen. She brought them in and set them on the coffee table in front of the couch. Then she sat down near the other end of the couch.

"*She could have sat a little closer*," he thought.

They both pretended to focus their attention on the Jack Benny Show. Susan laughed in a way that emphasized her wonderful sense of humor.

After the show ended, and the root beer-float glasses were emptied, Susan said, "Here's an article that I thought you'd like to see. It appeared in today's *Times*." She inched closer to Robert, inviting him to read it as she held it.

Robert read the article, a short one. He steadied Susan's hand as he read. The article was in a column on the editorial page, entitled "University News." It read as follows:

2, 4, 8...(Destiny of the Human Species)

A relatively new face in campus politics is that of Robert Welton. He is the recently-elected President of the Friends Of The Environment, a student group that focuses on ways in which our natural surroundings are being harmed by pollution caused by human activities in general, and by industrial processes in particular. We wish him well in his quest for solutions to the problems that he is illuminating, although we think that the status of the environment is much better than he claims it to be.

Robert could have released his hold on Susan's hand, but the sensation of hers against his told him that she was just as interested in maintaining contact as he was. She put the newspaper article on the coffee table with her other hand, then snuggled against Robert's shoulder. That sent a thrill through him that he had never before experienced. Did he dare put his arm around her? He did. It was more than he had expected when she had invited him up for a root beer float and television. She turned her head, pressing her face against the side of his neck. It was just too much for Robert! He tilted her head back and pressed his lips lightly against hers. She sighed softly. He pressed his lips against hers more forcefully. She lightly pushed him a few inches away.

"I think we'd better say goodnight," she whispered. "This is fun, but it could lead to something that we might regret."

Robert ambled slowly back to his dorm, reliving the events of the evening.

Chapter 9

(3 months later)
Monday, January 15, 1951

"The meeting will now come to order!"

Robert Welton's voice echoed over the crowd of more than 200 people who had come to tonight's meeting of Friends Of The Environment. It had been necessary to move the meeting from their usual meeting place in Smith Hall to the auditorium in Meany Hall.

"I'm gratified to see such a large turnout. As most of you undoubtedly know, we're going to identify our key demonstration for this quarter. But first, we'll conduct our routine business."

Susan gave the report of the minutes of the last meeting. Her knowledge of environmental problems, plus her enthusiasm, had been keys to her being elected secretary of the organization. And, her being secretary was a big help to Robert, because he saw so much of her anyway, and that facilitated communication between the president and secretary, much to Robert's delight.

Jason Wong gave the treasurer's report. Their treasury had grown slowly, but steadily from additional membership fees, and it now had enough funds to permit the group to produce some high quality protest signs.

Under the heading of new business, Robert indicated that the entire remainder of the meeting would be devoted to identifying one primary target for peaceful demonstrations during the quarter.

"I'll now receive suggestions from the membership for topics to put on the ballot for the quarter's demonstration topic."

Bill Bloom raised his hand. "I'd like to suggest picketing the Catholic Church on 45th Street next Sunday. Their policies are definitely contributing to world overpopulation. They condemn birth control worldwide, in spite of the fact that many countries can't feed or care for their children."

"Susan, write 'Picket Catholic Church' on the blackboard, please."

"I'd like ta suggest that we picket the Internal Revenue Service office downtown," said Sarah Polito. "Their policy of givin' exemptions for every kid that anyone has is encouragin' people to have more kids than they can take care of. I think that some folks are havin' kids just to get more exemptions!"

A chuckle arose in the audience.

"Write ' Picket IRS Office,' please, Susan."

John Appleby stood up. "I think that we ought to march *in support of* the Careful Procreation organization. For a new organization , they're getting too much criticism from the press and the Catholic church. We could make a snake-line from their office on 15th Avenue, through the Quadrangle, and end up showing our support in front of the Pavilion. If we did it the night of the Husky-Cougar basketball game, it could attract a lot of attention."

"Write down 'March for Careful Procreation.'"

2, 4, 8...(Destiny of the Human Species)

Silence reigned. "Are there any more suggestions?" asked Robert.

No one offered anything.

"Well, I guess we'll have to vote on these three, then. But first, is there any discussion on the topics?"

An anonymous member of the audience, someone new, stood up. "I think that picketing the Catholic church could do this organization more harm than good. Almost all of the people who see us would be Catholics, and they pretty much believe the doctrine of the church, anyway. It's not likely that we'll change any minds."

David Coombs arose. "I agree with the previous speaker. And what's more, I don't think that it would do any good to picket the IRS, either. If we don't like their policies, we should be writing to our congressmen."

Helen Roberts raised her hand. "I think that marching *in favor of* Careful Procreation will be much better for our image than picketing *against* something."

Robert looked around the hall for other hands.

"Is there any more discussion before we vote?" No hands.

After the vote, Robert said, "Well, then, we'll march in support of Careful Procreation. Bob Gore, our demonstration chairman will have instructions for the demonstration at our next meeting. Please be here. The demonstration will be on Thursday, January 25th, the night of the big game."

Chapter 10

(3 months later)
Thursday, March 8, 1951

Things had been going well for Robert Welton lately. His friendship with Susan was progressing nicely, to the point that she felt comfortable with an occasional kiss on the lips whenever Robert got up the nerve. The Friends Of The Environment organization was having considerable success with its demonstrations for environmental issues. And his grades promised to be above a 3.0 if he could just do even average on the tests during exam week, which was coming up in only a few days.

However, he had been experiencing mild nausea frequently, and antacids didn't seem to help. Also, he often woke up in a sweat in the middle of the night. Furthermore, he had been feeling awfully tired the past few weeks. All of this was why he had visited the campus infirmary last week. The consulting doctor had ordered some tests, which the infirmary lab had performed on him. The usual things: urine sample, blood sample, blood pressure. Today he was supposed to visit the doctor to get the results of the tests.

"Good afternoon, Mr. Welton," said Dr. Mannfried.

2, 4, 8...(Destiny of the Human Species)

"Good afternoon, Doctor."

"How have you felt since I saw you last week?"

"About the same: nausea, sweats, tiredness," said Robert.

The doctor nodded as if to confirm the symptoms. "I think we know the cause of your problems. All of the test results point to a case of diabetes. Do you know what diabetes is, Welton?"

"Yes. Both my mother and dad and my grandfather on my dad's side had it. They had to take insulin every day, and had to avoid sugar."

"Well, it's genetic, you know. And it's not surprising that you have it, too."

Robert froze for a minute. He had heard about the genetic nature of diabetes in Genetics class, but he had never thought about the possibility that he could have it. It was a *genetic weakness* ! Here he was, concerned about the spread of defective genes in the population, and *he* had one!

"Yes," said Robert, "I learned about it in Genetics class. Does this mean that I'll have to take insulin? That's an awfully inconvenient process."

"Perhaps you can control it through proper diet, Welton. I have here a dietary list for you to follow for the next two weeks. Let's see whether your symptoms still persist after two weeks."

(The next day)
Friday, March 9, 1951

Tonight Robert had his first real date with Susan Ferguson. In fact, it was his first real date with anyone, *ever* . And it really was no big deal. They were just going to see the movie *Kind Hearts and Coronets* at the Varsity

2, 4, 8...(Destiny of the Human Species)

Theater, then have coffee at one of the small coffee shops on "The Ave," before calling it a night. Up until tonight, Robert's sole contact with Susan had been in classes, a few Cokes at the HUB, or meetings of Friends of the Environment, followed by his usual walk with her to her apartment door.

The movie was funny and stimulating. Alec Guinness and Alistair Simms were superb actors. Robert and Susan held hands during most of the movie. Robert loved the softness of her skin and the warmth of her fingers.

After the movie, they went to the Lun Ting Chinese restaurant, and ordered tea, instead of going to their usual coffee hangout. Robert liked Lun Ting's, because it had atmosphere that was not found in the coffee shops. Most people who dined there ordered expensive meals, but Robert and Susan were both scrimping in order to just get financially through the year.

The tea was steaming as Robert put it to his lips. Susan added a little ice to hers.

"I found out something today, Susan, that makes me a little depressed."

"Really? What is it?"

"I found out that I have diabetes," Robert said, somewhat mournfully.

"Well," said Susan, "What's so depressing about that? A lot of people have diabetes, and they handle it o.k. just by watching their diet."

"I might end up having to take injections of insulin, like my mother and dad and my grandfather did. But that's not the worst part. It's depressing to think that I have a genetic defect."

"What do you mean 'genetic defect'?"

"Diabetes is caused by an abnormal gene, and it can be passed on to future generations through your genes if you have it. I wouldn't want to pass on a characteristic like that to my children. It makes me think that I should never get married and have children."

Susan looked pensive for a moment. "I never heard of anyone avoiding marriage because they had diabetes, Robert Welton. That's the silliest idea I ever heard of! Of course you want to get married!"

Robert really thought over that last statement. *Could Susan ever have enough interest in him to marry him?* The thought had never before entered his mind. Here he was, barely able to muster up enough courage to kiss her goodnight when he walked her home!

They left Lun Ting's and walked to Susan's apartment. At the door, Robert was ready to give her the usual goodnight kiss.

"Want to come in and cheer up before you go back to your dorm? I hate to see you go back in this state of mind."

Susan seldom invited him into her apartment, and then only for a few minutes. But, now, here she was, offering to "cheer him up."

"I can fix us a root beer float, Robert."

"That sounds great," he replied.

They sipped their floats, and watched the Burns and Allen Show. Susan's 12-inch TV was really great entertainment, even if it didn't have color like the newer movies. Susan sat unusually close.

Robert thought,"*If this is her way of cheering me up, it works.*"

He put his arm around her, and settled down deeper into the sofa. She leaned her head on his shoulder. The Burns and Allen Show was passing before his eyes, but Susan's closeness made the show a blur. He turned his head and kissed her on the lips. She held the kiss, way

2, 4, 8...(Destiny of the Human Species)

longer than she had ever held any of his kisses before!

Well, one kiss led to another, and another, and another. This time Robert was the one who said that maybe they ought to say goodnight. He had such an ache in his groin that he thought it was going to burst!

"You definitely cheered me up, Susan."

And Robert then walked slowly back to his dorm, reviewing every kiss in his mind.

Chapter 11

(5 weeks later)
Monday, April 16, 1951

Robert brought the meeting to order at exactly 7 p.m. The crowd in Meany Hall auditorium had grown to almost three hundred. Friends Of The Environment had dropped a blockbuster when it had announced its meeting agenda on the bulletin boards around campus. The proposed purpose of the meeting — to select a topic for the organization's emphasis during Spring quarter — was dramatized by articles in the *Daily* claiming that this "radical" organization was trying to stir up a hornet's nest over "irrelevant" issues. The topics that had been pre-suggested in the announcements included petitioning the university administration to put condom machines in all campus restrooms, a petition drive to force Seattle and other cities around Lake Washington to form a coalition to prevent the dumping of sewage into the lake, and picketing the Watson Pulp Mill in order to persuade it to cease dumping sulfite wastes into the Duwamish River.

It appeared that at least a third of the audience were non-members, who probably wanted to argue against one or more of the proposed topics. After all, every one of the three was controversial to a significant proportion of the student population on campus.

As the primary "new business" segment of the meeting began after the routine business, Robert said, "We have a lot of new faces in the audience tonight. We'll permit *anyone* in the audience to participate in the discussion of the issues, but the voting tonight will be limited to members. At the beginning of the voting process, our stewards will pass out ballots only to those who show their memberships cards."

As Robert had anticipated, there was a slight groan from a significant portion of the crowd — probably the non-member portion!

"As stated in the meeting announcements, 'new business' will be limited to the pre-designated topic, that of deciding on the one issue that'll be the focus of the organization's attention during Spring quarter.

"Rolf, will you set up the blackboard containing the three issues for consideration?"

The blackboard listed the three issues in summarized form:

1. Place condoms in all campus restrooms.
2. Picket Watson Pulp Mill.
3. Petition for clean-up of Lake Washington.

As Rolf Amundsen set the blackboard on its tripod, a low murmur started among the audience; then it grew into a cacophony.

"Order, please," shouted Robert, as he banged his gavel. The crowd quieted noticeably. "I'll now entertain discussion on these issues. Please state your name before commenting."

Several dozen hands shot up.

2, 4, 8...(Destiny of the Human Species)

After a long and heated discussion, which was punctuated at times by shouts of support, at other times by groans of disapproval, Robert announced:

"All right, we'll begin handing out the ballots. Please show your membership card in order to receive a ballot. Vote for the one issue that you think we should emphasize this quarter."

About a third of the audience got up and left, even before the ballots were distributed. This confirmed Robert's hunch that a large portion of the audience weren't members.

After the ballots had been collected and tallied, Robert announced the final result. "Condom machines received 49 votes. Picketing the pulp mill received 47 votes. Sewage diversion received 105 votes. The sewage diversion project has a majority, so it'll be the issue that we focus on this quarter. However, because such a large portion of the membership is interested in each of the other issues, I'm going to appoint a sub-committee to explore further each of those issues for consideration in a later quarter. The meeting is now adjourned."

Chapter 12

(6 months later)
Friday, October 26, 1951

Since last April, a lot had happened to Robert Welton. For one thing, he had graduated in June with a bachelor's degree in Biology. Whereas most of his fellow male graduating classmates had been inducted into the armed forces because of the Korean War, he had obtained a deferment because of his diabetes. That had enabled him to accept full-time employment with Enviro Inc., a Seattle fledgling firm that hoped to not only convince local and state government officials of the advisability of studying the effects of potentially environmentally-harmful policies, but also to persuade them to hire the company to conduct the studies.

One momentous decision that Robert had made was to undergo an experimental operation called a *vasectomy*. That was a procedure in which he was made sterile through the process of surgically severing his sperm tubes. Although the procedure was relatively unknown by the general population, Robert had identified a surgeon who was conducting the operation on an experimental basis through a grant from the U.S. Health Department. The decision to have the vasectomy resulted

2, 4, 8...(Destiny of the Human Species)

from Robert's intense feelings about not wanting to pass the defective diabetes gene on to offspring. He felt that the only way he could assure that outcome was to undergo this procedure. Afterward, he felt greatly relieved to know that he wasn't going to contribute to the spread of any defective genes.

Robert had left The Friends Of The Environment in good condition, handing over the presidency to Allison McKenzie, a junior who shared his concerns about overpopulation. The demonstrations of Spring quarter had nudged the cities in the Lake Washington drainage system to schedule an exploratory meeting to discuss the Friends concerns and proposal.

During the summer, Susan Ferguson had done her usual vacationing in her little Washington hometown of Ilwaco. Since Ilwaco was pretty much an out-of-the-way place, Robert hadn't had an opportunity to see her. However, tonight he had a date with her. She was back in her same apartment, and working on her senior year in Sociology. She had been re-elected as secretary for Friends Of The Environment. They were going to attend the performance by The Mills Brothers at the Orpheum Theater in downtown Seattle. Although the tickets were a bit expensive, Robert could afford them now that he had a full-time job. And Susan really enjoyed The Mills Brothers music. Since it was such a special occasion, Robert also was taking Susan to dinner at Ivar's, the nationally known seafood restaurant. He was driving the used, but reliable 1947 Oldsmobile that he had purchased, and it was a treat for Susan to ride in a car rather than the usual city transit transportation that most of her college dates relied on. The car had a lot of attractive chrome trim that the cars that were built during the war didn't have.

Dinner at a table overlooking the waterfront proved

2, 4, 8...(Destiny of the Human Species)

to be romantic. Susan said, "This is a real treat, Robert. Most of my dates take me to Dick's hamburger joint or something else like it. I've been dating occasionally, you know, but I actually haven't met any guy who interests me."

Robert thought, *"Should I ask her if I interest her?"* He was certainly interested in *her*, and that was magnified by her summer's absence. She looked even more appealing tonight than ever before. Of course, now that he had a steady job and didn't have to scrimp just to make ends meet, his thoughts turned more often to the opposite sex, specifically Susan. Finally, he said, "Well, *I* definitely enjoy being with you, Susan. I missed you a lot this summer."

Susan extended her hand across the table. "I missed you, too, Robert, and I'm glad we're together tonight."

It had been quite awhile since he held Susan's hand, and the softness of it sent a sensation of thrill through his body.

The waiter brought their main course. Robert was having the Ivar's specialty, steamed clams. Susan opted for a more traditional fare of broiled salmon.

Susan said, "How is your work going?"

"Just fine," answered Robert. "We're gradually building our clientele. We've been able to convince the officials of several of the Puget Sound area cities that their expanding populations and industries make it necessary for them to consider setting up pollution commissions and laws and ordinances for protecting the environment from damage that would lower the quality of life that their citizens expect. It's difficult to convince some officials of the need for that kind of action, because that could require limitations on the activities of some residents and some companies that could be inconvenient or costly, or

2, 4, 8...(Destiny of the Human Species)

both. But, the work is stimulating. Every day brings a new challenge. I'm definitely able to apply my biological knowledge to the job.

"How's school going, Susan?"

Susan replied, "It's exciting. Since I'm a senior, I have most of the non-major requirements out of the way, and I'm really getting into the heart of sociology and social work. My internship with Careful Procreation is working out well. I get to work with people who have a need for help with serious social problems — particularly teenage girls who are pregnant or who have one or more little kids. Their plight's so sad, Robert. It's a shame that they didn't come to Careful Procreation before they got pregnant. So many of the fathers of their children cut off the relationship with the girls once they got pregnant. And those poor girls are in a dreadful state of mind, not knowing what to do."

"And how is The Friends Of The Environment organization doing?" said Robert. "Are the meetings and the plans going smoothly?"

"Well, we've only had two meetings since last year, when you were president, you know. But Allison has a good head on her shoulders, and those two meetings went well. We're going to keep in touch frequently with the council of representatives of the cities around the Lake Washington drainage basin, so that they don't forget their resolution to consider sewage control.

"Also, we've taken on a new program that you might not have heard about. It's an attempt to get the federal government to consider requiring pollution controls on newly manufactured automobiles. The air pollution problem is especially bad in the Los Angeles area. They say that some days you can only see for about a half mile because of it. In Seattle on some days one can get a headache from the exhaust fumes, and we don't want a Los Angeles type of situation to develop here or elsewhere. So, we're contacting other environmental groups around the country to see if we can't put pressure on congress to do something about the problem."

Robert looked at his watch. "7:30," he said. "We'd better start for the Orpheum. The program begins at 8:00."

When they arrived at the theater, they noticed that the crowd included people from a wide range of ages. The Mills Brothers' music was appealing to those of many ages, and the bulk of the crowd ranged from late high school age to middle-age.

When the singing group finally appeared, they opened up with one of their perennial favorites, "Up A Lazy River." For the next hour and a half they cruised through old standards like "Bye, Bye Blackbird," "Heart Of My Heart," "That Old Gang Of Mine," and "Pennies From Heaven." One of their most well-received numbers was "Paper Doll," which they had first performed in 1942 on a record that stayed near the top of record sales for almost two years.

After the performance, Robert took Susan to Lun Ting's restaurant in the U-district. It was as much a sentimental gesture as anything, because they had spent so many enjoyable times there when all they could afford was a cup of tea.

Then Robert took Susan back to her apartment. He was hoping that she might invite him in, and she did. "Let's have a root beer float, just like old times," said Susan.

"Great," said Robert. "I'll see what's on TV. I see that your set still works like a charm."

He scanned the TV listings. It was 10:45. "It's pretty

late for any of the regular good shows." Then he said, "At 11:00 they're showing the movie *Casablanca* on TV for the first time. It's getting kind of late. Do you feel like watching it?"

"Well, I can sleep in tomorrow morning."

"So can I. Let's watch."

The movie had deeply romantic overtones, and it aroused the incipient passions that Robert and Susan both harbored. She sat close on the couch, and before long, he had his arm around her. As the interplay between Ingrid Bergman and Humphrey Bogart unfolded, Susan ran her hand over Robert's thigh, and he experienced a sudden thrill. She was leaning her head on his shoulder, and he turned and kissed her full on the lips. She responded by kissing him back, even more forcefully. Breath came quickly, and Robert's heart was pounding. Her kisses were the most passionate that he had ever experienced. Before long, he was stroking her thighs with his fingers, and exploring her curves and creases, his middle finger subconsciously probing for what men's middle fingers have sought in the women they have made love to for eons. When he felt the warm, lubricous moisture of the spot that his instincts had led him to seek, they both knew that she was his.

(The next day)
Saturday, October 27, 1951

Robert's phone rang several times before he realized what was happening. He leaned over the edge of the bed and groped for it. The clock said 8:15 a.m.

"Hi." It was Susan. In just one word, her voice sounded troubled.

2, 4, 8...(Destiny of the Human Species)

"I thought you were going to sleep in this morning," said Robert.

"I couldn't sleep any longer, because I was thinking about last night."

"Do you have any regrets?" Robert asked.

"In some ways 'yes,' in some ways 'no,'" replied Susan.

"What do you mean by that?"

"Well, it was a lovely experience. My first, you know. But, now I'm worried about getting pregnant. A pregnancy could *really* ruin my plans, Robert. I'm not ready for parenthood. There are too many things to do in life before settling down as a parent."

"Don't worry," said Robert knowingly. "I didn't tell you last night, but last summer I had an operation called a *vasectomy*. Have you ever heard of it?"

"No."

"It made me sterile. I did it because I didn't ever want to risk passing on my diabetes gene to children. I wasn't going to tell *anyone*, but I guess this is a good time to tell *you*.""

"Are you sure it worked?"

"My doctor checked me out and said that I'm not producing any living sperms. So I shouldn't be able to get anyone pregnant."

Susan breathed a sigh of relief. "Well, that makes me feel a lot better, Robert. I really did enjoy last night."

Robert was glad to hear that comment. "I enjoyed it, too, Susan. It was special. You're special."

"Am I the only 'special' one in your life, Robert?"

"Yes, you are, Susan."

Chapter 13

(4 months later)
Thursday, February 21, 1952

Robert and Susan entered the VFW Hall and took seats about midway from the front. The folding chairs creaked as they sat down. This was their first time on Mercer Island, and they had come by way of the floating bridge, an engineering marvel. The serene life of Mercer Island had been shaken by the addition of the bridge and the highway running across the island toward Bellevue, Issaquah, and eventually to Snoqualmie Pass.

The Young Republicans had rented the hall for their monthly meeting. For the past few months, Robert had been looking for a political organization to join, so that he could work through political circles to help preserve the environment. His job with Enviro, Inc. permitted him, of course, to do that kind of work professionally, but he was getting frustrated with the heel-dragging of city and county officials, who resisted adopting policies that would protect the environment. He felt that if he could have a voice in deciding who got elected or appointed to those positions, it would help. Consequently, after attending a couple of meetings of the Young Republicans, he had joined the organization.

2, 4, 8...(Destiny of the Human Species)

Eric Alden, the chairman of the group, convened the meeting. "The meeting will now come to order. Will the Secretary please read the minutes of the last meeting?"

After the reading of the minutes and the treasurer's report, Eric called for reports on "new business". He began that portion of the program by calling upon Amy Jorgensen to tell of her Elections Subcommittee's plans for the Republican caucuses in the spring.

"We're asking each one of our members to attend their precinct caucuses and to introduce the name of General Dwight Eisenhower on the ballot. We feel that he's the right candidate to support in this presidential election. Senator Robert Taft is claimed by conservatives to be the frontrunner, but we think that Eisenhower can win the nomination. After all, he's a war hero who is highly respected, even by most Democrats. In addition to the presidency, we have printed a list of 'acceptable' candidates for lesser positions. Note that there are more than one for some of the positions. In those cases, we weren't able to make a decision to support just one candidate, so it's up to you, as individuals, to support the candidates of your choice for those positions."

It was at that point that Robert sensed his opportunity to introduce the topic of environmental issues to the group. He raised his hand.

"Robert Welton," said Eric.

Robert began slowly, somewhat hesitantly. "Mr. Chairman........ and members........ I think that this group... could take the lead in an area that is just now coming to be recognized.... in importance. That is... the quality of our environment. If we could help to assure that environmentally conscious candidates get elected, even to the lesser offices, we could be doing a valuable service for our society. The rapid expansion of our population is

51

2, 4, 8...(Destiny of the Human Species)

threatening the quality of our water, the quality of our air, and the quality of our life in general. If we could support candidates who want to work to limit population growth, and who want to make sure that human activities don't spoil the environment, we could be helping future generations to have a quality of life just as good as the one that we are enjoying."

There was a murmur among those in attendance.

Eric looked irritated. He said, "We realize, Robert, that your professional job is dedicated to helping to preserve the environment. But, we'd appreciate it if you would leave that type of thing at work, and not bring it up at our meetings. After all, there's no indication that we have any need to worry about pollution. Our environment is so vast that there's little chance that we can harm the quality of our air or water to the point that it'll be noticeable."

A few members of the group clapped lightly at the end of Eric's remarks. Robert felt that everyone could see that he was red-faced, and he swallowed hard. Susan squeezed his hand in a gesture of support.

After the meeting, they drove back across the bridge to the U-district. They had a shake at Bartell Drugs, then walked to Susan's apartment. Usually, Robert stayed at her place for awhile after their dates, but he was terribly frustrated by what had happened at the meeting. "I'm really feeling tired, Susan. I think I'll just call it a night." He kissed Susan lightly on the lips, and walked back to his car.

FACTS OF LIFE!

1955 A.D

U.S. Population:
165,900,000 (up 13,600,000 since 1950)

Chapter 14

(4 years later)
Tuesday, February 21, 1956

Robert and Susan entered the auditorium in the Bellevue City Hall, and took seats about midway from the front. This space was regularly rented for the monthly meetings of the Eastside Young Democrats. Although they were called 'young' democrats, a few middle-aged people were among those already in the room. It was about ten minutes to eight, and the meeting was slated to begin at eight.

Robert was now the President of Enviro, Inc., partly out of default because of the resignation of three presidents in a period of only two years. The turmoil in the company was due primarily to a lack of business, resulting in economic troubles that forced a cutback in personnel. It had turned out to be more difficult than they had anticipated to get local, county and state officials to consider policies that would protect the environment. Although Robert had little enthusiasm for taking over the presidency, most of the remaining employees encouraged him to do it, because of his dedication to the environmental goals of the company.

Susan had graduated with her degree in Sociology in June of 1952. She was hired by the state to serve as a social worker in the Seattle area. That made both her and Robert happy because they could see that much more of each other. She had moved to a different apartment on Capitol Hill, overlooking Lake Union. Robert had taken up residence in an apartment on Queen Anne Hill. It not only had a breathtaking view of downtown Seattle, but also one could see all the way around from the saltwater of Elliott Bay on the west, to a little portion of Lake Union on the east. Actually, Robert and Susan could observe each other's apartments from across opposite sides of the end of Lake Union.

At precisely 8:00 p.m., the president of the group, Sharon Radovic, called to order the meeting of the Young Democrats. She efficiently steered the meeting through the routine reading of the minutes, the treasurer's report, and old business. The first item of 'new' business was a discussion of which candidates to support in the spring caucuses. Since the presidential elections were coming up next fall, the decisions about which candidates to promote in the caucuses and in the voting were unusually important. Robert had never lost his interest in promoting candidates who were environmentally conscious, and he perceived an impending opportunity to have some influence in that regard. After his embarrassing experience with the Young Republicans four years ago, he had left the party and joined the Young Democrats, who, it seemed, were more inclined to promote the interests of the working class, and less inclined to look out for business interests. At Susan's urging, he had taken great pains not to arouse the hostility of members of the Young Democrats group by being pushy about environmental issues. Of course, they all knew that he worked for an environmentally oriented company, and some quietly

2, 4, 8...(Destiny of the Human Species)

snickered behind his back about what they considered to be his exaggerated concerns about potential damage to the environment by the increasing population of the region.

When Sharon announced that the first item of new business would be decisions about which candidates to support, Robert was ready to foster his goals.

Sharon announced, "The executive board has narrowed the list of candidates to two for each position which we eastside Democrats will be voting for at the county, state, and federal levels. We'll be voting tonight in order to determine the names of those candidates that our organization will publicly support through newspaper ads. We'll start with a discussion of the candidates for the presidency of the United States. They are Adlai Stevenson and Estes Kefauver. I now invite comments on either of these candidates from any member in attendance."

The first person to comment was George Anderson. He started by saying, "Kefauver has had all of that experience in the Senate. He knows how to raise support for his programs, much more so than Stevenson."

Next Sharon called on Ilene Bronson.

"On the other hand, Stevenson has had the experience of being a governor, that Kefauver hasn't had. That gives Stevenson more experience than Kefauver at being an administrator."

Dorothy Jensen spoke next. "Stevenson has called for an end to the draft, and the stop of nuclear testing in the atmosphere. Ike opposes Stevenson on both of these issues, and I think that fact can get Stevenson elected much more easily than Kefauver, who hasn't taken a firm stand on either one."

Craig Nelson asked to speak next. He said, "Eisenhower has been a popular president. It's going to take someone with a lot of charisma to beat him. Stevenson has it, but Kefauver doesn't."

There appeared to be no one else wanting to speak. Sharon asked, "Does anyone else want to say anything in support of either candidate?

"No? Well, then, we'll take a hand vote. All in favor of supporting Adlai Stevenson, raise your hands."

She said to the secretary, Jane Monroe, "You count, too, so that we can confirm each other's number."

Jane said, "I count 32."

"I count 32, too," said Sharon. "Now, all in favor of supporting Estes Kefauver, raise your hands."

Jane reported, "I count 24."

Sharon said, "I count 24, too. So our public support will go to Adlai Stevenson."

Next, the discussion focused on the position of Democratic candidates for the U.S. House of Representatives. The two from the Eastside Young Democrats' area were John Deming and Phillip Ronstadt. Robert knew the political agendas of both of them very well. Deming had ties to big business, even though he was a Democrat. He didn't want any policies established that would restrict business operations, even if they had potential for harming the environment. Ronstadt, on the other hand, was an outdoorsman who appreciated nature in its unspoiled state. He had even delivered a speech to The Friends Of The Environment at the University.

Sharon asked, "Would anyone like to comment on either of these candidates?"

Robert didn't want to seem too eager to speak up, for fear that his enthusiasm might be interpreted as radicalism.

Jane Emery stood up. "I want to speak in support of John Deming. He's pledged to work to create more jobs

2, 4, 8...(Destiny of the Human Species)

in our state, and, as the incumbent, he's already made great strides in arranging more lumber and fish exports. We democrats in this state rely heavily on the employees in the timber and fishing industries for political support, and they've benefited tremendously from Representative Deming's efforts."

By this time, Robert felt comfortable in speaking. He stood up. "Actually, the work that Representative Deming has done in Congress has led to excessive degradation of our forest lands and salmon runs. On the other hand, Mr. Ronstadt has pledged to work for the funding of scientific studies that will determine just how much timber we can cut, and how many fish we can take each year in this state without endangering our quality of life in the long run."

Robert sat down.

Sylvia Roberts stood up. "I'd like to point out that Robert Welton is the president of Enviro, Inc., and that his company stands to benefit extensively if Phillip Ronstadt gets elected. I think that there's a conflict of interest here. Furthermore, I recommend that we reject Welton's arguments about degradation of forests and fish runs, because we have practically limitless resources of those types. No one has ever offered any proof that we're in danger of ever running low on the supply of these things."

Robert's ears were burning. He hadn't anticipated that anyone would suggest a conflict of interest on his part. It undercut the influence that anything else he might say tonight in support of environmentally conscious candidates would have. The rest of the meeting sped by in a blur, almost unnoticed by him. The discussions of one candidate after another left him limp. He could have pointed out significant differences in the environmental attitudes of several of the alternative pairs of candidates, but he was sure that no one would listen.

2, 4, 8...(Destiny of the Human Species)

After the meeting, he and Susan drove back across the floating bridge, and to her apartment. By now, Robert was accustomed to routinely being invited in by Susan after their dates, even the 'political' ones. Usually, Saturday was about the only night of the week that they could get together, because of their busy work schedules. But tonight, a Tuesday, was different because tomorrow was Washington's Birthday, a holiday at both the state offices and Enviro-Associates. Intimacy was becoming a regular part of their lives, enhanced by the fact that they both knew that Robert was sterile, and that there was no risk of pregnancy. They followed their now familiar routine of watching TV and ending up in bed together.

Chapter 15

(11 months later)
Tuesday, January 15, 1957

Robert stood at the podium and looked out over the audience. About 65 people were there, a much larger group than he had anticipated. Could it be that there was more interest in the Seattle area in environmental issues than he had assumed? He saw the faces of several of his old friends from The Friends Of The Environment.

"I'm gratified that so many of you have responded to my invitation to explore the setting-up of a new political party. As most of you know, we've been unable to get either the local or state Democrat or Republican organizations to acknowledge the need for concern about the increasing damage to the environment that is occurring as a result of population growth in the Puget Sound region. Therefore, I decided to consider the possibility of establishing a party through which we could express our concerns publicly, and through which we could gradually build enough membership to have political clout."

Robert paused as he noted several nods of agreement. Then he continued. "There's only one item on our agenda tonight. I'm going to present a tentative set of basic goals for the new party. They have been developed primarily by me, but on the basis of conversations that I have had with many of you over the past few years. I suggest that each of you examine this set of goals prior to the next meeting, which is scheduled for a week from tonight at 7:30 p.m. at this same location. At that meeting, we'll consider suggestions for modifications of the set of goals in ways that will result in a majority of the potential members being able to support them. After that, we'll enroll, as charter members of the party, all who feel that they can support the goals. Susan Ferguson and David Jensen will now hand out copies of the tentative set of goals for your consideration."

Susan and David passed along the ends of the rows, counting out copies of the goals and handing them out. As the copies circulated, a murmur arose among the crowd. Robert couldn't tell whether it was an expression of doubt or enthusiasm, but hoped that it was the latter. He said, "Take these home and look them over. Be prepared to offer suggestions for changes or additions at our January 22nd meeting."

(1 week later)
Tuesday, January 22, 1957

It was a chilly evening. The winter sky had darkened earlier than usual because of the heavy cloud cover. It looked like it might even snow before the night was over. Robert hoped that the weather wouldn't keep people away from tonight's meeting. After having one of his usual varieties of TV dinner, which he had popped in the oven, he sat down to review the list of goals that he had prepared prior to the last meeting.

2, 4, 8...(Destiny of the Human Species)

PARTY GOALS

1. We believe that all races and religions should be respected.
2. We believe that the rights and property of all people should be respected.
3. We believe that the primary purposes of most religions are to promote behaviors that lead to the preservation of the human species and the improvement in the quality of life of all people.
4. We are committed to promoting political policies that will enhance the preservation of the human species and the quality of life of all people.
5. We are committed to promoting policies that minimize the pain and suffering of all living things, as long as those living things do not reduce the quality of life of human beings.
6. We believe that the greatest threat to species survival and quality of life is human overpopulation, with the consequent degradation of the environment and population pressures that result in social upheaval.
7. We believe that the following policies and programs, if adopted by our government, will lead to the maximization of the quality of life and probability of preservation of our species.
    a. Required teaching of birth control in our public schools, accompanied by government distribution of birth control information and devices.
    b. Sterilization of individuals who have a proven genetic defect that could be passed on to offspring, and which could result in a lower quality of life for those offspring.
    c. Required government-supported Parent Edu-

cation for all pregnant women and their husbands.
- d. Government sponsored free healthcare for life for every citizen.
- e. Required classes in thinking skills for all public school students, in order to promote rational decision-making.
- f. Legalization of suicide for people whose quality of life is adjudged by themselves and medical doctors to be totally miserable and irreversible.

Robert put his copy of the goals in his briefcase, and prepared to head for the meeting. He was picking up Susan on the way. She had proven to be his greatest supporter, as well as an exciting lover.

When Robert and Susan arrived at the meeting hall on 15th Avenue, just across the street from the University campus, a din of conversation was emanating from the large crowd that was already there.

Robert thought to himself, "*I hope that all of this excitement is in support of the goals, and not against them.*"

As Robert was spied entering the hall, several people with angry looks on their faces rushed over to him, some shaking their copies of the goals in his face. That answered his question about the cause of the clamor.

He approached the podium, and said, "Well, it seems that there is a lot of excitement among you. As a first step, tonight, I want to see a show of hands of all of those who feel that they can support this set of goals as written."

Of the hundred or so in attendance, only about twenty raised their hands. He was disappointed. He knew, from looking over the group, that the majority were people that agreed with his general feelings about the environment and population growth. He said, "Well, that surprises me. We should probably explore the reasons why so many of you feel that you can't support these goals. I'll now entertain comments about them from the audience."

The discussion was much more prolonged than Robert had anticipated. Challenges to various items in the list of goals were more numerous than he had expected, and several heated arguments took place. Major modifications of the goals were suggested; some of them were personally objectionable to him. It took all of his parliamentary skills to control the debate.

Finally, after every audience member who had raised a hand had gotten an opportunity to speak, he asked, "Is there anyone here who couldn't support the goals as revised according to these notes on the blackboard?"

Robert was dismayed as almost half of the audience raised their hands.

"Well, then, I'm going to ask Lowell, Amy, Jeff, and Cheryl to serve on a committee to work on a revision of the goals. We'll have a new version for you to consider at a meeting a week from tonight, Tuesday, at 7:30."

Chapter 16

(1 week later)
Tuesday, January 29, 1957

As Robert Welton surveyed the audience from the podium, he estimated that about 60 people had shown up for the meeting. That was slightly fewer than the number at the previous meeting, but he was encouraged to know that no more than 5 or 10 of those who had attended earlier were apparently sufficiently disenchanted with his list of preliminary goals that they hadn't come back to see the revised list.

At 7:35 he called the meeting to order. "I'm pleased to see so many of you back. Those who were at the meeting last week know that several changes were suggested to the list of preliminary party goals that I submitted. Since then, Lowell Jackson, Amy Roberts, Jeff Culbertson, Cheryl Mason and I have worked to incorporate those suggestions into a revised list. Jeff and Cheryl will now hand out copies of the revision to you."

2, 4, 8...(The Destiny of the Human Species)

Goals Of The Humanitarian Party
(Presented for consideration on January 29, 1957)

Primary Goal:

To promote the maximization of the quality of life for all human beings, and the minimization of pain and suffering of all human beings.

Secondary Goals:

1. To promote humane treatment of all animal life, with priorities set in the order of position on the evolutionary scale when choices between different species have to be made.

2. To promote the maximization of the quality of life of all living things, as long as those living things don't interfere with the quality of life of human beings.

Robert pounded his gavel in order to hush the loud surge of voices that had built up as the copies had been handed out. He said, "As you can see, the committee has suggested calling our new party The Humanitarian Party. That name was brought up by Lowell, after we had finalized the list. The implication in it is that our goals can be summarized as ways in which to make this a more humane world. You have probably noticed that the list is much shorter than the list that was submitted last week. The committee felt that in order to promote our main goals, we needed to come up with a list that the majority of you could agree upon. They thought that there was no point in getting bogged down in debate over fine points which can be debated at the appropriate time by the full membership as we pursue the implementation of the primary and secondary goals. In a few minutes we're

2, 4, 8...(The Destiny of the Human Species)

going to take a hand vote to see how many of you now feel that you could support this list of goals as the basic principles of the new party, and would be willing to join the party. But first, I'll take questions from you about the rationale for any of the goals."

Karen Bachman stood and asked, "Why did you add the secondary goals, when they weren't even on the list last week?"

"I'll let Jeff answer that," said Robert.

"Well," said Jeff, "we thought that if we want to promote a humane world, we shouldn't think only in terms of human beings. If we want to reduce total pain and suffering, we should be thinking about all animal life, at least those that can experience pain and suffering."

Jeff sat down.

Robert said, "Are there any more questions?"

No hands were raised.

"Well, then, it's probably time to take a vote on the goals. If you can support this new list of goals to the extent that you're willing to join the party as a charter member, you should now raise your hand."

An overwhelming majority raised their hands.

Then, Robert said, "It seems to me that this vote encourages us to stick with this list. Well, we'll now adjourn the meeting in order to give you some time to fill out party enrollment forms and to pay your dues. The dues are $1.50 for the first year. If you have to write a check, make it payable to The Humanitarian Party."

With that, about 5 people left, and that disappointed Robert. But, he was encouraged to see that almost everyone else was filling out an enrollment form.

Susan came over to Robert and said, "It looks like you've got the ball rolling, Robert," and she gave him a soft kiss on the cheek.

Chapter 17

At the last meeting of the now-official Humanitarian Party, the election of officers had occurred. As expected, Robert Welton was elected Chairman. Other officers included Lowell Jackson, Assistant Chairman; Cheryl Mason, Secretary; and Jeff Culbertson, Treasurer. The constitution which had been adopted at the meeting of February 12th had set up those four offices.

The meeting room on 15th Avenue, across from the University campus, was advantageous because a large proportion of the members of the party were also University students and members of Friends Of The Environment.

Robert convened the meeting at 7:30 sharp. "Would the secretary read the minutes of the last meeting, please?"

With that, Cheryl read over the results of the elections, which were the sole item on the agenda last week.

"Thank you, Cheryl," said Robert. "Jeff, will you give the treasurer's report?"

"Mr. Chairman, we've received sixty-six one-year membership fees, at $1.50 each, for a total of $99.00. The rent for each of our last three meetings was $5.00 per meeting, or a total of $15.00. We had printing expenses of $1.75. That leaves us with a tidy balance of $82.25."

"Thank you, Jeff. Our main agenda item for this evening is that of deciding on ways to pursue our charter goals. I'll now entertain suggestions that we can put on a preliminary list, to be narrowed down if necessary."

Wade Martin raised his hand.

"Wade."

"I think that we'd do well to go back to Robert's original list of goals from January 22nd, and to pick two or three projects from that list. I have a copy here."

He held up his copy, then said, "As I recall, there was at least one objection raised to just about every item on that list. The general consensus seemed to be that almost every one of them was originally worded in a way that made them seem pretty radical. But some of them were revised at that January 22nd meeting, and seemed to be fairly acceptable to most of the people present. One of the more acceptable revisions appeared to be the idea of promoting government distribution of birth control information and devices. If we pursued that project alone, it could take all of our resources, and it certainly would be a key step in promoting our charter goals. Most of the other goals that were on that original list met with more skepticism, and that causes me to think that we would be better off to identify one project that we could concentrate on, and not get locked up in debate over more controversial projects at this time."

Polly Wilson raised her hand and waved it impatiently.

"Polly," said Robert.

Polly spread out her hands, palms up, and said, "I'd like to ask Wade to explain the connection between birth control and our charter goals!"

2, 4, 8...(Destiny of the Human Species)

Wade got up slowly. "Well, Polly, our primary goal is to improve the quality of life for human beings — all human beings — and to minimize pain and suffering of all human beings. Most of the members that I have talked to see overpopulation as being the greatest factor in the reduction of standard of living around the world. Look at many of the Asian and African countries, for example. Almost daily we see photographs of starving, diseased and dying people in those countries, where they just keep on having babies in spite of their inability to support them properly. Although that level of overpopulation hasn't hit this country yet, it could if we don't do something soon to decrease the birth rate."

"Oh," said Polly.

Then Hans Johnson stood up. "I'd like to echo Wade's suggestion about limiting our activities to one major project for now, so that we can concentrate on it and do a good job on it. I move that we limit our efforts to one project, and that it be the promotion of birth control."

"I second that," said Amy Roberts. "We can always go on to additional projects if our funds and time permit it."

"It has been moved and seconded that we limit our activities to working on the promotion of birth control. All in favor say 'aye.'"

There was an overwhelming response.

"It appears that the 'aye' vote is almost unanimous," said Robert. "Now we have enough time left this evening to develop a preliminary list of specific activities that could help to promote birth control. Who wants to start the list?"

Jeff Culbertson raised his hand.

"Jeff."

"I'd like to suggest that we ask every member to

2, 4, 8...(Destiny of the Human Species)

write to his or her state legislators to recommend funding of free birth control clinics in every county."

"Write down these suggestions as they're offered, please, Cheryl," said Robert. "Who has another suggestion?"

"I do," said Rob Travis. "We could sign up our members to help out at Careful Procreation. They're struggling, you know, and what's more, they're already making birth control devices available free."

"O.K.," said Robert. "Who else?"

Teresa Miller spoke up. "We could petition city and county administrations to put condom machines in every public restroom. That was suggested for the University at a meeting of Friends Of The Environment a long time ago, but it was rejected at the time as being too radical. It could be that its time has arrived."

"All right," said Robert. "Who else wants to add to the list?"

No one volunteered.

Then Cheryl Mason spoke up. "I think that we have enough resources to begin work on *all three* of the suggestions.

"I so move," said Bart Sandovich.

"I second that," followed Bill Upjohn.

Robert said, "It has been moved and seconded that we begin work on all three of the suggested activities. All in favor, say 'aye.'"

The majority responded.

"All opposed, say 'no.'"

About 3 people said 'no.'

"The motion passes overwhelmingly," said Robert, with a smile on his face. After all, overpopulation and birth control were two topics that were dear to his heart!

Chapter 18

(4 days later)
Saturday, March 2, 1957

Robert was on his way to pick up Susan. It was her birthday today. She was 28 years old. They were going to celebrate by having dinner at Rosellini's 410, one of the upscale restaurants in Seattle. Robert could afford that kind of treat, now that he was the president of Enviro, Inc. He had even purchased a new 1956 Chevrolet, that Susan liked especially well. It was the deluxe BelAir model, with a V-8 engine. He had negotiated a very good price for it: only $2200, $300 below the asking price.

He arrived at Susan's apartment on Capitol Hill about 5 minutes late. He knew that she wouldn't mind that, because she was usually a little behind schedule anyway. When she came to the door, she said, "Hi. I just have to put on some fresh lipstick, and I'll be ready to go."

She was wearing a slightly low-cut, short dress that was one of Robert's favorites.

They drove south to Madison Street, then west on Madison, to 4th Avenue. Robert didn't want Susan to have to walk very far in high heels, so he parked the car at one of the high-priced parking lots. It cost a whole

2, 4, 8...(Destiny of the Human Species)

dollar for the evening, but the convenience of it made up for the price.

For dinner, Susan ordered her favorite, Fettucini Alfredo. Robert, likewise, ordered his favorite, Spaghetti and Meatballs Italiano. He was a plain meat-and-potatoes kind of guy, and seldom ordered anything exotic.

They ate dinner at a leisurely pace. Susan talked of her job with the state social services department. She asked Robert how his company was faring.

He frowned. "Business has picked up a little, but we're still not operating up to our expectations. It's just so hard to convince officials that they need to take steps to cut down on pollution."

"At least your party work is going well, isn't it?" said Susan, pursuing further the topic of his activities.

He smiled. "Yes, that's really going quite well. I have several projects in mind for the party, but it's a good start to find a lot of interest on the part of the membership in promoting birth control. Of all the things we could be doing, that's probably the most meaningful to our goals."

They had been intending to go to the movie *Blue Moon* after dinner, but when they had finished, Susan said, "Why don't we just go back to my apartment, now?"

Robert was pretty sure what that meant.

At the apartment, they watched TV for a short while. Susan was in an unusually passionate mood, and she kissed Robert on the neck and face several times, stroking his thighs at the same time.

"Do you want to go to bed?" he asked.

"Umm hmm," Susan breathed heavily.

They went into her bedroom, hung their clothes on chairs on the opposite sides of the bed, and climbed in. In a moment, Susan had her legs entwined around Robert's.

2, 4, 8...(Destiny of the Human Species)

Their kisses grew more passionate, and soon they were in the extreme embrace.

After they had both experienced the ultimate sensation, Robert fell asleep briefly. When he awoke, Susan was still beside him. She said, "You always fall asleep. I don't think you love me."

"Of course, I love you, Sweetie. Haven't I told you so many times? Don't you know that it's normal for a guy to get sleepy right after he has an orgasm?"

"Well, it makes me feel sort of unloved," said Susan. "Do you love me enough to marry me?"

Robert was startled. In all of the time during their relationship for the past six years, neither one of them had mentioned marriage. It wasn't that he hadn't thought of it, though. He often fancied himself married to Susan. She would be the ideal wife for him. He just had never thought of himself as being ready for marriage. But, here he was 29 years old, and not getting any younger. He had a full-time job, a nice car, a comfortable apartment that was large enough for both of them.

He hesitated briefly, then said, "Of course I love you enough to marry you. Do you love *me* enough to marry *me?*"

"Oh, Robert, of course I do. Is that a proposal?"

Without hesitation this time, he said, "Yes, it is."

Susan wrapped herself around him and squeezed him tightly. "Oh, Robert, I thought that you'd never ask."

"There's one catch," said Robert.

Susan sat up quickly. "What's the catch?"

I can't father any children, you know. Would you be satisfied not to have any?"

"That's hard to say, right now," replied Susan. "Is it possible that we could adopt one or two?"

75

2, 4, 8...(Destiny of the Human Species)

"It's *possible*," he said. "We can talk about it later."

Susan said, "If we can adopt some children, I'm willing to settle for that. But right now I'm not sure that I *would* ever want to adopt any anyway."

"O.K., then. You think about a wedding date," said Robert.

Chapter 19

(5 months later)
Saturday, August 3, 1957

Robert was up at dawn. He didn't have to get up that early, but today was his and Susan's wedding day, and he was restless. Anyway, it was a gorgeous view of the sunrise from his apartment. The sun arose over the Cascade Mountains, and Mount Rainier shone like a white jewel on the southeastern horizon, far beyond Beacon Hill. The sky was absolutely clear, which is often the case in August, probably the most consistent month for good weather in the Seattle area.

Because neither he nor Susan were connected with a specific church, she had decided to hold the wedding in Bellevue, on the other side of Lake Washington, in Green's Chapel Of The Flowers, a non-denominational setting.

The ceremony, which was scheduled to start at 2 p.m., was going to be conducted by Paul Gregovich, a Unitarian minister who had joined the Humanitarian Party, and who steadfastly supported its goals.

Robert looked out his windows, at the sweeping view of the south end of Lake Union, downtown Seattle, and Elliott Bay. The Smith Tower stood out above all of the other buildings on the horizon. It was, after all, the tallest

2, 4, 8...(Destiny of the Human Species)

building in the city, and at one time was the tallest building west of the Mississippi River. He could see Pier 54, where Ivar's, one of their favorite restaurants, was located. Farther to the south, almost in line with Mount Rainier, the Marine Hospital on Beacon Hill cast a long shadow in the morning sun. Immediately below him on the south was the Denny Regrade area, which had been a hill at one time, but which had been levelled years ago by the use of water-pressure.

As he sat mulling over the commitment he was about to make this afternoon, he had no doubts whatsoever. Susan was the perfect mate for him. She was attractive, vivacious, intelligent and, best of all, interested in his work and his political activities.

About 9:30 a.m. the phone rang.

"Hi."

It was Susan. She sounded sleepy.

"Did you just get up?" Robert asked.

"Yes. And I had a very *good* sleep, too. How about you?"

"I was up at the crack of dawn. But I slept o.k. up to that point."

Susan asked, "Do you have any qualms about to-day?"

"Qualms? Not in the least. I think we were meant for each other."

"Me, too," replied "Susan. I have a lot to accomplish, so I'd better get off the phone. I just wanted to see how you were feeling."

"Fine," said Robert.

"All right, then. I'll see you at the chapel." And she hung up.

A few minutes after 2 p.m., the ceremony began. It

2, 4, 8...(Destiny of the Human Species)

was a little late getting started, as most weddings seem to be. Robert was lined up at the front of the chapel with the minister and his attendants. As he surveyed the audience, he could see that it was obviously dominated by people from Enviro, Inc., the Humanitarian Party, Careful Procreation, and the Seattle contingent of the state social services department. His best man was Lowell Jackson, a person whom he had come to trust and admire as a result of Lowell's work in the party. Ushers were Ralph Stone, who worked at Enviro, Inc., and Dave Robbins, who was another staunch member of the party.

As the music began, the first bridesmaid, Ann Lucas came down the aisle. Ann was one of Susan's fellow workers with the state social services department. Next came Sheila MacPherson, who had been in several classes with Susan at the University, and who was also a Sociology major. Finally, Susan's maid of honor, Cheryl Mason, marched in. Cheryl, who was very active in the party, and Susan had become the best of friends as a result of their activities together in the party.

As "Here Comes The Bride" started playing, Susan entered from the back of the sanctuary, on the arm of her father, Joseph Ferguson. She was unforgettable in her flowing, white gown. A few of the people in attendance might have had cause for snickering about her wearing white, but it didn't matter to Robert and Susan. They had cemented a firm relationship over the past few years, and had no doubts that they were right for each other.

After the ceremony, cake and punch were served in the lobby. The usual congratulations were extended to the bride and groom.

After shaking hands with Robert and Susan, Lyle Woodard, one of the best workers in the Humanitarian

2, 4, 8...(Destiny of the Human Species)

Party, said to them, "Well, now I suppose that you'll proceed to have a dozen kids, and counteract all of the efforts of the party to promote a decrease in the birth rate."

Little did Lyle know the truth about their chances of having children.

Chapter 20

(4 months later)
Tuesday, December 17, 1957

Since their wedding in August, Robert and Susan had experienced a four-month-long honeymoon right in their own apartment on Queen Anne Hill. Susan had moved out of her apartment on Capitol Hill, and in with Robert. It was an easy commute for both of them to their places of work downtown. The bliss of new marriage would have almost made them oblivious to the problems of the world if the problems of the world weren't what their jobs were all about.

Tonight's meeting of the Humanitarian Party was going to be exciting for both Susan and Robert. They were going to get reports on the progress made on the activities of the party during the past few months. Also, the party was going to consider moving into some new areas besides promoting birth control. Robert had already had some individual meetings with Lowell Jackson and Jeff Culbertson about proposing some of their favorite projects to the membership, which had already grown to over 100.

After the routine business was out of the way, Robert asked for a report from the Legislative Committee. Rich

2, 4, 8...(Destiny of the Human Species)

LeBlond, the chairman of that committee began his report.

"Our membership letter-writing campaign has gotten off to a good start. Seventy-six of our members have reported writing to their legislators, requesting the establishment of birth control clinics in each county of the state. Our committee also had a private meeting with Representative Lloyd of the 41st District. He's probably the most supportive person in the legislature at this point. He promised to work on a bill to be introduced in the next session."

Robert thanked Rich, then said, "Rob Travis, will you give us a report on the Careful Procreation Committee?"

Rob stood up. "Thirty-seven of our members have already helped out on a volunteer basis at the Careful Procreation office on 15th Avenue. Most have done only clerical work on an occasional basis because they have limited time, but two of our members, Jane Goodwin and Allison Forten, have actually gotten involved in counseling pregnant teenagers, and they have found the work to be very rewarding."

"Thank you, Rob," said Robert. "Teresa Miller, will you give the report of the Committee on Condom Machines?"

Teresa, though frail looking, had a booming voice. She said, "I had individual meetings with the mayors of Seattle and Bellevue, and the Director of King County Health Services. They were all courteous, but non-committal about my suggestion that they consider putting condom machines in all public restrooms in their jurisdictions. They all said that they would bring up the topic with their staffs and get back to me. I'm waiting for them to call."

2, 4, 8...(Destiny of the Human Species)

She paused. Robert started to thank her, "Thank you Ter....."

She continued, "There are still several public officials that I intend to contact about this project, though, and I'm hopeful that I'll get a positive reaction from some of them."

"Thank you for the report, Teresa," said Robert. Then he continued, "It seems like we've made reasonable progress during our first ten months of operation. We still have a nice sum in our treasury, and dues-time will be coming up before long, giving us even more income. The Executive Board has decided to recommend that we expand our activities beyond that of simply promoting birth control. So, at this time, I'll entertain suggestions from the membership about which activities to pursue."

Jenny Conant waved her hand excitedly.

"Jenny," said Robert.

"I'd like to recommend that the Humanitarian Party supplement the efforts of Friends Of The Environment by applying whatever pressure it can in order to get the cities in the Lake Washington drainage basin to work together to stop the flow of sewage into the lake."

Jenny was a former member of Friends Of The Environment, and was the person who originally suggested this project to The Friends.

She went on. "Largely because of the influence of The Friends, the local city and county jurisdictions have tentatively formed a group to study the feasibility of the project. They're calling the group The Municipalities Of Metropolitan Seattle, or Metro in shortened form. They're about to vote on whether to unite in a legally-binding group to work on the sewage project. This party could help to swing the vote by having its members contact the representative in each of their respective areas of residence."

"Well," said Robert, "that sounds like something we could do that wouldn't cost much, but which could have an important result."

Then he continued, "Does anyone else want to suggest a project?"

At that point, Lowell Jackson raised his hand. "Mr. Chairman, I'd like to suggest that the party undertake the project of promoting the legalization of doctor-assisted suicide in cases of pain-wracked terminally ill patients. One of our main goals is to help to improve the quality of life for human beings. Many of these people, in their miserable state, want to have a death with dignity, and not linger on for months or years in an unbearable condition."

"How do you propose we promote the idea of legalized suicide for those people, Lowell," said Robert.

Lowell thought about it for a few seconds, hand on brow.

"We could do several things," he replied. "We could write to our legislators. We could sponsor public speeches on the topic to any groups that were interested. And we could sponsor candidates in the next election who are sympathetic to this cause."

Robert responded, "This sounds feasible, Lowell. The only doubtful part is the sponsoring of the candidates. We aren't yet large enough, and don't yet have enough funds in our treasury to contribute a very large amount to any one candidate. However, we could publicly support them through press releases."

"Well," replied Lowell, "a little help would be better than none."

With that, Lowell sat down.

2, 4, 8...(Destiny of the Human Species)

"Does anyone else want to suggest a project for our consideration?" said Robert.

No one raised a hand.

"Does anyone want to dispute either of the two projects that have been suggested thus far?"

Still no hands.

"Then let's take a vote. All in favor of pursuing the Metro project, raise their hands."

An overwhelming majority voted in favor of it.

"Now," said Robert, "all of those in favor of pursuing the legalization of suicide for the terminally ill, raise your hands."

This time, it wasn't obvious whether more than half had voted.

"Please take a count, Cheryl."

Cheryl counted the raised hands, then said, "I count 64, Mr. Chairman.

"Now," Robert instructed, "All who are opposed to pursuing that project, raise *your* hands."

It appeared that not as many had their hands up this time. Cheryl counted, then said, "I count 53 'no' votes."

"The favorable votes predominate," said Robert, "so we'll adopt that as one of our official projects. That concludes this meeting. It's the last one until January. Everyone have a nice holiday season!"

Chapter 21

At the board meeting of Enviro, Inc., Alan Trumbull, the company accountant, gave his routine financial report. "We're headed for financial trouble if we don't find more work for the company. Our asset/encumbrance ratio is getting weak, and we have to get more contracts soon if we're to avoid laying off anyone."

At that point, Robert said, "The Metro construction project isn't giving us as much work as we had hoped. When the Municipalities of Metropolitan Seattle signed the Metro agreement last October, we assumed that it would result in the need for a lot of environmental studies that would mean contracts for us. But Metro has hired their own staff of environmental biologists to work with their construction engineers."

Then Ralph Stone added emphatically, "It's not just the lack of Metro contracts that is causing our problems, gentlemen. We're having difficulty getting any of the city, county, or state officials to share our concerns about the environment. As you know, we've tried to generate some concern about the garbage disposal problem, the sewage disposal problem, the auto-exhaust problem, air

2, 4, 8...(Destiny of the Human Species)

pollution from the smelter, and numerous other conditions that we all view as impending dangers. However, the solutions to all of those problems have financial implications that the governments aren't willing to undertake. The Metro project is the only one that has made any major progress in this area in regard to safeguarding the environment, and that has happened largely as a result of lobbying by Friends Of The Environment and The Humanitarian Party."

"Well," replied Robert, "Perhaps The Friends and the Party should be a bit more aggressive in lobbying for increased concerns about the environment among the general public."

(The next day)
Tuesday, May 6, 1959

About eighty members of the Humanitarian Party were present when Chairman Robert Welton called the meeting to order.

After the routine business, he called for reports from the standing committees.

"Rob Travis, will you report on the Careful Procreation Committee's activities?"

Rob stood up, and said, "We now have twenty-three members who are part-time counselors at Careful Procreation. Some of them go to other locations besides the 15th Avenue office. In addition, another seventeen members do occasional clerical work on short notice when there is a high clerical load, such as during times of special mailings. Careful Procreation is grateful for the help, and we feel like we're doing something that can have a significant impact on the rate of unwed pregnancies in this area."

2, 4, 8...(Destiny of the Human Species)

"Thank you, Rob. Now, would you give your report, Rich?"

Rich LeBlond arose. His 6'7" frame towered over those who were seated. "The principal activity of the Legislative Committee is currently that of myself and Diane Temple identifying those legislators that are most in agreement with our goals, and then assuring them of our support in their efforts to promote our agenda. We have contributed $30 each to the campaign funds of Representatives Davis and Borden, and Senator Symms. Over sixty of our members indicate that they have written letters to those three legislators, showing support for the idea of birth control clinics in each county. However, most legislators are very cool to the idea of birth control clinics. They contend that the clinics will simply be places where condoms are handed out to teenagers, and that this will result in highly increased promiscuity. On top of that, there is the resistance by that segment of the public that opposes outright the idea of birth control."

Rich sat down, his muscular thighs overlapping the sides of the chair seat.

"Your committee report, please, Teresa," said Robert.

Teresa's disappointment showed. "The Committee on Condom Machines has had little success. None of the officials in the cities in the Puget Sound area are willing to implement the idea of installing condom machines in public restrooms. They all cite high public resistance to it. The general public fears that it would just promote promiscuity among young people."

"Perhaps we need to obtain more government figures on venereal disease and rates of teenage pregnancies to give to those officials," Robert responded. "Thank you

2, 4, 8...(Destiny of the Human Species)

for your efforts, Teresa. We'll try to get that information for your committee to use."

Then Robert continued, "Jenny Conant, will you give us a report on the progress of the sewage diversion program for the Lake Washington drainage basin?"

"Well," began Jenny, "this project is the bright light in our environmental program. Since the Municipalities of Metropolitan Seattle, or 'Metro' as it is commonly known, had its first meeting in October of 1958, extensive progress has been made on plans for one of the greatest sewage diversion programs ever undertaken. If it's implemented as now currently planned, it'll be completed about 1967 or 1968, and will almost completely eliminate the entry of sewage into Lake Washington. Aquatic scientists tell us that our now-polluted lake should completely recover within a year or two of the completion of the project. Our committee members have been in frequent contact with the Metro council members, in order to let them know that we're aware of their progress."

"Thank you, Jenny," said Robert. "It appears that one of our main objectives, that of getting birth control clinics in every county, is meeting with a lot of resistance. Does anyone have a suggestion about what to do to promote the idea of the clinics?"

Len Montgomery raised his hand. "Mr. Chairman, I think that we need to get more aggressive in our promotion of this idea. We might make up some graphic signs about the impact of unwed pregnancies on teenage girls, and carry them in snake-lines in front of some of the city and county administration offices."

"Would you be willing to head up that project, Len?"

"Sure."

"Well, then," said Robert, "who would like to work with Len on that project?"

2, 4, 8...(Destiny of the Human Species)

Six members raised their hands.

"Would you get the names and phone numbers of those who have their hands raised, Cheryl?"

FACTS OF LIFE!

1960 A.D

U.S. Population:
180,700,000 (up 14,800,000 since 1950)

U.S. Municipal Solid Waste:
88,000,000 Tons

Chapter 22

(18 months later)
Sunday, October 8, 1961

Although Robert could have slept in, he arose about 7 a.m. because he was wide awake, and couldn't help but think about the problems at work, as well as the difficulties that the Humanitarian Party was having. Susan was still sleeping. The fog level was below the level of their apartment on Queen Anne Hill, so that the view was obscured, even though there was now enough daylight to see well outdoors.

He opened the apartment door and picked up the Sunday paper. He then settled down in his favorite recliner chair. He scanned the front page, then turned to the editorial page. One of the headlines gave him a jolt!

Radical Party Creates Havoc

The Humanitarian party, under the leadership of well-known environmental radical, Robert Welton, has been asserting itself in even more aggressive ways in recent weeks.

2, 4, 8...(Destiny of the Human Species)

> Two weeks ago, members of
> the party marched in a circle
> in front of the Seattle City Hall
> with graphic, distasteful plac-
> ards depicting abortions of
> unwed women. Then just last
> Wednesday, members of the
> party chained themselves to
> the doors of the King County
> Courthouse to publicize their
> demands that birth control clinics
> be established in each of the
> cities within the county. We're
> appalled at this kind of behav-
> ior. It merely reveals the true
> radical nature of the party.

Robert was stunned to see his party and himself described as "radical." Why didn't the media understand that the party's primary interest was the quality of life of *everyone*, and that those protests which they staged were attempts to help reduce the misery that was resulting from illegitimate births?

By 10 a.m. the fog around Queen Anne Hill was dispersing, and Robert could now see the downtown area. Immediately below their apartment was the location that had been designated for the construction of the 1962 world's fair site. The construction equipment was all idle because it was Sunday. He could see the rising supports for what they were calling 'The Space Needle', a 600-foot tower that was going to have a revolving restaurant on top. Around its base were the foundation works of the various new buildings that were going to house the many exhibits at the fair. The Century 21 Committee, as the fair committee was called, had voted to preserve the existing Armory and Memorial Field, and to incorporate them into the fairgrounds. His and Susan's apartment had an unobstructed view of the site, and they kept track of the weekly progress on the construction.

Susan opened the bedroom door, stretched, and said, "Good morning, dear. How are you feeling this morning?"

"Not too good," replied Robert. "You should see the editorial in this morning's paper."

He handed the paper to Susan.

After perusing the editorial, she said, "I can't believe that the paper would call you a radical! It's really unfair. Let's do something today that's kind of fun, so you can get your mind off it."

"What do you suggest?"

"They say that the salmon are migrating in large numbers through the fish ladder at the Ballard Locks. We could have breakfast at Denny's on Mercer Street, and then go to the locks. It's going to be a sunny day."

After their breakfast at Denny's, they drove over to the locks. There was a large crowd there, watching the locks being alternately filled and emptied, carrying the boats to and from the level of Lake Washington from the level of the saltwater in the Ship Canal. Robert and Susan walked across the bridge to the fish ladder. Looking over the railing above it, they could see fish large and small making their way up the steps of the ladder. It was one of the marvels of nature, this annual salmon migration.

Robert couldn't get his mind off the troubles at work and the difficulties that the party was having.

"Enviro, Inc. is being threatened with bankruptcy, you know, Susan."

2, 4, 8...(Destiny of the Human Species)

"What? No, I didn't know."

"Well, I've been telling you about our difficulties in getting any contracts. People just aren't convinced that we have to protect the environment. They don't realize the many ways that the population in this area is degrading it. Our getting contracts depends on the demand for environmental research studies and problem solving, but there's practically no demand for them."

"I knew that you were having a hard time getting contracts," said Susan, "but I didn't know that the company was near bankruptcy."

"Now there is this problem with the image of the Party. We can't seem to generate any support for our goals."

Susan reminded Robert, "What about your success in getting the region's cities to form Metro? That was a big accomplishment. In a few years, Lake Washington will be fit to swim in again."

"But there are so many other factors threatening the environment that need attention, and nobody's willing to acknowledge them. It all seems so futile."

Chapter 23

(3 months later)
Thursday, January 11, 1962

When Robert got home from work, Susan's car was in the garage. *"Unusual,"* he thought. "She always gets home after I do."

As he entered the door to their apartment, Susan was sitting at the dining room table, looking out the view windows. She turned, and her face seemed drawn.

"I think I'm pregnant!"

Robert was stunned. "What? That's impossible."

"Well, I missed my period last month, and the last two days, at work, I got awfully nauseated. Just like morning sickness, according to my co-worker, Evelyn."

"You haven't been with another man, have you?" he questioned.

"Of course not. How could you even think such a thing?"

"It's only natural to ask," replied Robert. After all, I *am* sterile, have been ever since the vasectomy. I sure couldn't have gotten you pregnant. You'd better make an appointment right away with Dr. Smuthers. Maybe there's some other explanation for your symptoms."

2, 4, 8...(Destiny of the Human Species)

(4 days later)
Monday, January 15, 1962

Again today, Susan was already home when Robert arrived. This time her face was ashen.

"The doctor confirmed today that I'm pregnant. How could that be? I definitely have not had a relationship with another man, Robert!"

"Well," said Robert, "either I've regained my fertility, or this is only the second virgin birth on record. I'd better make an appointment with the doctor who performed the vasectomy."

(4 days later)
Friday, January 19, 1962

This time, Robert was the one with the ashen face. Susan could tell as soon as he entered the apartment that he was greatly troubled.

"The doctor confirmed it! He said that I'm now producing viable sperm. He said that sometimes the sperm tubes grow back together after a vasectomy. So, I guess I'm the father, Susan."

"Oh, Robert, I'm so relieved. I felt that you were convinced that I had been unfaithful."

"But I'm not relieved, Susan," he said. "We can't allow the birth of a baby that could be carrying a defective gene! You've got to get an abortion."

"That's unthinkable, Robert," she asserted.

Robert responded, "Before I agreed to get married, you told me that you didn't care if we couldn't have any children of our own, and that you'd be satisfied adopting children."

"But I didn't know that you could get me pregnant!

2, 4, 8...(Destiny of the Human Species)

Now that I *am* pregnant, I want to have this baby! My biological clock is ticking fast. This is our chance to start our very own family. I'm excited!"

"Look, Susan, you agreed. You *have to get an abortion.*"

"It's out of the question , Robert. Besides, abortion is both illegal and dangerous. Think about my needs and welfare!"

Chapter 24

(8 months later)
Friday, September 14, 1962

Susan was still sleeping. It was 9:15 a.m., and Robert was sitting at the dining room table, looking out over the Century 21 fairgrounds. The Space Needle now dominated the view. The restaurant on top was at an even higher altitude than their apartment.

His doctor had prescribed an anti-depressant about a month ago, because he was so depressed, but the medication didn't seem to help much. Not only was Susan due to give birth in just a few days to a baby that might be carrying his defective diabetes gene, but there were also a lot of problems associated with his work and the party. Enviro, Inc. had been forced to declare bankruptcy in June. The staff's inability to obtain contracts for environmental work had forced them to reorganize. He was out of work, and Susan had to quit her job because the baby was due any day now. The Seattle newspaper had been ridiculing the party relentlessly, and now the *University Daily* was harassing The Friends Of The Environment. He reviewed the latest editorial from the Seattle paper.

2, 4, 8...(Destiny of the Human Species)

Humanitarian Party Continues Self Destruction

The laughing stock in political circles these days is Robert Welton, chairman of the Humanitarian Party, a splinter group that has been trying to promote radical ideology in relation to the environment. Their common method of drawing attention to their causes has been to disrupt the orderly conduct of business at area government administration offices. Some of their favorite causes are the promotion of birth control, demands for unreasonably expensive pollution controls, and legalization of suicide. We think it is time for them to cease their immoral activities.

Robert had decided several days ago that he couldn't take it any longer. It seemed to him that the human race was on a course of self-destruction. Hardly anyone was concerned with the long-term quality of life, or the survival of the species.

When Susan got up about 10 o'clock, Robert announced, "I made reservations for us to have dinner at the Space Needle tomorrow night. I thought that we should have one last special night out."

"What do you mean 'last'?"

"I mean before the baby arrives, Susan. The reservations are for 6:30 p.m so that we can see the sun go down over the Olympic Mountains during our dinner."

"Oh, that *will be special*," said Susan.

2, 4, 8...(Destiny of the Human Species)

(The next day)
Saturday, September 15, 1962

The Space Needle restaurant revolved as they enjoyed their dinner. During the course of their meal, they were able to see the phenomenal view that it offered. On the west, there were the Olympic Mountains and Puget Sound. On the south, the skyline of downtown Seattle, and in the distance, Mount Rainier. To the east, they could see the Cascade Range, almost devoid of snow because the fall snowfall hadn't yet begun. Of course, on the north the view was largely obscured by Queen Anne Hill, but they could even pick out their own apartment when they looked closely.

Midway through dinner, Robert extended his hand across the table, and took Susan's hand tenderly in his. "I love you very much, Susan," he said.

"Oh, I love you, too, Robert. This evening out has meant so much to me. We're going to be pretty busy after the baby arrives, you know."

She had no inkling of what was going to transpire before the night was over. As Robert looked at her, he mentally reviewed his plan, and decided that it was the only alternative.

After their dinner, they drove back to the apartment.

Robert suggested, "Let's watch some TV on our new set." They had recently purchased one of the new, deluxe 19-inch color sets.

"We can watch the Lawrence Welk program. It comes on in 10 minutes," replied Susan, as she went in to put on her robe.

"I'm going to mix us a special celebration drink,"

2, 4, 8...(Destiny of the Human Species)

Robert answered back.

"What kind of drink?" called Susan from the bed-room.

"One that one of the guys at work told me about. You'll like it; it's sweet, the kind you prefer."

Robert took the ingredients for the drink from where he had been hiding them in the back of the sink cabinet. He carefully measured out each one of the three, and methodically mixed them together. Then he poured some into each of their cocktail glasses and carried them over to the coffee table in front of the couch.

When Susan came out in her robe, she sat down beside Robert on the couch, and said, "The drink looks good, dear. I hope it tastes as good as it looks."

The Lawrence Welk show started, and Robert and Susan sat back, sipped their drinks. They especially enjoyed this program, with its musical numbers involving the great hits of the past.

After a few minutes, Susan said, "Dear, I'm feeling a little drowsy. Is it o.k. if I just rest my head on your shoulder?"

"Sure, sweetie." And with that, Robert put his arm around her and held her close. He, too was starting to get drowsy as the hemlock potion pervaded his system. In the space of less than 10 minutes, they both lapsed into eternal sleep.

Part 2

DISSIPATIUM

FACTS OF LIFE!

WORLD POPULATION

Year   Population

1975   4,000,000,000   (Up 1,500,000,000 since 1950.)
1980   4,453,000,000

UNITED STATES POPULATION

Year   Population

1965   194,000,000   (Up 13,300,000 since 1960.)
1970   205,000,000
1975   216,000,000
1980   228,000,000

U.S. MUNICIPAL SOLID WASTE

Year   Tons

1970   122,000,000   (Up 34,000,000 since 1960.)
1980   152,000,000

Chapter 25

(19 years later)
Saturday, October 31, 1981

Lisa was an attractive, dark-haired freshman at the University of Washington. Her lithe, but voluptuous body and model-like face caused her to be an attraction everywhere she went on campus. Although it was early in her freshman year, it looked like she would have no difficulty in getting a date anytime she wanted one.

On this evening, she was going to the annual Halloween Barn Dance at the Kappa Rho fraternity with senior Dave Barnes. Dave was no slouch when it came to looks, either. With dark, wavy hair and chiseled profile, he formed quite a pairsome along with Lisa. She had met him at a social at her sorority, Omega Tau, during the first week of the fall quarter, and they both appealed to each other right away. She was teased a bit about dating a senior, but that didn't particularly bother her.

Dave and Lisa entered the front door of the fraternity house. The doorway had bales of hay stacked high on each side, and was framed with a mock barn door constructed of laths and painted poster board. The two of them fit in with the motif; they had simple garb consisting of the straw hats that Dave had borrowed for them:

2, 4, 8...(Destiny of the Human Species)

a red scarf around the neck, blue jeans, and checkered shirt.

They could hear the country music blaring from the loudspeakers in the dining room.

Lisa shouted in Dave's ear, "I hope they turn down the volume before long. I don't think that I could carry on a conversation with anyone with the music that loud."

Dave shouted back, in her ear, "You don't have to talk with anyone but me, tonight, sweetie." He grabbed her hand, and led her between rows of bundled cornstalks, to the main dining room, which had been vacated of its usual furniture, and was serving as the dance floor.

They were late because Lisa had been asked to work late at her job in the Husky Union Building (HUB) dining room on campus. Several Kappa Rho's that she had previously met at weekend socials at the Omega Tau house were there with their dates, two of whom were also Omega Tau's like Lisa. Kappa Rho pledges, in overalls, were serving as waiters. They weren't allowed to bring dates to fraternity social functions until their pledge period was over.

Ron Graver, the fraternity vice-president was an amateur square-dance caller, and he announced that the next song would be a square-dance tune.

Dave said to Lisa, "This ought to be fun."

She wasn't so sure. She had never square-danced in her life.

But, Ron, knowing that many of the participants had little or no square-dance experience, started out by giving them some simple instructions.

Then, as the music started, Dave and Lisa formed a square with three other couples, and began going through the simple routine that Ron had shown them.

2, 4, 8...(Destiny of the Human Species)

"This is turning out to be easier than I thought it would be," said Lisa.

"I knew you'd enjoy it," Dave replied.

As the evening progressed, it began to get warm inside the frat house. That probably was exacerbated by the presence of all of the jack-o-lanterns that were placed in various locations. Each pledge had been required to carve one. And their candles gave off considerable heat.

Finally, someone opened the patio doors to cool things off, so Dave and Lisa walked out onto the patio, which was also ringed with the grotesque smiles of cleverly-carved jack-o-lanterns, giving an eery light to the scene.

"Having fun?" Dave said.

"Yes, lots," responded Lisa.

As the disc jockey started to play Ann Murray's recording of Tennessee Waltz, they went in and proceeded to do the customary dance steps of slow country music. Dave had his arms around Lisa, with his hands draped behind the back of her waist. She had her arms circled around the back of his neck. It was the usual way to dance to this type of music nowadays, but her foster-mother looked upon it as sinful for unmarried guys and girls to dance that way. Even couples who had just met for the first time danced that way!

After the Tennessee Waltz ended, Lisa said, "Whew, it's really hot in here."

"Well, we could go out to my car and cool off," he said. And then he led her back between the rows of cornstalks, and out onto the street. His car was parked about half a block from the Kappa Rho house.

He held the passenger door open for Lisa. The car was a fairly new 1980 Chevrolet, one of the flashy two-

2, 4, 8...(Destiny of the Human Species)

tone two-door models. She got in, and then he went around to the driver's side and got in.

Dave began the conversation by asking Lisa about her classes for fall quarter.

"I'm not sure of my major at this point," she said, "so I'm just getting some of the requirements out of the way. You know, things like English 101, Biology 101, Sociology 101. You might call me 'the 101 kid.'"

"I went through the 101 period, too," said Dave, "except that I knew, when I started as a freshman, that I wanted to be a pre-med major. My dad's a doctor, you know, and he told me that if I would study medicine, he'd give me a free ride through college as long as I maintained a B average."

"We're both fortunate," said Lisa. "My foster-parents are paying my way, too, except for spending money. I have to earn that myself. That's why I work at the HUB."

She began to shiver from the coolness of the crisp autumn night.

"Here, let me warm you up," said Dave, and he moved closer and put his arm around her.

"*Nice excuse*," thought Lisa.

Dave wasted no time in pursuing the opportunity of the moment. He began to plant soft kisses on Lisa's face and neck, and his hands started to wander over her breasts.

She abruptly pushed him away, and said, "I think we'd better go back inside."

"What's the matter? Are you going to be unfriendly?"

"I think it's a little bit soon to be getting *too friendly*," she replied.

"Well," said Dave, "an unfriendly attitude is going to get you nowhere fast among the fraternity crowd. That kind of reputation travels like wildfire on campus." Then he tried to move closer again.

"Let's go inside," she insisted.

"O.K., but I don't think that you want the word to spread that you're just a tease."

"I've got plenty of time to get serious about boys," she pointed out. "If the fraternity guys can't respect a girl who has high moral standards, that's their problem."

With that, they went back inside and joined the partiers.

Chapter 26

(2 weeks later)
Friday, November 13, 1981

As the Biology 101 lecture ended, Dr. Lehman called to Lisa. "Miss Billings, could I talk to you for a minute?"

She nodded, and walked up to his desk. She was surprised that he already remembered her name from among the hundred or so students in the class.

"You aren't by any chance the daughter of the late Robert Welton, are you?"

"Why, yes," said Lisa, surprised that he would know that. "How did you know?"

"Your father was a student of mine in 1950. I was in my first year in the Biology department that year. He stood out because of his political activities on campus. After he graduated, I kept track of his progress. He got a job in the biology field, you know. Was one of my best students. You have many of his features. I read about the circumstances surrounding the death of him and your mother, and then I later read about how you were adopted by the Billingses."

"I never did know my father," she said, a little embarrassed.

"I know about that, too," replied Dr. Lehman. "I

114

thought a lot of Robert, and was fairly sympathetic to his environmental cause. He was a 'man before his time,' you know. If there is any way I can help you out this year, please let me know."

"I will. I have to hurry now to my English class." Lisa thanked him, then left the lecture hall.

When she got back to the sorority house after the English class, she pulled out the scrapbook that her mom (actually her foster-mother) had made up for her. She turned to the first page, where the article about her real father and mother's death was glued.

RADICAL POLITICIAN DIES
September 16, 1962

Last night, Robert Welton and his wife, Susan, were found near death in their apartment on Queen Anne Hill. Robert was pronounced dead-on-arrival at Harborview Hospital.

Susan, who was pregnant, remained in a coma for several hours, before succumbing at 9:15 this morning. Susan was almost nine months pregnant, and doctors were able to save the surprisingly healthy baby girl by Caesarean section. Police are not sure at this point whether the deaths were a double suicide or a murder-suicide.

The pair died from a lethal dose of chemicals, which they appeared to have consumed voluntarily. The baby girl has been placed under county supervision until she can be placed in a foster home.

2, 4, 8...(Destiny of the Human Species)

(Two weeks later)
Wednesday, December 4, 1981

Again, at the end of Biology 101 lecture, Dr. Lehman called to Lisa Billings. "Do you have time to talk for a few minutes now, Miss Billings?"

"Actually, yes I do. It's just a coincidence, though. My English class for today was cancelled because the instructor has the flu."

"That's good," said Dr. Lehman, "because I wanted to talk to you some more about your father and his philosophies. I was one of the more supportive faculty members for the ideology of the Humanitarian Party."

"What's the Humanitarian Party?" she asked.

"You mean you don't know?" he asked, somewhat surprised. "That was the environmentally-oriented political party that Robert Welton formed in the late 1950's. I suppose the fact that I was a biologist made me more sympathetic to their cause. Most people in the Seattle area thought that Robert was a radical, and that the Humanitarian Party was on the outer fringe of politics."

"But you didn't think so?

"Not necessarily. I thought that they went a little overboard, especially in respect to some of their protest tactics. But their basic goals were respectable and logical. They essentially wanted to improve the quality of life for humans. Some of their methods for attaining that turned off a lot of people. Those same methods today wouldn't seem particularly radical. They held a lot of peaceful protests and sit-ins, the kind that are pretty commonplace now."

Lisa asked, "Do you think if my father were alive now, his ideas would be accepted by the general public?"

"Probably," answered Dr. Lehman. "You see, the

2, 4, 8...(Destiny of the Human Species)

publication of Rachel Carson's book, *Silent Spring*, in 1962 opened the eyes of a lot of people to the kind of environmental damage that was resulting from chemical pollution of the water and atmosphere. That book discussed primarily the effects of a chemical called 'DDT', but it left implications about the potential hazards of industrial wastes in general. That might be called the official beginning of the environmental movement."

"I think that I might want to declare an Environmental Science major," Lisa said. "It's a pretty hot topic right now, and I think that people with expertise in that field should be able to find work quite easily."

"I agree," concurred Dr. Lehman.

"Well, thanks for the chat, Dr. Lehman. I'll see you in class on Friday."

Chapter 27

(One day later)
Saturday, November 14, 1981

"Mom, did you know that my father was the leader of a political party called The Humanitarian Party?" Lisa asked.

Susan addressed her foster mother as "mom" because she had never known her biological mother. "Mom," or Cheryl Mason Billings, had been Susan Welton's best friend. Shortly after Susan died, Cheryl and her husband, Brad, had adopted baby Lisa.

"Why, yes, dear," answered Cheryl. "Actually, I was on the executive board of the party for a time."

"Was my father called a radical by some people?"

"Yes, that's true, Lisa," Cheryl said. "He was a man before his time. Many of the policies that he advocated are now more acceptable, although some are still considered to be at least unconventional."

"What kinds of things did he believe in?"

Cheryl stepped over to the bookcase at the side of the living room. She pulled a somewhat worn book off one of the shelves, and removed some folded papers from inside it. "I've never before felt inclined to show this to you," she said. "But, I guess it's time."

2, 4, 8...(Destiny of the Human Species)

Cheryl then handed the papers to Lisa. The top page was entitled "The Goals of the Humanitarian party." Lisa read on, absorbing the information with a mixture of astonishment and tremulousness.

After reading the complete list, Lisa sighed deeply. "Well, he had some really far-out ideas, didn't he?"

Cheryl replied, "Some of them don't seem as 'far-out' now as they did when he was alive. Of course, even now some of them are resisted by the majority of the populace. Your father was a kind man, Lisa, one who never did anything to intentionally hurt anyone, as far as I know. He felt that the human race was bent on a course of destroying itself and all other life unless it adopted those principles."

"Well," said Lisa, "I'll read them again when I'm in a better mood. Right now I'm tired, and not very receptive to any 'radical' ideas."

Chapter 28

The phone rang. Lisa picked it up and answered, "Zoology Department, Lisa Billings speaking. How may I help you?"

Lisa's shift as the receptionist in the Zoology Department was just about over for the day. She glanced at the clock as the caller asked to speak to Dr. Williams, the instructor for Zoology 127. It was 4:30 p.m., only a half hour before she could leave and start getting ready for her big date with Hal Joplin. Hal was planning to treat her to a birthday dinner at the Space Needle.

Lisa was now in her third year as an Environmental Science major. After she finished the Biology 101 class in 1981, Dr. Lehman had found this great job for her, so that she could make some extra spending money to supplement the basic funds provided for her college expenses by her mom and dad. The job also provided her with great contacts with a lot of people in the environmental field, and enhanced her opportunities to discuss and explore the principles that her biological father, Robert Welton, had espoused before his death in 1962.

Hal picked up Lisa at her apartment on 13th Avenue,

2, 4, 8...(Destiny of the Human Species)

just off University Way, at 6:30. "We're scheduled for dinner at 7, so I guess we'll have to hurry!" he said.

Hal was just one of several guys that Lisa dated from time to time. Her striking appearance led to no shortage of potential dates. In fact, attentive men were often a bother to her — guys who valued a girl's looks more than her mind. She had no difficulty in striking up a conversation with just about any man that she met, but she was selective about whom she dated. She wasn't ready for an advanced relationship with anyone yet.

As they were led to their table and sat down, Hal said, "You look great tonight. Actually, you look great every time I see you. I wish I could see you more often."

Lisa thought for a moment, evaluating Hal's statement. *"Should I be flattered by that comment, or is Hal just another guy who's interested primarily in sex? "*

The waiter asked whether they wanted a cocktail before dinner. "I think I'll have a Vodka Collins," Lisa responded. "I'm 21 years old today, so I might as well celebrate it. But only one."

Lisa generally avoided drinking alcoholic beverages. Although she just today reached the legal drinking age, there was no shortage of those types of drink at the frat houses around the campus. Once in a while she would sip a cocktail or a glass of beer, but only a sip, because she was well acquainted with the fact that guys felt that if they could get a date drunk, it would be easier to end up in bed with them.

"It was nice of you to bring me here for dinner, Hal," she offered. "Although you aren't aware of it, I'm sure, this is the place where my biological mother and father had their last meal before they died".

"Oh, Lisa, I'm *sorry!* If I had known that, I would've suggested some other restaurant for dinner."

2, 4, 8...(Destiny of the Human Species)

"Don't let it bother you, Hal. It doesn't bother me. Actually, I never knew my biological mother and father. They died the day that I was born."

"That probably makes dining at this place even more painful. I'm sorry for bringing you here," said Hal.

"No. I'm really sort of glad that we're eating here tonight. In the last couple of years, I've been studying the lives of my parents, and being exposed to places they went or things they did doesn't bother me."

Hal looked quizzical. "How did they die?" he asked. "I thought that your mom and dad were your biological parents."

"No. Mom and Dad adopted me when I was only about two months old. Did you ever hear of Robert Welton?"

"No," Hal replied. "Was he well-known?"

"I don't know if 'well-known' is an accurate description, but apparently there were quite a few people in the Seattle area who knew about him during the last few years of his life," she began. Then, she went on to give a sketchy description of Robert Welton's philosophy and political activities.

Meanwhile, the waiter took their order.

"Well," said Hal, "I guess that explains a lot about something I was wondering about. This club that you're secretary of on campus, The Humanitarians, has caused quite a stir among the student body. In fact, some of the guys in my frat chuckled when I told them that I was dating you. They've gotten the word that you're a little 'radical'; they've even used the word *weird* a time or two. I told them not to believe the gossip that they hear, that you're really a lovely person, and fun to be with. They laugh and tell me that I'm going to get the same kind of

2, 4, 8...(Destiny of the Human Species)

reputation as you have if I continue dating you. They're afraid it'll reflect on the fraternity."

"I'm glad that you don't let their opinion of me keep you away," sighed Lisa. "A couple of the guys that I used to date haven't called me lately, and I think that it could be because of my club activities. Some guys just can't handle a serious topic of conversation."

After dinner, Hal and Lisa went to the Top Of The Hilton for a few minutes of dancing. Then he drove her back to her apartment. He walked her to the door. She kissed him lightly on the cheek, and said, "Goodnight, Hal. Thanks for the lovely evening."

"Aren't you going to invite me in?" he asked.

"Not tonight, Hal. I think it's not wise to have guys come into my apartment."

"Well, jeez, Lisa, you ought to be more friendly to a guy that treated you to a dinner at the Space Needle. I'd better tell you that your club activities aren't the only thing that turns guys off. The word has also gotten around that you're just a tease. You won't let any guy get beyond your front door, or beyond 'first base' as they say."

"Goodnight, Hal."

Hal shrugged his shoulders and headed back for his car in disgust.

Lisa entered the apartment, locked the front door, and proceeded to get ready for bed. It had been a long day, she was tired, and on top of that, Hal's comments depressed her. She wanted to get as much rest as possible during the next two weeks, because the Fall Quarter began on October 3rd.

Chapter 29

(Four weeks later)
Monday, October 17, 1983

Seattle was experiencing an unusually warm and dry October, the kind that came around only every five or six years. Lisa basked in the sun on a ledge in front of Johnson Hall while waiting for her 1:20 p.m. Limnology class to begin. Limnology, the study of lakes, was just one of several courses that were required during the junior year of the Environmental Science major.

As she sat in the warmth of the mid-day sun, John Spencer approached. "Hi," he offered.

"Hi," Lisa replied.

"You enjoying the Limnology class?"

"So far," said Lisa. "I never before realized that lakes had so many different factors that affected their purity and productivity."

"It's been an eye-opener for me, too," replied John. "Here we are, studying one small segment of the environment, and I'm beginning to think that a person could spend a whole lifetime just on this one subject."

Lisa had met John in the Limnology class on the first day that it convened in early October. At that time, he happened to take a seat next to her in the classroom. They had only exchanged pleasantries on that day, but since then their conversations had gotten more and more detailed and personal. John didn't appear to be interested only in Lisa's looks, the way a lot of other guys did. He was able to carry on an interesting conversation on just about any topic that she brought up. In addition, he could initiate an interesting conversation very easily, too.

About 1:15 p.m., Lisa and John walked into the classroom and took their seats. The next hour was spent in listening to a fascinating lecture by Dr. Schonstein on the topic of temperature-layering of the water in lakes. At the end of the class, Lisa said ,"John, would you be interested in attending a meeting of The Humanitarians tonight?"

John looked at her questioningly. "The Humanitarians. That's that radical environmental club, isn't it?"

Lisa squirmed a little. "Well, some people on campus call it 'radical,' I guess, but it's just the kind of club that an Environmental Science major like you would enjoy. A large portion of our approximately seventy-five members are Environmental Science majors, too. I'm the secretary, you know!"

John looked surprised! "No, I didn't know that."

"We're meeting tonight and the third Monday of every month in Johnson Hall, Room 120, at 8 p.m. I think that you ought to come. We discuss just about any event or situation that affects the environment of living things. I think that you'd have fun."

"Well, o.k. I'll see you there."

(4 days later)
Friday, October 21 1983

As the Limnology class ended, John Spencer came up to Lisa as she was about to exit the doorway to the

125

classroom. "You were right. I enjoyed the meeting last Monday night. Your club isn't as radical as some of the campus rumors indicate it to be. In fact, the word *radical* doesn't even fit. It seems to me that the pollution issue that you discussed at the meeting was fitting. The argument that both sides presented seemed to be completely logical. I'd like to learn more about the club's overall goals. Maybe I'll become a full-time member."

"I have a list of our goals right here in my three-ring binder," said Lisa. "I never know when someone who finds out my role in the club will challenge me about it's being radical. So I give that type of person a list of the goals. They usually back off after they read it, and admit that it doesn't look all that radical."

Lisa opened her binder and removed a printed sheet. She handed it to John.

He scanned it quickly.

Goals of The Humanitarians

1. To promote the maximization of quality of life for all human beings, and to minimize pain and suffering of all human beings.

2. To promote the humane treatment of all animal life.

"It looks pretty simple and logical to me," he said.

"That's what most people say when they read it," replied Lisa.

"You're one of the most interesting girls that I have ever met, Lisa," John offered.

Lisa thought. *"Hmmm. I've heard that before. It sounds like an old fraternity line."* But it just could be that John was

2, 4, 8...(Destiny of the Human Species)

different. After all, they had had some fairly serious conversations about various aspects of life.

"I thought maybe you'd like to go to the Husky-Stanford football game with me tomorrow. After the game, we could have a sandwich at Doug's Coffee Shop."

Lisa mulled over the offer. Could she afford the time? She *did* have a test in her Soc. 212 class on Monday. But, she could study for that most of the day on Sunday. "Sure. That sounds like fun. You can meet me at my apartment about 12 noon. Then we'll walk down to the stadium. I have an ASB pass for the game. You have one too, don't you?"

"You bet." He took down the address of her apartment, and they parted company.

(The next day)
Saturday, October 22, 1983

The Husky-Stanford game was a rout, 35 to 7, in favor of the Huskies. The unusually warm, dry weather had continued, making the afternoon in the football stands very enjoyable. Lisa detested sitting in the rain for a football game. Last year, it rained for almost every home game, and she gave up attending after the first two.

After the game, Lisa and John walked to Doug's Coffee Shop. John offered to pay, but Lisa insisted on 'dutch treat'. She didn't want to get herself in the position of feeling obligated to anyone she knew for as short a time as she had known John.

Lisa ordered a club sandwich on rye, and John ordered a hamburger. As they sipped their coffee and consumed the sandwiches, John said, "I was surprised at how innocuous the list of Humanitarian club goals is. From rumors that I had heard amongst the students in my

127

2, 4, 8...(Destiny of the Human Species)

dorm, I was expecting something a lot more extreme. Promoting quality of life of people and humane treatment of animals seems pretty logical and down to earth. Of course, I realize that many of the students that I meet in my classes seldom think about those kinds of topics. Any thoughts of that type may seem 'radical' to guys whose thoughts center primarily on who their next date is going to be, or the rushing statistics of the league running-backs."

"Well," replied Lisa, "most people think the way you do about our major goals. It's when they find out the details about some of our methods of achieving the goals that they begin to wonder about us."

"Like what kind of details?"

"Actually, one of the most controversial is our aggressive advocacy of birth control, and our fervent support of organizations that promote birth control."

"I'll go along with that. Are there any that are more controversial than that?"

Lisa thought for a second, then said, "Some of our members would like to promote a few more controversial concepts than that, but we're afraid that our overall goals would be rejected if we publicly advocated anything more extreme than birth control."

John got up, and pulled out Lisa's chair for her. "I've got to get back to the dorm. I have to spend some time on my report for my Embryology class. Tomorrow, I have to work on some embryo slides with the microscope. The time that they give you in the regular lab sessions just isn't enough for me to get all of the lab work done."

"I know what you mean," said Lisa, recalling the many extra hours that she had spent in the Embryology lab last spring. "You don't have to walk me back to my apartment," she said. "I don't mind going back by myself.

2, 4, 8...(Destiny of the Human Species)

That way, you can save yourself some time."

John nodded in agreement. That made Lisa think that here was an unusual guy: he wasn't trying to make his way into her apartment, where he could pursue romantic inclinations. At least not yet!

Chapter 30

Today was the beginning of Winter Quarter at the University of Washington. As Lisa munched some toast and sipped orange juice for breakfast, she looked over her schedule.

Winter Quarter, 1984
Student: Lisa Billings, #2237564

Class	No.	Sect.	Room	Days	Time	Credits
German	102	B	Dn 203	MWF	8 a.m.	3
Bacteriol.	111	M	HS 334	MWF	10 a.m.	3
Bacteriol.	Lab.	C	HS 302	TTh	10 a.m.	2
Env.Sci	.236	G	Rip 133	MF	1 p.m.	2
BusLaw	112	A	Sm 124	TTh	2 p.m.	2
Chem.	235	L	Bag 133	MWF	2 p.m.	3
Chem.	Lab	H	Bag 221	MW	3 p.m.	2

A chill engulfed Lisa. *"A heavy load this quarter,"* she thought. But her adviser, Dr. Lowell, approved it, because she felt that Lisa's academic ability should be

2, 4, 8...(Destiny of the Human Species)

challenged. Lisa was trying to avoid having to go to summer school at any time, because she needed the complete break from class routines in the summer, in order to recuperate from the school year's hectic schedule, and also to put in more hours at her receptionist's job, so that she would have enough spending money.

After breakfast, Lisa put her books in her backpack and headed off in the chilly air to the first session of her German 102 class. She thought to herself, *"An eight-o'clock on Monday morning isn't exactly everybody's dream class!"*

About two minutes before 2 p.m. on the same day, Lisa entered the Environmental Science classroom. The first session involved mainly a preview of the quarter's topics, and handing-out of supplementary printed materials that would be needed during the course. While all of that was going on, Lisa spied John Spencer on the other side of the room. He had noticed her, too. She hadn't seen him since before Winter break, and was eager to see how his vacation had worked out. The last time she saw him, he was planning to ski-bum to Vail, Colorado during the break. He had very little money for luxuries or vacations, but had joined together with three other college buddies to share the expenses of driving to Vail. They were going to try to find a few odd jobs there, in order to pay for their lift tickets.

After class, John came over to her, and said, "You're looking good. Did you have a nice vacation?"

"Boring but relaxing," replied Lisa. "My mom and dad insisted that I help them entertain various out-of-town guests that came and went during the holidays. It was fun, but not exciting. Did your trip turn out the way you had been hoping?"

2, 4, 8...(Destiny of the Human Species)

"It was great. It turned out that the ski resort needed replacement lift helpers, so we ended up making more money than we spent. The skiing was fabulous. It's hard to get back to classes now. Would you like to get a cup of coffee or Coke with me at the HUB?"

The invitation pleased her, but she said, "Sorry, I have to hurry to get to my Organic Chem class. But I'll take a rain check."

With a wave, she walked off in the direction of Bagley Hall. *"Too bad,"* she thought. *"If I didn't have a chem class after each Environmental Science class, I'd get more chances to visit with John."* But it surprised her that such a thought would enter her head. She had never before actually looked forward to frequent encounters with any of the guys that she had met. Of course, she sometimes eagerly anticipated dates with some of them, but only because it offered relief from regular routines. John was a different kind of guy from the norm. He wasn't at all self-centered, and he was better looking than the average man on campus. He hadn't aggressively pursued her since they first met in October. In fact, he hadn't paid her as much attention as she would have liked. Again, this thought was of a new kind for her.

(One week later)
Monday, January 16, 1984

Precisely at 8 p.m., Eli Roberts, the president of The Humanitarians brought the meeting to order. After the routine opening procedures, Eli introduced the evening's speaker, Gerald Watts, of Careful Procreation (CP). Watts proceeded to thank the club members for their support for CP - both financial and demonstrative. Although The Humanitarians' membership was comprised largely of relatively non-affluent students, they nevertheless had been able to make a small donation each quarter to CP. Their most effective support, however, was the series of discussions about CP which they sponsored, and their signing-up of volunteers to help out in CP clinics.

First Watts reviewed both the major goals and activities of Careful Procreation for those not completely acquainted with them. Then he went into some details about each goal and activity - the kind of thing that would only be presented to an obviously interested group like The Humanitarians.

Then Watts said, "Careful Procreation's programs and influence are expanding at a rate that exceeds our most optimistic expectations. However, we have encountered one major point of contention between our organization and a large percentage of the general population in the Seattle area. That is our belief in the right of women to terminate pregnancies through abortion. What most people don't realize is that abortion is a choice of *last resort* when we are counselling pregnant women. Our primary goal is that of maximizing the quality of parenting, with the resulting enhancement of standard of living of children and assurance of an upbringing and preparation for life that will increase the promise of a happy, healthy life beyond infancy and adolescence. One of our main goals is to help prevent pregnancy among people who are not qualified or ready for parenthood. But, if a woman gets pregnant, and the circumstances surrounding the expectant mother are such that inadequate care for an infant is almost unavoidable, then, and only then, do we counsel for consideration of abortion. This limited application that we make of the concept of abortion is skewed by the news media and pro-life organizations, so that the general public tends to ignore all of the positive things we do to make life better for people."

"What could The Humanitarians do to help the situation, Mr. Watts?" said a voice from the back of the room. Lisa Billings was in attendance, and she was surprised to observe that the voice was that of John Spencer. He had been attending club meetings sporadically since October, but had not, thus far, participated actively.

Gerald Watts replied, "You could do a variety of things. We have prepared leaflets that emphasize our major goals, and which demonstrate that abortion plays only a minor role in our program. Your members could help to distribute those leaflets among people of college age in this area. Another thing that you could do would be to hold a campus-wide meeting on the topic of the good things that CP does to help improve quality of human life — I mean the non-controversial things that we do. And, third, since your influence on campus is growing, you could help by simply continuing to recruit members and continue to do the positive things that your club does to stimulate interest in the environment and quality of life."

Gerald Watts then thanked the group for inviting him to speak, and took his seat in the front row. Eli thanked him, then asked for a motion to adjourn the meeting.

As the crowd filed out of the exits to the room, John sidled alongside Lisa. "Want to go have a cup of coffee?"

Lisa thought about her Bacteriology lab report that was due the next day, and apologetically said, "Sorry. I'd like to very much, but I have a lab report that I still have to finish tonight in order to hand it in tomorrow. It seems like I'm always turning down your invitations. Believe me, I'd *really* like to have coffee with you. Let's do it some other time, *soon*."

John nodded, "Some other time, soon," and they went their separate ways.

Chapter 31

(3 months later)
Thursday, April 19, 1984

The phone rang four times before Ramona, Lisa's roommate, answered.

"Hi, this is John Spencer. Is Lisa there?"

"She's in the shower, John. Can I have her call you back?"

"Sure," said John. "My number is 623-4553."

"O.k.; she should be out of the shower in five or ten minutes," said Ramona.

When Lisa emerged from the bathroom, bundled in a terry-cloth robe, Ramona said, "John Spencer called. He wants you to call him back. His number's there on the end table."

"John Spencer? He's never called me here before. I wonder what's on his mind."

After blow-drying her hair, she sat down and dialed John's number.

"Dorm C, Kyle Kimura," said a high-pitched voice.

"Would you call John Spencer to the phone, please?" Lisa requested.

"Sure. I'm his roommate. I know right where he is. Hang on a second."

2, 4, 8...(Destiny of the Human Species)

Lisa could hear the typical sounds of a men's dorm rec room in the background: the click-click of a Ping-Pong ball; raucous laughter now and then. Then footsteps approaching.

"This is John Spencer."

"Hi, this is Lisa Billings. You called?"

"Yes," said John a bit shyly. I haven't seen you yet this quarter, since we don't have any classes together. And, of course, there was no meeting of The Humanitarians this month because of Spring vacation. So, I was wondering if you would like to take in a downtown movie with me on Saturday night."

John was right. They hadn't seen much of each other for the past month. During Winter quarter they had been able to have a Coke or coffee at the HUB now and then because John had a different chemistry class the same hour as hers in Bagley Hall. They encountered each other now and then after class on Fridays, and since they both had the ensuing hour free, they would slip over to the HUB. John had proved to be a very pleasant conversationalist, particularly because he and Lisa shared many of the same interests, and had experienced many of the same classes during the past two-and-a-half years.

She was delighted that he had called her. "Sure," she said. "I'll look forward to it."

After Lisa hung up, Ramona queried her. "Who is John Spencer?"

"He's a guy who's an Environmental Science major. I'm sure I must have mentioned him some time or other. Don't you remember? I went to a football game with him last fall."

"Oh, *that* John. The one who ignores you most of the time," said Ramona.

"I've never said he ignores me," Lisa flashed back. "I

2, 4, 8...(Destiny of the Human Species)

only said that he hasn't acted as interested in me as a lot of the other guys I meet in my classes."

"I think that bothers you," said Ramona.

(2 days later)
Saturday, April 21, 1984

John arrived at the apartment about 6:15. He announced, "I brought the movie section of the newspaper. We can pick out the one that you want to see."

Lisa looked surprised. "I thought we would just walk over to the Neptune, and see whatever is playing there," she said.

"Well, ordinarily that might be the case, but my roommate, Kyle lent me his car for the night. So we can go to whatever theater meets your fancy."

Together they looked over the movie listings.

"Have you seen *Terms of Endearment*? I hear that it's really good. Shirley MacLaine got the Oscar for Best Actress in it," said Lisa. "But, it's clear over at the SeaTac Theater. And besides that, it's probably pretty expensive."

"No problem tonight!" said John. "As long as I have the loaner car, we can get there o.k., and I'm treating for the admission, too. My dad sent me twenty dollars for my birthday."

"Do you think we can make it by the 7:30 starting time?" asked Lisa.

"I'm sure that we can," replied John.

On the way to the movie, John was preoccupied with his driving, and said very little. But silence with him didn't bother her as much as it did around some dates. She remembered the saying that she had received in a

138

2, 4, 8...(Destiny of the Human Species)

fortune cookie: "True friendship exists when silence between two people is comfortable."

During the movie, they sat as close together as the lounge seating would permit, but John never once reached over for her hand like most of her previous movie dates had done. She was just slightly aware of his shoulder brushing against hers now and then.

On the way home from the movie, John suggested that they stop at Dick's Drive-in for a burger and shake. Lisa was agreeable to that idea, and as they sat consuming their food, Lisa said, "Your roommate must be a trusting soul, to let you use his car like this. He sounded very young on the phone, too."

John responded with a chuckle. "Oh, Kyle? His last name's Kimura. He's of Japanese ancestry. A real brain. Graduated from high school two years early, and enrolled in Environmental Science. We have a lot of the same classes. He's a physical exercise fanatic — works out in the weight room every day of the week."

Then John changed the subject. "The elections of the officers for The Humanitarians for next year will be coming up soon. Have you thought of running for office?"

"This may surprise you, but I've been thinking of running for president," Lisa said haltingly.

"That's a great idea," said John. "You're well respected among the membership. Besides that, the knowledge that you've built up about the environment and environmental problems is as extensive as just about anyone on campus. I think you'd be a shoo-in!"

"My mom's afraid that I'll end up being ostracized by the mainstream of students on campus, and that I might hurt my chances of getting a good job after I graduate.

2, 4, 8...(Destiny of the Human Species)

After all, I *do graduate* in just a little over a year, you know."

"Nonsense. For every employer that might be turned off by your activities, there'll be two or three environmentally oriented companies that would *love* to have you on their staff. You have the grades, the experience — and the *looks, too.*"

"What do looks have to do with anything?" asked Lisa.

"Well, you know what I mean. Companies want brains, but beauty is a close second, when it comes to selecting employees."

That was the first time in a long time that John had said or done anything to indicate to Lisa that he was even slightly aware of her good looks. *"Maybe he's normal, after all,* she thought to herself.

After they had finished their burgers and shakes, John drove her back to the apartment. He walked her to the door, and said, "Goodnight, Lisa. I had a great time."

"I did, too," she replied. At that point, she half expected him to give her a goodbye kiss, but he just ambled back to the car.

When Lisa slipped inside the apartment and locked the door, she found Ramona sitting on the couch, reading a paperback novel.

"Did you have a good time?" Ramona said.

"It was nice," said Lisa, "but John is sure shy. He didn't even try to kiss me goodnight."

"I still think he bothers you — in a nice way, I mean."

Chapter 32

Eli Roberts opened the meeting at 8 p.m. sharp. A larger than usual portion of the registered membership had arrived at the auditorium in Meany Hall. That was probably because the meeting was to be devoted to campaign speeches by those running for the various offices of The Humanitarians for 1984-85. Also, the speeches were to be followed by question-and-answer sessions with each candidate, and then those present would get to vote for their selections before the meeting ended.

Only two candidates had filed for the position of president: Lisa Billings and Carol Jennings. Although they both supported the general goals of the club, Carol was less inclined toward confrontation than Lisa was. For example, on the issue of industrial pollution, Carol preferred meeting with the executives of local industrial firms to inform them of environmental concerns associated with their activities, and to find out whether there were any minor modifications in their manufacturing processes that might eliminate the environmental problems. On the other hand, Lisa advocated more aggressive tactics, such as petition drives to firmly persuade those

kinds of companies to change damaging processes. She
was even willing to organize picket lines, if necessary.

After Carol had finished her speech, Lisa took the
podium. She said, "John Spencer is passing out the printed
statement of my platform. I think that in comparing it
with the platform that Carol has presented, you'll understand why I should be your preference to lead this organization for the next year."

She gave the audience a few moments to scan the
handout.

LISA BILLINGS FOR PRESIDENT
Platform Statement

1. I fully support the major goals of The Humanitarians.

2. Activities which I intend to promote and pursue if
   I am elected president of The Humanitarians are as
   follows:

   a. Petition drives and/or picket lines to convince
      companies that produce environmentally harmful
      waste products that they should strive to re-
      duce those harmful materials.

   b. Active and aggressive support of legislative
      candidates who have proved that they are in-
      terested in sponsoring legislation that will help
      to protect the environment.

   c. Financial and political support for organizations
      that promote family planning. One of the most
      notable is Careful Procreation.

2, 4, 8...(Destiny of the Human Species)

d. Support for legislation that would provide for birth-control counselling available to every student above the elementary school level.

e. Support for the idea of free health care for all Americans.

f. To support legislation providing for the punishment of anyone convicted of causing unnecessary pain or suffering of any animal.

After ample time for everyone in the audience to scan the handout, Lisa said, "I don't think that it will be necessary for me to give a lengthy speech. We can just go directly to the questioning. Does anyone have a question to ask me?"

Numerous hands were raised. Lisa wasn't surprised. She called on a girl near the back of the room.

"In conjunction with the last item on your platform, do you feel that animal experimentation in our Health Sciences Department should be abolished?" the girl asked.

"That would be an extreme interpretation of what I intend to support," Lisa answered. "I think that there are situations in which a certain amount of pain must be inflicted on a lower form of animal life in order to develop methods of improving the quality of life of human beings. But, we should make sure that the process involves the least amount of animal suffering that is possible to insure. If I had to choose between enhancing the quality of life of humans or rats, I would choose humans every time."

A chuckle arose among members of the audience.

"That man in the second seat from the end, over there," said Lisa, pointing.

2, 4, 8...(Destiny of the Human Species)

The young man stood and said, "Don't you think that organizing picket lines could damage the image of our club?"

"Some people already consider us to be a radical organization," she replied. "Among that group, our image couldn't sink any lower. No, we have to take unconventional action when companies that damage the environment form unyielding positions. One of our biggest tasks is to publicize the ways in which environmental damage affects all citizens, and to gain public support for our methods in that way."

There were only three hands still raised by now. Lisa called on a primly dressed young woman in the front row.

"I think that your idea about birth control counselling in the schools is abhorrent. Don't you see that a program like that will give the message that we condone illicit sex among young students? We should be promoting the idea of abstinence, not birth control."

"Actually," responded Lisa, "there's a lot of promiscuity among students in the middle schools and high schools already. The statistics on teen pregnancies confirm that. It appears that many students *don't even know what causes pregnancy!* In addition to that group, there are girls who want to have a baby just to have someone who gives them unconditional love, and who depends on them. They need counselling to make them aware of the responsibilities that fall upon an unmarried teenage mother."

There were widespread nods of agreement to Lisa's last statement.

No more hands were raised, so she sat down, and observed while the candidates for lesser positions gave their speeches.

At the end of the campaigning activities, all club

members in attendance were given ballots for voting. After the ballots had been collected, President Eli Roberts and Vice-president Wally Boehmer counted the votes. Then Eli wrote the results on the chalkboard at the side of the stage.

President:
Carol Jennings – 43
Lisa Billings – 72

Vice-president:
Joy Lucas – 39
Raul Montez – 71

Secretary:
Julie Johnson – 56
Jay Schwartz – 63

Treasurer:
William Bays – 121

A large portion of the audience clapped, and then almost everyone arose to leave even before Eli could say, "Meeting Adjourned!"

Several people came to the stage to the front of the auditorium to congratulate the winners. John Spencer walked up to Lisa and said, "Congratulations!" Then he leaned over and kissed her lightly on the cheek, a bold move, indeed, for *him*.

(2 days later)
Wednesday, May 18, 1984

News Item From A Seattle daily newspaper:

2, 4, 8...(Destiny of the Human Species)

Our University reporter informed us that history is repeating itself on the University of Washington campus. A club called The Humanitarians on Monday elected Lisa Billings as their president for the 1984-85 academic year. Lisa happens to be the daughter of Robert Welton, who died in 1962.

Our older readers might recall that Welton was a radical student activist while at the University. He was president of an environmental group there, and later formed an offshoot political party called the Humanitarian Party. Welton eventually became the laughing stock of politics in this area, and committed suicide as a result of his depression that followed.

Chapter 33

(7 months later)
Saturday, December 1, 1984

Lisa was waiting for Mel Favre to pick her up. He had said that he would be there at 7 o'clock, but it was now ten after, and he hadn't yet arrived.

She reviewed the events of the past couple of months as she sat by the front window of the apartment. Fall quarter had begun very well, indeed! Most of her classes were in her major field because of the fact that she was in her senior year. All of the Environmental Science, or "EnSci" classes were especially interesting, but along with them, she had to take an advanced Biochemistry course and an advanced Statistics course. The latter two had proved to be less boring than she had anticipated, however. The advanced Biochemistry turned out to relate directly to her EnSci classes. And, the advanced Statistics class made her aware of the desirability of conducting life and career by using probabilities to the best advantage, and by not always trying to "beat the odds", as some of her acquaintances seemed to always be doing.

In EnSci 321, she had met Mel. Subsequently, he had attended both of the monthly meetings of the Humanitar-

ians, and had participated substantially in those meetings. He seemed to have a good head on his shoulders,
despite the fact that her roommate, Ramona, thought that
he was "kind of rough around the edges." It was true that
his language was a bit crude at times, but he was basically
a kind and gentle person. After having a Coke at the HUB
on several different occasions between classes, they had
dated twice in the last month. He knew how to give a date
the right amount of attention and luxury, in addition to
being able to converse about the kinds of topics that Lisa
was interested in. He obviously was attracted sexually to
Lisa, unlike John Spencer, who continued to be a faithful
friend and fellow member of the Humanitarians. John
just didn't seem to be attracted to Lisa the way that most
other guys on campus were. Although she was sometimes aggravated by the wolf-whistles and suggestive
comments that even total strangers made to her, she
occasionally wished secretly that John would show at
least a little bit of that kind of attraction toward her.

Her responsibilities as president of The Humanitarians took almost all of the time that wasn't tied up with
studying for her classes. At the October and November
meetings, the members of the club had been very receptive to the ideas that she had expressed in her platform
last spring, and had shown a lot of support for the various
implementing activities that she proposed. Several committees had been appointed to concentrate individually
on each of those activities.

Lisa looked up just in time to see Mel approaching
the front door of the apartment. She got to the door before
he could knock, and said, "Hi!"

"Sorry I'm a little late," Mel said. "As president of
the frat house, I have ta deal with an emergency situation
now and then. The 'emergency' this time was one of our

2, 4, 8...(Destiny of the Human Species)

pledges who chug-a-lugged one too many beers and he was botherin' some of the other guys at the house. We finally got 'im to bed, so he could sleep it off."

"How did a freshman get beer?" Lisa queried.

"A couple of 'em do it all the time. They stand in front of a convenience store and wait until a likely prospect comes along. Then they offer 'im $10 if he'll buy 'em $5 worth of beer. It's pretty easy to do."

"Well, I'm glad you're here. I'm looking forward to the concert!"

They were going to see a live performance of "The Easy Rockers", a group that played many of the early rock-and-roll tunes, like those that the Beatles wrote. Lisa didn't care much for the newer "hard-rock" music, and Mel knew that.

At the theater, on 5th avenue, they sat near the front of the main floor. Mel knew how to make a girl feel special, and this time he had done it by getting especially nice seats. As Lisa looked around, she noticed that most of those attending were quite well dressed — not in jeans and T-shirts like the crowd at the only "hard-rock" concert she had gone to. As the band played one old hit after another, the audience clapped and swayed in their seats, but no one got over-emotional or out of control. The whole scene made her feel an affinity for Mel, because of the fact that he had set up such an enjoyable evening for her.

After the concert, Mel drove in the opposite direction from that of her apartment. "Where are we going?" she asked.

"I thought we'd drive up to the view point on Duwamish Head. There's a great view of downtown from there. We c'n talk for a while before I take ya home."

When they arrived at the viewpoint, Mel pulled the

2, 4, 8...(Destiny of the Human Species)

car into a parking spot so that they had a wide view of the Seattle nighttime skyline and the waterfront across Elliott Bay. "You havin' a good quarter in your classes?" he asked.

"Yes, very good!" Lisa replied. "I'm really enjoying my EnSci classes, especially, including the two that we're taking together. They make me realize how important the activities of The Humanitarians are as a way of bringing about significant changes in public policies."

"I was hopin' you wouldn't bring up The Humanitarians tonight, Lisa."

"Why?" she asked.

"Well, every time we start talkin' about The Humanitarians and their various projects, you get all stirred up. I'd like just a little quiet time together." He tugged on her arm, and pulled her lightly toward himself.

"This is one advantage of having one of those cars with a bench seat," he chuckled.

She complied, and quicker than a cat can blink its eye, his arm was around her. She didn't mind, though. Mel was a nice guy, and she felt stimulated by his closeness. On their previous date, they had shared several passionate kisses. The whole thing had left her feeling very feminine.

Mel kissed her softly on the neck, and rubbed the back of her neck gently. She responded by squeezing his upper arm, and drawing him more tightly to her. He kissed her full on the mouth, and she acknowledged it with moist lips. She could hear and feel his breathing quicken, as they shared long, sensuous kisses. His left hand brushed across her breasts. She didn't recoil, but sighed softly. Immediately he lightly squeezed her right breast, then her left. She didn't recoil as he thought she might, and her lack of negative reaction spurred him on.

2, 4, 8...(Destiny of the Human Species)

His left hand dropped to her knee, and his fingers gradually moved with a gentle massaging action up her thigh, under her dress.

She abruptly pulled away from him. "I think that's enough for tonight, Mel."

"Gee whiz, Lisa. You get a guy all turned on, then cut him off at the knees. That's torture for a guy, ya know."

"It's enjoyable, Mel, but I don't want to get carried away." Lisa had decided some months ago that there was no such thing as safe sex, and she didn't want to get lured into a situation that she would be sorry for. It appeared to her that the only way to avoid an unwanted pregnancy was to practice abstinence. And, in order to do that, it was best to avoid getting into a position in which her emotions might cause a lapse in her good judgement. If she was going to be an effective leader of The Humanitarians, and pursue a successful career, she had decided that it was best to forego the pleasures of intercourse, even though a lot of her dates applied pressures such as those she had just experienced with Mel.

FACTS OF LIFE!

1985 A.D

WORLD POPULATION

4,850,000,000 (Up 397,000,000 since 1980)

UNITED STATES POPULATION

238,000,000 (Up 10,000,000 since 1980)

U.S. Municipal Solid Waste

164,000,000 tons (Up 12,000,000 since 1980)

Chapter 34

(6 weeks later)
Wednesday, January 22, 1985

EnSci 322 class had just ended. John Spencer walked out of the lecture room with Lisa.

"Would you like to get a Coke before your next class?" he asked.

"Sure," answered Lisa.

At the HUB, as they drank their Cokes, Lisa said, "After my last class tomorrow, I'm going over to the Career Center. They have counsellors there that help students plan job searches. Maybe you should come with me. After all, we graduate at the end of May, you know. Have you started looking for a job, yet?"

"Not really," replied John. "I've been so absorbed in all of my class studies and club activities, that I haven't done much thinking about life after graduation."

"Well, I think you ought to come with me, John. Although they say that there are a lot of job possibilities for Environmental Science majors, it'd be a good idea to start applying early."

"O.k.," said John. "I'll meet you at the Career Center at 3:10."

2, 4, 8...(Destiny of the Human Species)

(The next day)
Thursday, January 23, 1985

John was right on time. He met Lisa at the front door to the Career Center, and they both walked in together. The receptionist eyed them over the rim of her reading glasses.

"How may I help you?" she asked. "I'm Mrs. Hopkins."

"We're both Environmental Science majors who will be graduating in May," said John. We've never been in here before, so we'd like to hear what kinds of services you offer."

Mrs. Hopkins took two identical packets from a file cabinet behind her desk. "The first thing you should do is read over the materials in this packet. It will probably take close to an hour to do that. Why don't you take them home with you, and then call for an appointment with one of our counsellors when you have finished looking them over."

"Thank you," said John and Lisa in unison.

"Thanks, Lisa, for asking me to come along today. It looks like there's some pretty important material in these packets. I'll see you in class tomorrow." Then he squeezed her hand, and they parted ways and headed toward their respective living quarters.

(1 week later)
Thursday, January 30, 1985

Lisa approached Mrs. Hopkins, who was sitting at her desk in the lobby of the Career Center.

"I'm here for my 3:30 appointment with Mr. Helling," she announced.

"I'll take you right in," said Mrs. Hopkins.

2, 4, 8...(Destiny of the Human Species)

Mr. Helling was a kindly looking, portly gentleman. He extended his hand. "I'm Dick Helling. I understand that you're an Environmental Science major who'll be graduating in May. Are you looking for immediate employment at the time of graduation?"

"If I could get a job that I really liked, I'd take it as soon as possible," said Lisa. "But, I could also wait for a few months, if it looked like the ideal position would open up. I have a part-time job as a receptionist in the Zoology Department, and I could work almost full-time at that for at least the summer months."

"Well, not being desperate for an immediate opening helps," said Mr. Helling. "Actually, the positions that are available for Environmental Science majors are plentiful and varied. We're in a period of great environmental awareness, you know."

"That was one of the reasons why I selected that major," replied Lisa.

Mr. Helling continued. "Because there are so many openings for people with your major, it might be wise to think in terms of where your main interests lie before we zero in on available openings. Here's a breakdown showing where the jobs are that are usually of interest to Environmental Science majors. While you read it, I'll look over your resumé."

He handed her a one-page list. She perused it.

**Positions Related To The Field
Of Environmental Science**

Pollution
    Air
    Water
    Visual/Aesthetic

2, 4, 8...(Destiny of the Human Species)

Waste Disposal
   Sewage
   Solid Wastes
Plant Preservation
   Forests
   Marine Plants
   Aquatic Plants
Animal Preservation
   Wildlife
   Fish
      Marine
      Freshwater
Population Issues
   Family Planning
   Quality of Life

Types of Employers

Private
   Industrial
   Philanthropic
Governmental
   County
   State
   Federal
   International

When Lisa appeared to have surveyed the entire page, Mr. Helling said, "As you can see, there's considerable overlap between various parts of this list. Do you see any there that appeal to you more than others? Any that you have little interest in?"

"I've been excited over just about all of the various

2, 4, 8...(Destiny of the Human Species)

aspects of environmental protection and control that I've learned about in my classes the last four years," she said. "Up until now, I never really thought about having to make a choice for a career. One thing that I want to avoid is to get stuck in a routine job, where the responsibilities never change, day in and day out. I'd like to be in a field where I can apply creativity to the solution of problems. I guess I'd prefer to be on the research and development end of things, rather than to just be a technician following orders."

Mr. Helling responded, "I see from your resumé that you have made outstanding grades over the four years here at the University. That should help you considerably when it comes to competing for jobs. I also notice that you were very active in campus activities, especially in the club called The Humanitarians. Ordinarily, active participation in extracurricular activities also helps one to get the job of her choice. In the case of The Humanitarians, I'm not so sure. Some of the staff here look upon that club as being a bit radical, you know."

"I'm aware of that," responded Lisa.

"Many of the environmentally-oriented jobs are offered by companies that need environmental experts to defend their questionable practices. In other words, they want to hire people who can do a good job of countering the arguments of extreme environmentalists. On the basis of your background, I would doubt that any such companies would want to hire you. However, you probably wouldn't want to work for them anyway. Am I correct?"

"Definitely yes!" said Lisa.

"Looking on the bright side," said Mr. Helling, "there are a few employers who are specifically looking for people with your kinds of attitudes and experience. But, first you have to decide what general segment of environmental work appeals to you."

"Fish and wildlife protection and conservation appeal to me a lot. but, I'm aware of the fact that many of the other aspects that are on the list are interrelated with these aspects. Also, through my work with The Humanitarians, I've realized that almost all of the major social and environmental problems in the world are a result of too high a birth rate and overpopulation. If I wanted to do the greatest possible good in helping to solve the most important of all environmental problems, I should probably work in the area that deals with the effects of overpopulation on the environment."

"You've told me enough to help me identify some positions that should interest you," said Mr. Helling. "Why don't you make an appointment for this same time next week. By then I should have a list of openings for you to consider."

"Thanks for your time, Mr. Helling. I'll see you at 3:30 next Thursday, then."

(1 week later)
Thursday, February 7, 1985

Because of the rapidly falling snow, it was a challenge for Lisa to walk the distance from Johnson Hall to the Career Center. When she got there, she shook the snow off her stocking cap and scarf before entering the lobby.

"Mr. Helling is expecting you," said Mrs. Hopkins, and she led Lisa to his office. "Miss Billings is here, Mr. Helling."

"Have a seat," offered Mr. Helling. "I came up with four well-paying positions and one moderately-paying

2, 4, 8...(Destiny of the Human Species)

position that I thought you might be interested in applying for. Here's a one-page summary for you to look at. If
you want to pursue any of them, we can get you more
details about them."

Lisa looked over the list.

Lisa Billings: Openings of Interest

1. Environmental Specialist I
   Montana State Department of Fisheries
   Location: Missoula, Montana
   Responsibilities:
   > Collecting and interpreting data gathered
   > by field biologists. Data include records
   > of observations by biologists, anecdotal
   > evidence from residents, and technical
   > data from our research technicians
   >
   > Composing reports on the above, to be sub-
   > mitted to the Director of Fisheries
   >
   > Salary: Beginning at $16,500; possible rise
   > to $27,000 after seven years.

2. Biologist II
   Missouri Department of Wildlife
   Location: Jackson, Missouri
   Responsibilities:
   > Do field collections of data on effects of
   > farming and industrial activities on game
   > animals in the Setawnee National For-
   > est. Publish department reports on in-
   > terpretations of said data for consider-
   > ation by state officials planning legisla-
   > tion affecting game animals.
   >
   > Salary: Beginning at $14,000, but rising by
   > $1000 per year for the first ten years,

with satisfactory supervisor evaluation.

3. Environmental Specialist I
   Pro-Enviro (Private environmental consulting firm)
   Location: Placentia, California (Orange County)
   Responsibilities:
   > Process environmental data collected by our field biologists. Assist Environmental Supervisors in quantifying and analyzing data statistically.
   > Salary: Beginning $18,300; progressing to $23,000 in 3 years, with possibility of rising to $32,500 within 10 years, if supervisory evaluations are excellent.

4. Assistant Director
   Careful Procreation (Non-profit Family Planning Agency)
   Location: Seattle, Washington
   Responsibilities:
   > Assisting Director in management of agency activities, planning overall programs, and supervising employees.
   > Salary: Beginning at $14,500, with possible rise to $19,000 within 5 years.

5. Coordinator of Environmental Analysis, Population Division
   Careful Procreation (Non-profit Family Planning Agency)
   Location: Seattle, Washington
   Responsibilities:
   > Serving as primary specialist in environmental aspects of overpopulation, in order

2, 4, 8...(Destiny of the Human Species)

to promote public awareness of the need
for our programs.
Salary: Beginning at $12,800.

Lisa expressed some of her thoughts about the list to
Mr. Helling.

"None of them is perfect. Each has its drawbacks. The
Montana opening pays really well, but it sounds like the
work would be mostly that of a technician, with little
opportunity to help affect environmental policies.

"The Missouri job doesn't appeal to me at all. From
what I know about that state, I wouldn't enjoy working
there. The Pro-Enviro position offers very good pay, but,
again, it just sounds like mainly technical work. The two
positions with Careful Procreation both sound like they
would involve interesting work, but the pay is relatively
low. But, on the other hand, they're both right here in
Seattle, and I love this place."

"Ordinarily, I wouldn't recommend an Environmental Science major for the Assistant Director's job," said
Mr. Helling. "However, your experience with The Humanitarians not only makes you more qualified for that
job than the average Environmental Science major would
be, but it also gives you an advantage in the competition
for the position."

"Do you think I could take this list with me and have
a week to think these over?"

"That's perfectly all right with me, Lisa. Do you want
to make an appointment for 3:30 again next Thursday?"

"That'd be great," said Lisa, and she put on her coat,
scarf and hat before heading back out into the falling
snow.

2, 4, 8...(Destiny of the Human Species)

(The next day)
Friday, February 8, 1985

Lisa could hardly wait to talk to John Spencer after class. As he approached, she said, "Hi. I've got some interesting news!"

"Let's talk about it over a hamburger and soda at the HUB," replied John.

As they consumed their hamburger and soda, Lisa showed John the list of positions that Mr. Helling had given her. After scanning it, he said, "Well, are you interested in any of these?"

Lisa thought for a minute. "The out-of-state jobs don't appeal to me for a variety of reasons. But the two positions with Careful Procreation sound interesting. I'm not sure I could handle the Assistant Director's job, but I don't think I'd have any trouble with the other one. Mr. Helling thinks that I'd have a good chance at landing either one."

"They both sound pretty good to me, too," said John. "I haven't yet made an appointment with a counsellor at the Career Center. Which of those two jobs would you rather have? Do you think that it would be o.k. for me to apply for the other one?"

John's comments surprised Lisa. She wasn't sure what to say. After all, John was her best friend now. She had never thought about the possibility of working with him in the same organization as a career, even though they had hit it off beautifully. in their work for The Humanitarians.

"I don't really care which one I get, if I can even get *one* of them," she finally replied. "We each have very similar qualifications. Maybe we should both apply for *both* of the jobs. It wouldn't bother me to have you as my

2, 4, 8...(Destiny of the Human Species)

supervisor. Would it bother *you* to have *me* as *your* supervisor?"

"Not at all," said John, smiling.

"Well, then, let's both go to my next Thursday appointment with Mr. Helling, and tell him what we'd like to do!"

As they stood up to leave the cafeteria, John gave Lisa a firm hug. It caught her off guard, because John didn't do that kind of thing ordinarily. But, it pleased her immensely!

Chapter 35

(6 months later)
Wednesday, July 10, 1985

Wendy Martin, the Director of the Seattle Division of Careful Procreation, convened the weekly staff meeting. The bright morning sun had already warmed the office building to a slightly uncomfortable 73 degrees, even though it was only 10 a.m. The summer had started out typically for Seattle: rainy throughout June, right up through the 4th of July. Then, about July 6th, the clear skies started to dominate.

As usual, Assistant Director Lisa Billings was in attendance at the staff meeting, as were several of the coordinators, including John Spencer, Coordinator of Environmental Analysis. After Lisa had accepted the Assistant Director's job, John had been offered the coordinator's position. They were both extremely pleased with that arrangement. John didn't mind the fact that Lisa was technically his supervisor. It all seemed just like a logical extension of the roles that they had performed in The Humanitarians at the University. Only, now they were getting paid as full-time employees, and they could both make professional decisions that mattered. They saw each other almost every day at the office, but that didn't

166

2, 4, 8...(Destiny of the Human Species)

keep them from having an occasional dinner together at one of several downtown restaurants that they liked. The dinners were strictly platonic, though. Lisa thought of John only as her best friend, and never as a romantic connection. Perhaps that was because he had never shown any romantic inclinations toward her, except for a hug or a friendly kiss on the cheek now and then.

After the staff meeting, John asked Lisa to accompany him on a coffee break. "I have something interesting to tell you," he announced.

As they sat sipping their coffee, John continued. "I talked with Carol Perkins yesterday." Carol was president-elect of The Humanitarians at the University. "She said that the club wants to expand into an official political party, registered with the State Public Disclosure Commission. The Executive Board has been looking for someone to chair the new party, and they think that you're the logical person for the position."

Lisa was taken aback by the notion. "I have a full-time job right here, and I'm enjoying it very much. I really don't think that I would have time for that type of work. Anyway, what made them decide that they should do any more than what they have been doing effectively as a campus club?"

"They're aware of a significant increase in public support for their goals. Quite a lot of legislation has been passed at both the state level and the national levels - the type of legislation that encourages them to seek a stronger, expanded organization. I agree with them that you're the right person to chair the new party. As far as I can tell, you perform your responsibilities here at Careful Procreation extremely well, and still have a lot of extra time to do other things after work and on weekends. You could schedule the party activities so that they didn't interfere with work. What do you say? I told them that if you would chair the party, I would serve on the Executive Board. After all, we've been a great team for quite a while now, you know."

Lisa mulled over the idea. She had never made it known to anyone, but she secretly believed in most of the goals that her father, Robert Welton had listed for himself in the 1960's. Being chairperson of a new party like this could give her an opportunity to pursue some of those goals with official backing.

"Have they thought of a name for this new party?" asked Lisa.

"They think that the logical name would be The Humanitarian Party," John replied.

It hit her like a bullet between the eyes! "Did you know that my biological father was the chairman of a political party called The Humanitarian Party in the 1950's and '60's?" asked Lisa.

"No, I've never heard that," replied John.

"It caused him a lot of grief. The party's goals, which were largely composed by him, were way ahead of their time. He ended up committing suicide because of the stress!"

"Does that fact cause you to reject this idea about chairing a new party having the same name?" asked John.

"Not necessarily. Times have changed. A lot of ideas that were socially unacceptable then have gained wider acceptance now. Some of those original goals of his are now espoused by the both the Careful Procreation organization and The Humanitarians. My father was a man before his time, I guess. Let me think this over. I should also talk it over with Wendy. She might frown upon my taking on such a publicly visible role while I'm working here. We have enough public criticism to deal with without stirring up any more. I'll let you know tomorrow."

(The next day)
Thursday, July 11, 1985

When it was time for the 10 a.m. coffee break, John stopped by Lisa's desk. "Want to have a cup of coffee with me?" he asked.

"Sure. I want to tell you my thoughts about the political party offer anyway."

Over coffee, Lisa told John briefly, without detail, about her father's original goals, and how they tied in so closely with what The Humanitarians today wanted to achieve. Then she added, "I talked with Wendy after work yesterday. I told her about the offer to chair the new party, and I was surprised at her reaction. She doesn't think that it would interfere in the least with my work here at the office. In fact, she views it as an opportunity to further the goals of Careful Procreation by working in political circles in a way that CP, itself, can't. And, I guess you're right. I probably do have time for it, as long as I delegate responsibilities properly and don't set up any kind of schedule that interferes with my work at CP. So — I guess my answer is 'Yes.' But I want to talk with the Executive Board of The Humanitarians myself before making the final decision. I want to see what kind of detailed plans they have for the structure of the party, and I want to make sure that I would have a strong hand in composing the goals for the party."

"Great! I'll call Carol, and ask her to set up a meeting for you with the Executive Board," said John enthusiastically.

FACTS OF LIFE!

1986 A.D

WORLD POPULATION

4,936,000,000 (Up 86,000,000 since 1985)

UNITED STATES POPULATION

241,000,000 (Up 3,000,000 since 1985)

U.S. Municipal Solid Waste

171,000,000 tons (Up 7,000,000 since 1985)

Chapter 36

(10 months later)
Friday, April 25, 1986

"Wendy, I'll be coming in to put in a couple of extra hours tomorrow morning," Lisa announced.

"Is your work load getting to be too much?" Wendy asked. "I hope that your work with the Humanitarian Party, along with your work here at CP hasn't added up to more than you can handle."

"No problem. I just want to put the finishing touches on the annual CP report for the Citizen's Advisory Council before it's presented to them on Monday evening."

Wendy queried, "Do you think that they'll be positively impressed?"

"Well, there's isn't much negative news to put in the report," Lisa answered. "As I've told you, all of our activities have met with considerable success during the past 12 months. Our counselling successes are up 12%; our clientele has increased by 8%, which indicates that word about the advantages of our services is spreading among the population that needs them. Our funding is up by 26%, which means that we can improve our staff-to-client ratio significantly. The Pro-Existence group has

2, 4, 8...(Destiny of the Human Species)

been relatively quiet, too. They didn't even bother to picket our last two clinic open houses."

"It sounds good," said Wendy.

"I agree," said Lisa. "By the way, I have another date with David Trammel tomorrow night. You know, the one who is president of Environment, Inc."

"This is your third date in a month with him. It sounds like it's getting serious."

About that time, John Spencer walked into Wendy's office and waited to speak to Wendy.

"Not really, Wendy," said Lisa. "Not yet, at least. We're going to have dinner at Benjamin's in Bellevue, then come back to town for a little dancing at The Garden Court in the Olympic Hotel."

"Sounds like fun," Wendy said.

Lisa glanced at John as she left the office. If he cared at all whether she was having a date with someone else, it didn't show on his face.

(The next day)
Saturday, April 26, 1986

The dinner at Benjamin's was superb. Lisa and David had a seat by the west windows, so that they could look across Lake Washington at the Seattle skyline. David was easy to talk with. He was always interested in what Lisa was doing, where she was going, how she felt. He was quite handsome, too. At thirty-seven, he was thirteen years older than she was, but the age difference didn't bother her. She enjoyed his maturity. She had met him at a Humanitarian Party luncheon for legislators. He happened to be at the capitol on that same day, lobbying for some environmental legislation that would benefit his company.

174

2, 4, 8...(Destiny of the Human Species)

After the waiter took their order, David asked, "How are you holding up under the heavy load that you've set up for yourself?"

"It's really not that bad. Many former members of The Humanitarians at the University have volunteered to take on chairmanships of the various Humanitarian Party committees. That has made it easy to delegate a lot of the responsibilities, so that my personal work load with the party isn't as great as I had originally feared it would be. And, my work at Careful Procreation is going very well, too. The Pro-Existence group has organized statewide, however, and they've taken every opportunity that they could to harass our organization lately. But, as long as I see them for the emotionally oriented group that they are, their activities don't bother me much. I'm even planning to take up another activity next week. My friend Georgia Perkins took me to a meeting of the Women In the Nation last week. You know, WIN."

David nodded with a slight smirk.

"Do you have negative feelings about WIN, David?" Lisa asked.

"Well, it seems to me that they're going a bit overboard on this women's liberation thing. It's all right to exert pressure for women's rights, but to insist on affirmative action programs for the employment of women goes too far. They also want an increase in salaries for what has typically been women's work, like being secretaries. I say that if they want to compete head-to-head with men for men's types of work, let them. But they shouldn't want the same pay for secretarial work or clerking that a plumber or truck driver makes!"

"The reason for affirmative action, David, is that, just like blacks, women have been discriminated against for such a long period of time, that it's going to take special action to remedy the disparity in salaries that now exist between men and women in the *same* kinds of jobs."

David winced, but then relaxed. "I have to agree with most of your positions on issues, Lisa. You usually can bring me around to your way of thinking on just about any topic, if I give you an opportunity to apply logic. That's one of the things I like about you the most. You can apply logic to the interpretation of most problems, much better than most of the other women I know."

Their dinner was splendid, definitely up to the quality for which Benjamin's was noted. After dinner, they got into David's 1986 Cadillac, and drove back across the Evergreen Point Bridge, and to the Olympic Hotel.

At the Garden Court, a 5-piece band was playing the old standards. David was an exceptionally good dancer, and Lisa enjoyed every number that was played.

After several dances, she exclaimed, "Whew. I'm getting a little tired. It's fun, but hard on my calf muscles."

"We could go back to my apartment for a drink and a few snacks," he suggested.

"Maybe just one small drink to sip on," said Lisa. "But snacks sound good."

David's apartment was only a few blocks away, on Capitol Hill, just up the hill from the Olympic. He must have been doing very well salary-wise, because he had a penthouse with a beautiful view of downtown, Queen Anne, and Elliot Bay.

"You can see my apartment from here," Lisa pointed out. "Look, right down there, just to the left of the Space Needle."

"I know," said David. "I've seen you through my telescope a couple of times, standing by the window."

That made Lisa wonder. *"Hmm. I wonder just exactly what he has seen of me and my apartment."*

2, 4, 8...(Destiny of the Human Species)

"What kind of drink do you want?" David asked.

"Vodka Collins, light on the vodka," Lisa answered, sitting down on the couch.

David mixed a martini for himself, and then brought the drinks and a tray of luscious looking hors d´oeuvres and set it on the coffee table in front of the couch.

"You and I could benefit each other, you know. Professionally, I mean. In your work with the Humanitarian Party and Careful Procreation, you make a lot of contacts with business people and public officials who are in a position to hire out the services of my company. And, during my frequent lobbying activities, I meet many legislators who are in a position to sponsor legislation that's supportive of your organizations' goals."

"As long as I don't do anything unethical, you might be right," Lisa responded. "We could mutually benefit each other in a lot of ways. It's nice to have a date with someone who's interested in a lot of the same topics that I'm interested in, David."

He sat down on the couch, next to Lisa, and put his arm around her shoulders. Up to this point, the only intimacy they had shared was a goodnight kiss after each date.

"You're a lovely woman, Lisa. Both beautiful and talented."

He kissed the side of her neck, then the front. His kisses sent shivers up her back. He kissed her softly on the lips, and she reciprocated. Then he kissed her with more fervor, and, again, she cooperated. The passionate kisses of someone so handsome and mature gave her a thrill.

He slowly eased her blouse from inside her skirt, then slid his hand behind her and deftly unsnapped her bra.

2, 4, 8...(Destiny of the Human Species)

"*He must have had quite a bit of practice at this,*" she thought to herself.

He gently massaged her back for a few moments. Then his hand moved around to the front, under her bra, and he softly massaged her breasts. A feeling of excitement rushed through her, and she sighed. She didn't resist in any way. Then, almost before she realized it David's hand was under her skirt and on her thigh. It jolted her back to reality.

"No activity below the waist, please, David!"

David recoiled slightly, with a somewhat shocked look on his face.

"You're not going to get prudish on me are you?" he asked mockingly.

"I'd rather that you keep your hands above the waist," she retorted.

"I can't believe this," he exclaimed. "Most women who will let a man fondle their breasts will let him go all the way."

"Do you know that from *experience* or rumor?" she queried.

"One or the other," he answered, sidestepping the question.

With a questioning look on her face, Lisa asked, "Haven't you ever thought of the risk of pregnancy or AIDS if you 'go all the way?'"

"I don't worry about those kinds of things when I'm with a beautiful woman," he replied.

"I think you had better take me home, now, David. I've enjoyed the drink, the snacks, and your company up to now."

David sheepishly accompanied Lisa back to his car. When they arrived at her apartment, he walked her to the door, but didn't offer the customary goodnight kiss. He

2, 4, 8...(Destiny of the Human Species)

simply said "Goodnight, Lisa," and got back into his car.

Lisa entered the apartment, took her high heels off her aching feet, and sat down in her La-Z-Boy chair.

"It's the same old story," she thought. *"I meet a nice guy, he likes me, we date, and about the third date he tries to get too friendly. Then I never see him again."* She was pretty sure that David wouldn't ask her on another date.

FACTS OF LIFE!

1987 A.D

WORLD POPULATION

5,000,000,000 (Up 64,000,000 since 1986)

UNITED STATES POPULATION

243,000,000 (Up 2,000,000 since 1986)

U.S. Municipal Solid Waste

178,000,000 tons (Up 7,000,000 since 1986)

Chapter 37

(13 months later)
Thursday, May 14, 1987

"Angie!" Lisa called frantically. Angie was Lisa's new secretary. Since taking over the Director's job following Wendy's departure in March, Lisa had hired three personal secretaries already. The first two resigned after only a couple of weeks because they couldn't handle the heavy work load that Lisa assigned to them. Actually, she didn't expect any more of them than she expected of herself, but it was difficult to find truly dedicated help. Finally, Angie seemed to be working out.

Angie responded to Lisa's call immediately.

"Angie, will you call Wendy at organization headquarters in D.C.? I know that she's probably very busy with her job, but I desperately need to ask her a couple of questions before I can get anything done today!"

Wendy had been promoted to the position of Assistant National Director of Careful Procreation. That had left the Seattle area directorship open, and Lisa stepped into it easily. Not only that, but she had subsequently been able to appoint John Spencer as her new Assistant Director, and that pleased both of them very much!

2, 4, 8...(Destiny of the Human Species)

"Miss Billings, Miss Martin's on the line now," Angie announced.

"Hi. Wendy? Is your job as hectic as mine is right now?"

"Probably," replied Wendy. "What's on your mind?"

Lisa took a deep breath, and started on a series of questions concerning methods that Wendy had previously used in dealing with various benefactors of Careful Procreation. When her questions and Wendy's answers had terminated, Wendy said, "I hear that you've revved up the pace at the Seattle office."

"Well," said Lisa, "the problems of overpopulation continue to mount, you know. We're aggressively approaching potential contributors in order to raise more funds for our projects. Besides that, the Pro-Existence bunch have zeroed in on our support for women's choice in matters of terminating pregnancies, and they've managed to cause our abortion referral program to be interpreted completely out of proportion to its minor role in our overall operations. We're planning a new series of commercials to explain to the public that we only refer people for abortions after all possible avenues of assuring quality parenting have been exhausted. Those commercials take a lot of funds, you know. In addition, we're planning a new type of presentation for public schools. It's based on the figures on birth rate and population growth, and is intended to give students a realistic view of the multitude of problems that result from too high a birth rate. We'd like to send crews to film scenes of the horrible living conditions in some of the countries where the birth rate is highest."

"We ought to be able to help with that last item,"

2, 4, 8...(Destiny of the Human Species)

Wendy said. "It really shouldn't be the responsibility of a local group to fund that kind of thing. Especially when all of the locals nationwide could use that same type of film. I'll check our budget, and see how much we can help."

"Many thanks," said Lisa. "I'll call you again when I need help or advice. And, that shouldn't be too long." She chuckled, and hung up the phone. She handed Angie a list of names and phone numbers. "Would you call each of the persons on this list and set up an individual appointment with each of them for me. They're some of our most reliable contributors, and I want to talk to each of them personally."

"Yes, Miss Billings," Angie replied.

(The next day)
Friday, May 15, 1987

Lisa was scheduled to preside at the meeting of the Humanitarian Party in Olympia that evening at 7:30. She had just barely enough time to get home from work, change clothes, and, with John Spencer, drive the fifty-eight miles to the meeting.

They arrived at the auditorium about 7:15. There was already a sizeable crowd, nearly filling all of the seats. This was an especially important meeting. Besides serving to discuss ongoing committee activities, it was being held for the benefit of party representatives from all over the state, who were here in the capitol city to participate in a weekend of lobbying-training and a brushing-up on fund-raising techniques. The party was planning to have several candidates for the legislature on the statewide

2, 4, 8...(Destiny of the Human Species)

ballot in only 19 months, and they wanted to be sure that they could raise enough funds to adequately support their candidates. Following the meeting on Friday, many party members were going to stay in Olympia for part of the next week in order to lobby for favorable legislation.

At 7:30, Lisa convened the meeting with the pledge of allegiance. She then directed the procedures through a long list of committee reports:

> The Committee on Free Distribution Of Birth Control Devices
> The Committee on Reproductive Counselling in Public Schools
> The Committee on Tax Disincentives For Large Families
> The Committee on Genetic Screening
> The Committee on Parent-Education
> The Committee on Thinking Skills Education
> The Committee on Legalization of Suicide
> The Committee on Health Care
> The Committee on Free Housing For The Homeless
> The Committee on Hunting and Trapping
> The Committee on Medical Experimentation With Animals
> The Committee on Sterilization of Household Pets

Anyone who had seen the list of Robert Welton's original goals for the Humanitarian Party in the 1950's would have thought the list of committees to be the list of Welton goals reincarnated.

Lisa was gratified by the overwhelming support shown

2, 4, 8...(Destiny of the Human Species)

by the membership for the committee activities. After the reports, she turned the gavel over to John Spencer, who was to preside over the training sessions. During the past couple of years, John and Lisa had become even closer friends, if that is possible. Between their work together at Careful Procreation and their frequent work together on Humanitarian Party projects, they saw a lot of each other, but never tired of it. In fact, John was going to take her to watch the opening day boat parade the next day.

(The next day)
Saturday, May 16, 1987

It was the kind of day for which the boaters and viewers alike had hoped. The temperature by 10 a.m. was a comfortable 67 degrees, under cloudless skies. John parked the car on one of the side streets just off Montlake Boulevard, and they walked to the south side of the Montlake Cut, where it was especially good for viewing the boat parade. Once alongside the water, they spread a sports blanket, and dismantled a basketful of assorted snacks.

Once the parade began, there appeared one brightly-decorated boat after another. They ranged in size from 6-foot prams to 60-foot yachts, each sporting decorations that supposedly fit the "World Capitols" theme. It took a lot of ingenuity on the part of the owners of some of the smallest boats to come up with enough decorations to subtly suggest a world capitol, without simply labelling it as such.

As Lisa and John lay there on their blanket, enjoying the passing parade and the beautiful weather, she sur-

2, 4, 8...(Destiny of the Human Species)

veyed John surreptitiously and thought, *"Here is a man that I could truly love. He's handsome, kind, considerate, sensible, down-to-earth, interested in the same kinds of things that I am. What else is there to ask for? But, whereas all of the other men that I date end up getting too 'friendly' John isn't 'friendly' enough to my way of thinking. He shows absolutely no romantic interest in me."*

FACTS OF LIFE!

1988 A.D

WORLD POPULATION

5,100,000,000 (Up 100,000,000 since 1987)

UNITED STATES POPULATION

245,000,000 (Up 2,000,000 since 1987)

U.S. Municipal Solid Waste

184,000,000 tons (Up 6,000,000 since 1987)

Chapter 38

(8 months later)
Friday, January 15, 1988

The work day was just about over when John stopped by Lisa's office. "I guess you must be getting pretty excited about your trip to Cabo San Lucas."

"That's for sure. Not only can I use the rest, but I can also stand some heat and sun. It's been so *cloudy* here lately."

"Well, that's typical Seattle weather in January," replied John. "Will you be travelling with anyone I know?" he asked. He wasn't sure whether she was going alone or with someone, and that piqued his curiosity.

"No one you know," replied Lisa. She thought she'd let John stew about it a bit.

He *really* was curious to know whether she was going with a female friend or a male friend. He seriously doubted that she would take off on a trip like that with a man, but he was smarting to know for sure.

Eyeing his piteous look, Lisa finally said, "Oh, it's my friend Sharon Schumacher. I met her at one of our Humanitarian Party meetings about a year ago, and since then we've done several things together, but this is our first long-distance trip. She's fun. Has a lot of the same

2, 4, 8...(Destiny of the Human Species)

interests that I do. The fact that I met her at a Party meeting would probably indicate that."

"How many days you going to be gone?" John queried.

"A full nine days," Lisa answered. "I'll be back a week from next Monday."

"I'll miss you, Lisa," John said somewhat shyly.

Lisa thought, *"That's the first time he's ever said that to me. I wonder if he'll really miss me."*

(The next few days)
Saturday, January 16 - Sunday, January 24, 1988

The week in Cabo San Lucas passed by much too fast. Lisa and Sharon spent at least an hour each day alternately lying in the sun and dipping in the pool. One cloudless day followed another, and their suntans got richer with each passing day. Of course, they couldn't spend very much time in the sun, for fear of getting burned. So, they sat in lounge chairs in the shade of the hotel veranda, reading some of the interesting books that they had brought along.

"This is sure a good way to catch up on reading," Sharon opined.

"Yes, I brought along three good books that I had been wanting to read for a long time. One is on the history of the populating of the earth; another is on the topic of the interdependence of various living species; and the third is on business management techniques. I could use a little brushing-up on all three."

For a while each day, they would browse among the tourist shops along the main street. The Mexican men that they encountered lavished attention upon them. Lisa and Sharon, in their short skirts and halters, presented a

192

2, 4, 8...(Destiny of the Human Species)

much more exciting spectacle for those men than did their own native women, in long, baggy dresses.

One day, they visited the local glass factory, which was only a few blocks away from their hotel. The temperature in the factory was almost unbearable, and they wondered how the workers could stand it for very long.

On Sunday morning, the 24th, they had to begin packing their bags for the flight back to Seattle. Luckily, they were going to fly non-stop. It was difficult to fit everything into the bags. As most other tourists discover, they were going to have to have a large amount of carry-on luggage in order to take all of their souvenirs back home.

(The next day)
Monday, January 25, 1988

In a way it was good to be back at her desk, yet somewhat disappointing to realize that her relaxing vacation was over. Phone messages from the past week were stacked high in the middle of the desk, and Angie had a long list of questions that needed answering.

Within a few minutes of her arrival at work, John stuck his head in her doorway and said, "Missed you, Lisa," and the look on his face convinced her that he really had missed her.

"It's good to see your face, again, John," she said. "Have we had any disasters while I've been gone?"

"Nothing serious," he replied. "We had some pickets from Pro-Existence in front of the building on Tuesday. They were protesting our program for birth-control counselling in the public schools. They notified the news media that they were going to picket, but only one insignificant radio station sent anyone. Not a single TV photographer showed up. I think that the news media are getting fed up with Pro-Existence's ranting and raving."

"Are you prepared for tomorrow night's meeting of the Party at the Olympic Hotel?" Lisa asked. "I hope that those guests from Detroit and Augusta are favorably impressed with our discussions and reports. They're trying to get party chapters established in their cities. We need to give them all of the support that we can."

"I'm ready for my part of the program," John replied. "Are you ready for yours?"

"My part isn't any problem," retorted Lisa. "All I have to do is keep the proceedings flowing. I'm going to be very interested in what our guest speaker has to say. He's Dr. Arnold Volmer. He's an expert on solid waste problems, you know. He asked to be on the program at this meeting, because he's so concerned about the rapid accumulation of solid wastes in this country, and the effects that it can have on our quality of life over the long term. He feels that our party can be more effective in getting legislation adopted in relation to that whole set of problems, than either of the two major parties can. They're so widely lobbied by groups that oppose alternative ways to deal with solid wastes, that they can't get anything meaningful done. In the meantime, we're running out of landfills for disposing of the wastes."

"I know what *you mean!*" John stated emphatically. "Besides that, everyone wants their garbage shipped off to some place else. The NIMBYs are really out in force on this issue. It's unfortunate but true — most of the NIMBYs don't see the connection between the high birth rate and the threat of the garbage dumps that they're always fighting."

Lisa looked at her watch. "I have to get started now on my report for the Citizen's Advisory Committee on

2, 4, 8...(Destiny of the Human Species)

Wednesday evening. I see that you've prepared a rough draft for me to use, so it shouldn't take me long to put the finishing touches on it."

"I'll see you later, Lisa. Again, it's nice to have you back. You're a bright and shining star for everyone around here."

Lisa grinned sheepishly. "Did you know that I'm leaving again on Friday night for Los Angeles?"

John was surprised. "Why, no!" he said, trying not to look disappointed. "What are you going to do in Los Angeles?"

"I'm representing Region IX at the national conference of Women In the Nation. It's a great honor, you know. The members in this region voted for me at our regional meeting in December in Portland. My activities in WIN give me a chance to promote the idea of *equal quality of life for men and women*. WIN is the only organization that's been publicly outspoken on this issue, and the only one that's been willing to stand up to the male-dominated political groups in this country."

"You do keep busy, don't you," John said with a sigh. "I was hoping that we could do something fun together next weekend. Well, maybe the weekend after that."

FACTS OF LIFE!

1989 A.D

WORLD POPULATION

5,200,000,000 (Up 100,000,000 since 1988)

UNITED STATES POPULATION

247,000,000 (Up 2,000,000 since 1988)

U.S. Municipal Solid Waste

191,000,000 tons (Up 7,000,000 since 1988)

Chapter 39

(15 months later)
Thursday, April 13, 1989

Angie stepped into Lisa's office and laid an envelope on her desk. "Here are your plane tickets, Miss Billings," she said.

Lisa opened the envelope and took out two packets of tickets. One read "Seattle-Dallas/Ft. Worth: Ms. Lisa Billings." The other read "Seattle-Dallas/Ft. Worth: Mr. John Spencer."

"Angie," Lisa said, "we're counting on you to keep this office on an even keel while we're gone."

"I'll do my best, Miss Billings!"

"With both John and me gone, Boyd will have to take over administrative responsibilities, but he isn't on top of all of the things that John and I do. So, he'll need all of the help that you can give him. We'll actually only be out of the office one work day — tomorrow — so I don't expect any problems that you and Boyd can't cope with."

"Well, you and Mr. Spencer have a *nice* time in Dallas, and don't worry about things here at the office."

Lisa wasn't sure what the tone of *nice* was supposed to mean. "This is strictly a *business* trip, you know, Angie. John and I have *separate* rooms, of course."

2, 4, 8...(Destiny of the Human Species)

"I understand, Miss Billings."

Lisa still wasn't sure that Angie understood *correctly*. Actually, it probably did look a bit suspicious: a beautiful, single business executive and a very eligible, handsome bachelor going off on a three-day trip together. Lisa thought that just about everyone at the office knew about the strictly platonic nature of the relationship between her and John. Although they were best friends, no romantic encounter had ever occurred between them, even though Lisa might not have actually minded one.

"Hi!" It was John. He walked in Lisa's office door, and sat on one corner of her desk. "Do you have things ready to leave behind here without worrying about them while we're gone?"

"Angie and Boyd can take care of office matters with no problem," Lisa answered."

John glanced at his watch. "It's five after 5," he said. "I'm going to leave now. I have quite a bit of packing to do before I go to bed tonight. I'll see you at the Delta check-in counter about 7:15 in the morning. I'm going to try to get to bed a bit earlier than usual tonight; this 8:10 a.m. flight means I'm going to have to get up a lot earlier than my regular schedule."

"Me, too," said Lisa. "I'll see you about 7:15."

(The next day)
Friday, April 14, 1989

As Lisa stood in line at the check-in counter, John approached.

"Good morning! Did you get any sleep last night?" he asked.

"A little," Lisa replied, "but much less than I usually do. We can board in about twenty minutes. The flight

200

2, 4, 8...(Destiny of the Human Species)

takes about 3½ hours, so I can get a good nap in before we land at Dallas. Once we get there, the schedule is going to be pretty hectic for the next three days, you know."

"I'll say," John answered. "Your speech to the General Session is one of the first. After the General Session, we're both scheduled pretty tightly in one Concurrent Session after another until noon on Sunday. Those sessions should be fairly relaxing for us, though, except for the one that you have to conduct on Saturday, and the one I have to conduct on Sunday."

This annual National convention of the Humanitarian Party was the largest ever. Membership had grown so fast, that it took a place like the Dallas Convention Center to house all of the meetings this year. It seemed like a long time ago that Lisa had accepted the chairmanship of the original chapter of the Humanitarian Party in Seattle. Now there were chapters in almost every major city in the country. Party candidates, although not yet dominating state legislatures or congress, nevertheless had gotten into position in those legislative bodies to cast the deciding votes on numerous issues that were critical to the goals of the Party.

As the plane finally levelled off at flight altitude and the seatbelt sign went off, John asked Lisa, in the seat next to him, "Are you nervous about your speech this afternoon?"

"Not really. It's just a slight modification of the ones that I gave at the WIN National Convention in September and the Careful Procreation National Convention in St. Louis in October."

"We could call you the 'NC Gal,'" John chortled. "National Conventions, I mean."

"Well, the audiences have been fairly mutually exclusive, and each so far has seemed to appreciate my message. The goals and activities of WIN, CP and the Party overlap so extensively, that a very similar message is appropriate for all of them. I mean, population issues, women's rights, and quality of life are all interrelated to the extent that my speech on that interrelationship is pretty well accepted by the kinds of people that attend these conventions."

"That's for sure," John replied.

"I think I'll get a nap now, John. Do you mind?"

"Not at all. I think I'll do the same."

Within a few short minutes they were both dozing in their reclined seats. Lisa's head gradually shifted toward John, and his toward her. Before long, their heads were pressed lightly against each other. Each of them was half-consciously aware of the other's presence. Neither made any effort to eliminate the titillating contact.

Once the plane had landed at Dallas/Ft. Worth, they picked up their baggage and hailed a shuttle.

"The Adolphus Hotel," said John, as he gestured toward his and Lisa's baggage sitting on the curb.

Lisa enjoyed tremendously travelling with a take-charge man like John. When she was travelling with various women friends, she never was sure how much authority to exert.

The Adolphus was one of Dallas's older, but finer hotels. They approached the check-in counter. John presented both his and Lisa's room reservations.

"Miss Billings, Room 314; Mr. Spencer, Room 316."

John asked a bellman to transport their luggage up to their respective rooms, and then he and Lisa took the elevator to the third floor.

2, 4, 8...(Destiny of the Human Species)

As they walked down the third floor hall, Lisa said, "Here they are, 314 and 316, right next to each other. That's great!"

After she had said it, she wondered whether John might wonder what she meant by *great*. *"But, then, being in a room right next door to mine probably doesn't mean much to him,"* she thought.

"I'm going to get into some better clothes," Lisa said.

"Me, too," John responded. "I'll knock on your door when I'm ready. We can just walk over to the Convention Center. It's only two blocks away. It would take us twice as long if we took a cab."

As they entered the Main Hall from the concourse, Lisa gasped. "This is enormous! I'm afraid I'm going to get cold feet about making a speech in *here*," she exclaimed.

"It's not that much bigger than the halls where you gave your speeches to WIN and CP, is it?"

"Well, no, not really," she answered.

They walked to their respective seats. John's was several rows back, near the middle, but Lisa's was right up on stage, with the other General Session speakers.

After the conference had been convened by the national chairman, each of the three main speakers took their turns addressing the General Session. John was proud of Lisa. Her speech was applauded numerous times. He felt that the applause was truly sincere, not just the polite type.

When the three speakers had finished their speeches, the General Session was adjourned, and the thousands of delegates headed toward the various concurrent sessions of their choice. Before Lisa could even step down off the stage, three reporters surrounded her, and blitzed her with eager questions.

"You were stupendous, Miss Billings," said one. "Could you give me a 'one-liner' that I could use to head up tomorrow's column?"

"Of course," Lisa replied. "To sum up my speech, you might quote me as saying 'Population Control, Women's Rights, Man's Humanity to Man: The Three Principal Keys To High Quality Life.'"

All three reporters hastily scribbled some notes on their notepads, then said in unison, "Many Thanks," and hurried off.

The Friday afternoon concurrent sessions went smoothly and effortlessly for Lisa and John. The topics which they had respectively selected were exciting, and they gained many tips for new approaches they could use in their own Party chapter, as well as in their CP work. They agreed to not try to meet for dinner, but to get a meal on their own, since the sessions went on into the late evening. Both were exhausted as they returned separately to their respective rooms, and they retired shortly thereafter.

(The next day)
Saturday, April 15, 1989

The phone rang several times before Lisa realized where she was. She picked it up.

"Hi," John said. He sounded amazingly alert for so early in the morning. "My first concurrent session begins in less than an hour, so I'll get breakfast by myself, if you don't mind. Good luck on your presentation this afternoon. Why don't we meet back here about 6 p.m., after the last concurrent session. Maybe we can have dinner together."

"Fine," said Lisa.

The schedule of concurrent sessions proved to be just as interesting as those of yesterday. Lisa's presentation at 1 p.m. drew an overflow crowd. Her topic was "The Effects of Tax Disincentives on Family Size." She presented a comparison of compiled statistics from states that had those kinds of disincentives and those that didn't. The applause that she received indicated that her interpretations of the data were persuasive.

After her last concurrent session ended at 5:45, she walked back to the hotel. After entering her room, she called John's room.

"This is John Spencer," he answered.

"This is Miss Lisa Billings," she replied with a chuckle. "I just got back. Do I have time for a short nap and time to changes clothes before we have dinner? It will only take me about 45 minutes."

"Sure," replied John. "That will give me a little time to look over my outline for tomorrow. Just give me a call when you're ready."

At five minutes to seven, John's phone rang. "John Spencer."

"I'm ready for dinner now. Did you hear of any good places to eat?"

"A couple of people who have stayed here told me that the hotel restaurant has outstanding food, and not too expensive, either. I called for reservations, but they

2, 4, 8...(Destiny of the Human Species)

said they didn't take them, and that we should have no trouble getting in, anyway."

"O.k., I'm practically out my door," said Lisa.

They both left their rooms at the same time, and took the elevator together to the lobby level. Then they proceeded to the hotel restaurant.

"A table for two," John requested.

"Would you like to dine in the main restaurant or the lounge?" the receptionist asked.

"What's the difference," asked John.

"You may order from exactly the same menu in both places," the receptionist said. "However, if you like to dance, there is a combo playing tonight in the lounge."

John looked at Lisa. "You like to dance?" he asked.

"Very much," said Lisa, surprised by the fact that in all of the time that she and John had known each other, they had never danced together. Maybe people in a platonic relationship didn't enjoy dancing as much.

"We'll take the lounge," John indicated.

The receptionist led them to a dimly-lit table at one side of the room, but right alongside the small dance floor.

"Would you like a before-dinner drink?" a voice asked. It was the cocktail waitress.

"What do you think, Lisa?" John asked.

Lisa rarely consumed alcoholic beverages, but it was not a typical occasion, so she said, "I'll have a Vodka Collins, easy on the Vodka."

"I'll have the same," John said.

Shortly thereafter, a waiter took their order.

"How did your presentation go this afternoon?" John asked.

2, 4, 8...(Destiny of the Human Species)

"Very well, I think. I was interrupted several times by applause, and a lot of those in attendance came up to me afterward with good questions and compliments. How did your day go?"

"Very well, too," John replied. "This conference is very exciting for me. It's nice to be among people that share the same philosophies. Being here can almost make one forget that the majority of the U.S. population doesn't actually agree with many of our policies."

"You're definitely right about that," said Lisa.

During their meal, they exchanged stories about the various concurrent sessions that they had attended during the day. John was very handsome in his blue suit, and Lisa was stunning in her red velvet dress. They made an extremely attractive couple.

The combo played a continuous selection of old favorites, the kind of music that you didn't hear in very many lounges. They performed some of the songs that had been hits by great bands like Artie Shaw, Glenn Miller and Tommy Dorsey; and great vocalists like Andy Williams, Perry Como, Frank Sinatra, Tony Bennett, Ella Fitzgerald, Doris Day, and Jo Stafford. Those were songs that had been popular during an earlier generation, but both Lisa and John enjoyed the music immensely.

When they had finished their meal, John said, "Care to dance?"

Lisa was almost surprised by the invitation. She had never known John to dance anytime previously. But, when he started leading her to the tune of "Stardust", she was secretly overjoyed at his feel for the music and their coordination of motion. John held her at a proper distance during the entire number. Then, when they began playing "Moonlight Serenade," he pulled her a little

207

2, 4, 8...(Destiny of the Human Species)

closer, and eventually his cheek was touching hers. Lisa felt a bit flushed from the experience.

As romantic tune after tune came from the instruments of the combo, John and Lisa kept dancing in that same cheek-to-cheek fashion. A feeling of mutual attraction welled up in both of them. John tightened his arm around Lisa's waist, and she put her hand on the back of his neck.

The band stopped playing at 11 p.m. John looked at his watch, and exclaimed, "Gee, it's a lot later than I thought. I guess we'd better get back to our rooms. The first session tomorrow comes pretty early."

They held hands in the elevator, as it went up floor-by-floor. This was the first time that either of them had ever had any inclination to do so. When the elevator door opened at their floor, John walked Lisa to her door. She unlocked it, and opened it.

"Goodnight, John," she said softly. "I had a wonderful time. You're a great dancer. Why haven't I known that before now?"

"I never had the chance to show you," he said, and he gently nudged her inside her door and closed it behind him. Then he pulled her toward himself, and to her great astonishment, he planted a kiss full on her lips. It was a novice-like kiss, but Lisa cooperated, and held it for a couple of seconds. He looked deep into her eyes. It was a look that she hadn't seen in him before. He kissed her again, this time more passionately, and again she didn't resist.

"You're an excellent dancer, too," he said. "That was the most fun that I've had in years."

He kissed her again, this time placing his hand on the back of her neck.

2, 4, 8...(Destiny of the Human Species)

John's behavior caught her by surprise, but she actually enjoyed it. *"After all,"* she thought, *"isn't this the kind of thing I have secretly been longing for from John for a long time?"*

The kisses were sweet, but eventually Lisa said, "Don't forget that early session tomorrow, John," and she drew away from him and shooed him politely out of the door to her room.

(The next day)
Sunday, April 16, 1989

John called Lisa's room at 8:30. "I had just a roll and juice for breakfast. I'm heading for my first session now. I'll see you back here after the end of the 11 a.m. session. Wish me luck on my presentation this morning." He made no mention of what had transpired the previous evening.

"All right, I'll see you here about noon. We'll have to hurry in order to get to the airport in time for our flight back to Seattle." She, too, didn't mention last night.

At 11:45, John called Lisa's room. "I'm all packed and ready to go."

"Me, too," said Lisa. "I'll meet you in the hall."

At the curb in front of the hotel, John paid a bellman for bringing their luggage to the shuttle, and they climbed aboard. It took only fifteen minutes to arrive at the Delta check-in counter. From there, they walked in silence to their designated departure gate, and waited until the announcement to board the plane. During the wait, John read over some of the notes that he had taken during one of the sessions, and Lisa read from a book on the environ-

2, 4, 8...(Destiny of the Human Species)

ment that she had brought along. When the announcement to board came over the loudspeaker, they again walked in silence to their seats, which were side-by-side. During the 3½-hour flight home, not much was said. They were both tired from the hectic schedule at the conference. But, the silence wasn't uncomfortable for either of them. John slipped his hand into Lisa's, and they both fell asleep in their seats, heads touching ever so slightly.

(The next day)
Monday, April 17, 1989

Angie was already at work when Lisa arrived at 8 a.m. "Did you enjoy the trip?" she asked. "It was great! Very interesting and exciting! I got a lot of good ideas for us to use here in our local operations." *If Angie only knew all of the exciting things that had happened*!

About 8:15, John stuck his head in Lisa's office door. "Good morning. How does it feel to be back?"

"A little anticlimactic," Lisa replied.

After that, neither of them brought up the topic of what had happened on that Saturday evening.

Chapter 40

(5 months later)
Saturday, September 16, 1989

John picked up Lisa at 7:15 p.m. They were going to the 8:05 showing of *Rain Man* at the John Danz Theater in Bellevue.

"Are you ready for the state conference of Careful Procreation next week?" he asked, as he drove across the Mercer Island Floating Bridge.

"Not entirely," she replied. "I can't complete my reports until you give me the preliminaries. Can you have them by Monday?"

"No problem. I'll be able to finish them up tomorrow. I'm going in to the office, Sunday or not."

"How has your outside life been going, John?" Lisa asked. "I mean, outside of work." She was curious about whether he was dating anyone. Since the episode in Dallas last April, he and she hadn't been on a real date — only coffee breaks at the office, and an occasional conversation over lunch at the nearby sandwich shop.

"I've been enjoying life pretty well," he replied. "I'm in a racquetball league at the U of W on Tuesday and Thursday evenings. That's been great fun. Then there's the cycling club that I belong to. We tour at least one day

211

2, 4, 8...(Destiny of the Human Species)

almost every weekend, rain or shine. And, I've done some hiking with my former roommate, Kyle Kimura, into several mountain lakes for fly-fishing during the last three months. Kyle's been working for King County since graduation, but has just been offered a job with a prestigious Atlanta company that specializes in solving environmental problems."

"It sounds as though you're keeping fairly busy," Lisa responded. Secretly, she thought to herself, "*It doesn't sound like there are any _women_ in his life at this point,*" and she was surprised to find herself feeling somewhat relieved.

The movie lived up to its reputation. Dustin Hoffman showed why he had won the Oscar for Best Actor. It was a real tear-jerker. Lisa had her handkerchief out much of the time. The experience left her emotionally wrung-out, and she was feeling a little dependent toward John on the way home. She wriggled until she was up close to him on the car seat. John didn't put his arm around her, the way she had hoped he would. He just kept both hands on the steering wheel, and kept a conversation going about the projects at the office.

When they reached Lisa's apartment, John walked her to the door. She unlocked it, and asked, "Do you want to come in for a coke before you leave?"

"I don't think I'd better," said John. "After all, I do have those reports to work on tomorrow."

And with that, he kissed her lightly on the cheek, and returned to his car. Lisa entered the apartment, locked the door behind her, and got ready for bed, a little disappointed that John had declined the invitation to come in.

(5 days later)

2, 4, 8...(Destiny of the Human Species)

Thursday, September 21, 1989

The state conference of the Careful Procreation Association was convened at 3 p.m. in the Main Auditorium of the Puget Power building in Bellevue. Jolene Lipton, the director of the Spokane office presided. There were two or more representatives from every office in the state - a total of 125 in all. From the Seattle office, there were Lisa and John, as well as Jeremy Watson, the Coordinator of Student Counselling, and Anne Bates, the Coordinator of Reproductive Services. Each was scheduled to preside at one of the section meetings of personnel having their similar responsibilities.

The main speaker was Brad Ervin, the director of the Tacoma office. He had compiled data sent to him by each of the local offices statewide, and his primary purpose was to show what progress Careful Procreation had made in the past five years. The first transparency that he displayed on the screen showed the pattern of revenues. **(See chart on next page)**

Brad scanned the image with his pointer. "As you examine the figures on this chart, it becomes obvious that the general trend in Careful Procreation revenues in this state has been on the increase. Many people have been taking advantage of the opportunity to designate which specific organizations should receive the charitable deductions that are given from their paychecks. We have obviously been a beneficiary of that policy. As you will see in the next few charts, the increase in revenues has enabled us to increase our services significantly."

He then proceeded to display a series of charts summarizing a variety of financial data: Reproductive Services, Counselling Services, Referral Services, ParentEducation,Education, Pregnancy Education, and School Clinics.

Revenues, 1984 to 1989

State Region Revenues, in thousands of dollars

	1984	1985	1986	1987	1988	1989
Bellingham	23	26	28	27	32	38
Everett	28	31	32	32	35	41
Seattle	67	73	84	92	103	105
Tacoma	43	46	42	54	67	79
Olympia	27	29	32	40	43	44
Chehalis	21	24	30	28	32	36
Vancouver	35	34	39	42	45	51
Spokane	45	51	53	52	58	64
Yakima	24	25	23	28	31	36
Walla Walla	21	23	22	26	28	34

"To sum it all up, ladies and gentlemen, we can accurately say that the services provided by Careful Procreation statewide have been making significant gains. We can be proud of the fact that we have helped thousands of men, women, and teens who were in need of services of the types that we provide."

2, 4, 8...(Destiny of the Human Species)

The audience applauded enthusiastically as he returned to his seat.

"Thank you, Brad, for that encouraging presentation," Lisa said. "We'll now divide up into our Section Meetings. You'll be in your same section meetings the rest of this evening and tomorrow." With that she adjourned the auditorium gathering.

Lisa, John, Jeremy and Anne all went their separate ways to their section meetings. Lisa's section was scheduled to meet in Room 112. When she entered the room, there were about a dozen other office directors there. She knew almost all of them by name, and spent several minutes sharing tidbits of news with various ones. Then, since she had been designated to preside at this section, she said, "Would you all find the seat of your choice, and we'll get started."

Everyone scurried for a seat, and when all had settled in, she said, "Brad Ervin's presentation shed a very favorable light on our progress over the past few years. In this section, we want to develop a list of ways in which office directors can help to expand that progress even faster and farther. I'm going to help you to get in the proper frame of mind by asking you to list on a sheet of paper every new idea you can think of for improving our organization's ability to attract clientele and to serve the clientele more effectively and more efficiently. Remember, we're thinking in terms of what we can do as *directors*. The personnel in the other sections will be going through a similar process related to their specific job titles. After five minutes, I'll ask you to hand in your lists. Then, I'll read the ideas, one-by-one, and we'll have a discussion of the potential, the pros and the cons of each one."

2, 4, 8...(Destiny of the Human Species)

As it turned out, all of the evening's time, and that of the next day were filled with the discussion that Lisa had referred to. The lists of ideas were so extensive that the section group was barely able to get to all of them before the meetings ended at 3 p.m. on Saturday. When Lisa talked to John, Jeremy and Anne on Monday, she found that they had experienced the same phenomenon. They were all gratified that their groups had so many enthusiastic members who had submitted the wide variety of ideas for discussion. They agreed that the time at the conference had been well spent.

Chapter 41

(3 weeks later)
Friday, October 13, 1989

Lisa opened the General Session of the Washington State Division of the Humanitarian Party with a bang of the gavel. It was being held in the main auditorium of the new Washington Trade and Convention Center in Seattle. Delegates from all of the legislative districts in the state were in attendance. The party's rise in the state had been so successful that every district had at least one delegate, and some had more than a dozen.

Lisa began by announcing, "Our main order of business at this convention is to affirm our party's goals. Since our convention last year, the National Executive Board has proposed several additions and modifications. The ushers are passing out ballots at the left end of each row in each seating section. Please take only one, since there are exactly the same number being handed out as there are delegates in the row."

As the ushers proceeded to hand out the ballots, Lisa continued. "The primary changes from last year are as follows. Items 1-b and 1-g have been reworded. Items 2-d and 3-a, 3-b and 3-c have been added. With those exceptions, the goals are identical to what the party has affirmed previously." She was reading from her copy of the ballot.

The Goals of the Humanitarian Party

1. To promote the maximization of the quality of life for all human beings, and the minimization of pain and suffering of all human beings.

    a. To promote a decrease in the human birth rate

        1. through government dispersal of free birth control information and devices to all who want them.

        2. through government sponsored school birth control counselling programs every year for all girls who have reached puberty.

        3. through government tax disincentives for having large families.

    b. To promote the principle of genetic screening of all aspiring parents for genetic defects, and to promote the principle of mandatory birth control for all girls and women until they have passed genetic screening.

    c. To promote the idea of mandatory government-supported Parent Education Classes for all pregnant women and their spouses.

d. To promote the idea of requiring classes in thinking skills for all students, so as to maximize the probability that life decisions will be made on a rational basis rather than an emotional basis.

e. To legalize suicide for people who are living an intolerable life.

f. To provide free health care to all humans.

g. To provide minimum housing and other basic necessities of life for all who lack them.

h. To provide a free K-16 education to all who want it.

2. To promote humane treatment of all animal life, with priorities set in the order of position on the evolutionary scale when choices between different species have to be made.

a. To outlaw hunting and trapping of animals.

b. To outlaw medical experimentation of animals if it results in any pain or suffering.

2, 4, 8...(Destiny of the Human Species)

      c. To require sterilization of all house-
hold pets except those for which the
owners obtain an official "Breeder's
Permit."

      d. To establish punishments for anyone
convicted of causing the pain or suffering of any animal.

   3. To promote the maximization of the quality of life of all living things, as long as
those living things don't interfere with
the quality of life of human beings.

      a. To promote the preservation of the
habitat of all living things.

      b. To require stringent inspections of all
locations where animals are raised
for food, to insure humane treatment
of those animals.

      c. To promote the gradual shift in the
human diet from one consisting partly
of animal tissue to one consisting entirely of plant tissue (vegetarian).

What most of the delegates didn't know was that Lisa
had been very influential in making the decisions about
the new changes and additions. As a member of the
National Executive Board, she was in a position to do
that. She was gratified by the fact that she had been able
to inject some more of her father's ideas into the party
platform. Robert Welton would have been proud of her.
The proposed list of party principles was almost identical
to the one that he had privately espoused in the late
1950's and early 1960's

2, 4, 8...(Destiny of the Human Species)

After all of the ballots had been handed-out, Lisa announced, "John Spencer, a member of the Executive Board of the State Chapter of the Party will now give a brief explanation of the reasons for the changes and additions."

John walked to the podium. He had developed an exceptional amount of poise in recent years, and radiated confidence as he spoke. "The reason for the change in Item 1-b is that within the past year, the technology has been developed that permits genetic screening and long-term birth control. The reason for the changes in Item 1-g is that the previous wording 'to provide a minimum standard of living for all humans' was too vague to allow a favorable majority vote. The reason for the addition of Item 2-d should be self-evident. The entire section 3 was added because the Executive Board felt that we should be promoting humaneness not only to humans, but to all living things."

John sat down, and Lisa again took the podium. "We will now adjourn this General Session, and you will move into your small group sessions for discussions of the ballot items. A member of the State Executive Board will preside at each small group session. At the end of those sessions tomorrow, you will vote by writing either a 'Yes' or a 'No' preceding each lettered item on the ballot. The results of this voting will be considered by your delegates to the national convention next April. This session is now adjourned."

(The next day)
Saturday, October 14, 1989

Alec Dexter, the chairman of the ballot committee approached Lisa and John about an hour after the small group sessions had adjourned, and most of the delegates had left the Convention Center. "Well, we got some pretty clear-cut results in the voting," he announced. An overwhelming majority affirmed almost all of the goals. The only exceptions are 1-g and 3-c.

Lisa and John glanced at copies of the ballots to see just what those items were.

Lisa said, "It looks like we need some orientation work in regard to those two items. I can understand why people may have voted against them. Let's get the word out to the local chapters that we have to explain those items better, then present another ballot on just those two items before the national convention in Kansas City next April. If members of our state executive board will visit each of the local chapters before their balloting, in order to explain these two items, I think we can get a favorable consensus."

FACTS OF LIFE!
1990 A.D.

World Population: 5,294,000,000 (Up 94,000,000 since 1989)

U.S. Population: 250,000,000 (Up 3,000,000 since 1989)

U.S. Municipal Solid Waste: 196,000,000 tons (Up 5,000,000 since 1989)

News Item, March 16, 1990

Washington - If the tropical rain forest is felled in the Amazon River basin of South America, the loss of trees would permanently change local weather and a sharp decline in area rainfall could, in turn, change the global climate, a study says....

A computer model of the effects of deforestation along the Amazon River shows rainfall would decline by more than 26 percent, the average area temperature would rise, and evaporated moisture in the Amazon basin atmosphere would decline by 30 percent.

Once this new, drier pattern is established, the loss of the Amazon basin forest would be irreversible; such a steep decline in rainfall could change the global climate

News Item, November 6, 1990

Geneva - Eighteen European nations on Monday agreed to keep carbon dioxide emission in their nations at 1990 levels to curb the threat of global warming.

Scientists have identified carbon dioxide as the main contributor to the so-called greenhouse effect, induced by heat-trapping gases.

Chapter 42

(6 months later)
Friday, April 13, 1990

John and Lisa presented their tickets at the check-in desk. The clerk directed them to put their baggage on the scale. This trip to the National Convention of the Humanitarian Party was going to be exciting, indeed. Lisa was slated to give the keynote speech this evening to the General Session. This entire week she had been practicing over and over in her head what she was going to say. John was going to conduct one of the Concurrent Sessions again.

The check-in clerk processed their baggage, then pointed them in the direction of their departure gate. There was only about a ten-minute wait before the announcement came over the PA system that their flight to Kansas City was boarding. They entered the door of the plane. A flight attendant smiled and welcomed them aboard.

"What are your seat numbers?" she asked.

"12-A and 12-B," John replied.

"About a third of the way down the aisle," the flight attendant said.

2, 4, 8...(Destiny of the Human Species)

John let Lisa have the seat by the window, and he took the one next to the aisle. "More security," he said. "We don't want to have some of these overzealous guys on the plane coming by and intentionally brushing against you just because you're so gorgeous."

Lisa thought to herself, "*My, he's being unusually complimentary.*"

As the plane lurched from its last contact with the runway, Lisa tensed for a moment, then relaxed and settled back. The previous day had been a nightmare, trying to get things squared away in the office so that no emergencies should arise. Then, last night she had been up late packing her bags. As the plane levelled off, she reclined her seat back to the maximum, and closed her eyes, ready to get a good nap in preparation for her opening speech later that evening. She had barely closed her eyes when John slipped his hand into hers without saying anything. She held onto it tenderly, and fell asleep in that position.

"We're now descending for our arrival at Kansas City International."

The voice of the captain boomed over the loudspeaker. Lisa awoke with a startled look on her face, until she realized where she was.

Outside the baggage claim area, after they had gotten their bags, John hailed a cab.

"Hotel Franklin," he requested.

"We'll be there in about 15 minutes," the cabby replied.

At the hotel, John and Lisa approached the manager's desk.

2, 4, 8...(Destiny of the Human Species)

"How may I help you?" a pert young woman asked John. She was practically staring at him. Lisa could hardly blame her. John was a handsome, impressive figure.

"Here are our reservations," John said.

"Mr. Spencer, Room 1012; Ms. Billings, Room 1014."

They ascended in the elevator, and got out at the tenth floor.

"The sign there indicates that 1012 and 1014 must be down this way," he said, gesturing to the left.

"Here they are," exclaimed Lisa. Right next to each other, just like last year."

"I requested that arrangement when I made the reservations," John responded.

Lisa considered that comment with interest, then said, "I need a shower before I go to the Convention Center. I'll give you a call when I'm ready. We don't have a lot of time, so I'll have to hurry. The General Session begins at 7 p.m., so we only have an hour, and that includes having to take a taxi."

"O.k., give me a call. I'll be ready," said John.

As the General Session was convened by the Convention Chairwoman, Marsha Tuttle, John and Lisa and all of the other Concurrent Sessions chairpersons were seated on the stage.

Marsha opened the session with the pledge of allegiance. Then she said, "As you undoubtedly know, one of our primary purposes at this convention is to vote on the party principles. With that in mind, I want to introduce our keynote speaker. Lisa Billings is the Chairwoman of the Washington State Chapter of the Humanitarian Party. She is also the Director of the Seattle office

2, 4, 8...(Destiny of the Human Species)

of Careful Procreation, and a national delegate to Women in the Nation. Please welcome Lisa Billings!"

There was an appropriate level of polite applause as Lisa approached the microphone.

"I want to say a few things about the principles that we will all be voting on before this conference ends on Sunday. You have all received sample copies of the ballot containing the list of principles. I will begin by speaking to the topic of major challenges that we have been confronted with in the last few months, and to review the purposes for some of our long-accepted goals. Then I want to say a few things about some of the new or revised goals that we will be voting on.

"But, first, I want to give you some statistics that are related to our principles. One is that the world population this year will have reached approximately the 5,294,000,000 mark, up 94,000,000 from just last year. Next, the U.S. population reached 250,000,000 this year, up 5,000,000 from last year. And last, the U.S. municipal solid waste tonnage reached an annual rate of 196,000,000 tons this year, up *5,000,000 tons* from last year. The U.S. population is predicted to reach 276,000,000 by the year 2000, and 300,000,000 by the year 2010. Ladies and gentlemen, I don't have to remind any of you who are in attendance at this convention, that the environment is not infinite!"

Vigorous applause ensued. As she went through her speech, section by section, she received enthusiastic applause at the end of each segment.

Lisa continued, "During the first half of the twentieth century, the primary concern of population experts was the question of how to feed the burgeoning population of the earth. Extensive efforts were undertaken to increase the productivity of the world's farms and farmers, and to increase the food supply in other ways, also. Little thought was given to cutting down on the birth rate, and to thus keep the population level from straining the food supply. During those years, people tended to look upon the earth as an infinite environment: one that could support unlimited population growth. In recent years, however, it has become apparent that the environment is not infinite.

"One important way to measure the progress of the human race is in terms of their standard of living. Up until recent years, the standard of living of any group of people was closely related to both their control of the environment and to their utilization of various aspects of the environment, including raw materials. As long as the environment was 'effectively' infinite, that approach was reasonable, but now we have to examine other alternatives for preserving and enhancing our standard of living. No longer can we enhance it by plundering the environment, because there are so many of us on earth now, that every time one group over-utilizes the environment, there is one or more adverse effects on some other group. One fairly familiar example is the interdependence between our forestry and fisheries industries. For years we logged off the trees as though there were no end to the supply. As a result, the rate of water run-off from former timberlands increased extensively, causing two primary effects. One was the rise in the temperature of streams. The other was an increase in siltation of the stream beds due to soil erosion on the denuded lands. The higher temperatures have resulted in extensive loss of fish life in the streams, and the siltation has caused a loss of much of the prime fish spawning areas. The logging of the timber created numerous jobs for people, but the lowered fish population has eliminated numerous other jobs in the fisheries industry. That is only one of many examples that I can think of which illustrate the interdependence between various segments of our environment, and what happens when the human population over-utilizes one segment of it. If we had an infinite environment, the human population could spread out widely throughout it, and thus humans might not have any significant negative effects on each other. But, the environment is not infinite; therefore, the more that the population increases, the greater the effects that humans have on other humans.

"I think that it's safe to say that a finite environment cannot support an unlimited human population, and it's time that world leaders acknowledged that fact.

"Next, I want to comment on one of the greatest problems that has resulted from a combination of too high a birth rate and the breakdown of the family unit. That is the giving birth to an unwanted baby, which I contend is one of the world's greatest sins. That sin is compounded frequently by mothers who actually end up murdering their newborns. We read about such incidents frequently in reports such as those about dead babies being found wrapped in plastic bags in dumpsters. The world is quick to decry such an act, but you hardly ever hear anyone condemn giving birth to an unwanted baby, who may very well continue life for years in that same unwanted mode. Scientific studies of child development and child-rearing practices have shown that people are more likely to reach their full potential for physical, emotional and social development if they have received an appropriate amount of nurturing during their early years. By *nurturing*, I don't mean only the instinctive maternal coddling that is most likely to be administered by the majority of mothers. I also mean the assistance in skill development and knowledge attainment, and frequent expression of the kind of love that goes beyond the instinctive level.

"The birth of an unwanted baby who continues on as an unwanted infant, toddler, and adolescent condemns that child almost certainly to a second-class position in society and to a relatively unhappy life. It is extremely unfortunate that the desirability of policies to prevent the birth of unwanted babies isn't given at least as much emphasis as abortion gets. That fairly common practice is condemned by a significant portion of the human population. Cries of shock, disgust, and anger are routinely expressed as a result of disclosure about abortions that have occurred. And there are, of course, some highly organized large groups that aggressively pursue the opposition to abortion as their primary focus. However, when we compare the seriousness of the two crimes of abortion and giving birth to unwanted babies, I'm not sure which is more grave.

"Of course, a way out of this dilemma is to implement methods other than abortion for preventing the birth of unwanted babies. Many of the abortion opponents with whom I speak refer to adoption as being a major answer, but I'm confident that if you compared the numbers of all of the unwanted babies in the world with the numbers of qualified adults wanting to adopt babies, the latter number would seem minuscule.

"Because most of the pro-existence segment of the population considers the beginning of human life to be the point at which conception occurs, and because those same people interpret any interference with the survival of the organism beyond that point to be abortion, it is advisable to develop and expand birth control methods preventing conception. Furthermore, it might be prudent to make those methods available to all potential parents, free of charge. It seems undeniable that such an approach would reduce significantly the number of births of unwanted babies.

"Of course, when we mention birth control, the first method that comes to mind in the thoughts of our hormone-driven teenagers is 'condoms.' Some zealous birth-control advocates have been promoting the idea of handing out free condoms in schools. Actually, that practice is too likely to convey the message that premarital sex is condoned, even encouraged! Not only that, most kids are like most adults: offer them anything free, and they'll grab it up. Then they'll try to figure out what to do with it. In the case of condoms, 'what to do with it' is just a matter of doin' what comes natcherly' for most teenagers.

"No, let's not distribute free condoms. Instead, let's put a condom machine in every public restroom in America. Yes, condoms in all public restrooms would help to avoid the permissiveness connotation of free condoms.

"Many opponents of easy condom availability point out that any kid who really wants a condom can get one at just about any drugstore. Well, most of the teenagers that I know would rather risk almost certain death from AIDS than to face the piercing stare of the drugstore clerk when they take their condoms to the checkout counter.

"Next, I want to point out an irony of tremendous magnitude that exists in our society. Of all of the human tasks that warrant the development of a set of preparatory skills, probably none is more critical than that of being a parent. Ironically, parenting is one of the few skill-demanding endeavors for which there is no test of skills that must be passed before embarking on the task. We're all familiar with the multitude of tests which must be passed before one may pursue various vocational, educational, and recreational activities. For example, there

2, 4, 8...(Destiny of the Human Species)

is the bar exam for a law degree, the oral exams for a PhD degree, the SAT tests for entrance into college, the CAB test for prospective operators of radio-controlled model airplanes, and the Cosmetology Board Exam for those wishing to pursue a career as a cosmetologist.

"Unfortunately, the primary task which the vast majority of human beings end up undertaking requires no prior test of skills. It is sad to realize that a human being with absolutely no skill in child-upbringing can become a parent. It certainly isn't because parenting skills aren't important. Actually, the more one learns about such skills, the more important they seem to be. The more books and magazines one reads about parenting skills, the more that one realizes the magnitude of the task of proper parenting. In fact, we might make great strides toward causing post-puberty human beings to delay pregnancy if we would just require every pre-puberty individual to read at least one of the leading books on parenting.

"If we were not trying to perpetuate a civilized society, parenting skills might not be so consequential. But, an appropriate level of skill in bringing up children is essential if we want the majority of our citizens to believe in democracy and to be able to successfully participate in it. Could it be that the recent deterioration of our society, as indicated by things such as crime statistics and poverty, is related to the increasingly common phenomenon of 'children having children?' By the former, I mean socially immature, inadequately educated young people, who not only have no parenting skills, but few skills of any other kind.

"One solution to this type of problem might be to require the passage of a parenting test by any woman before she could become pregnant. In order to implement such a policy, it would be necessary to first develop a

2, 4, 8...(Destiny of the Human Species)

contraceptive that could be irreversibly inserted into the female body prior to puberty, and which would last over the rest of her reproductive-capable life unless an antidote were administered. If this entire idea seems ridiculous, think of how ridiculous it is that one of the most skill-demanding tasks in the world is undertaken routinely by millions of people who currently could never pass such a test.

"Not only are unqualified people becoming parents, but people who have defective genes are also becoming parents. Today, many humans are able to survive and reproduce successfully despite having genetic abnormalities that would have prevented their survival in periods of human existence prior to about the last 100 years. One single, simple example is diabetes. I feel safe in mentioning it, since most of the members of the last two generations of my ancestors had diabetes. As far as we know, diabetes is caused by a genetic abnormality which may have resulted from a gene mutation far back in the development of the human race. Before insulin and its substitutes were discovered relatively recently in human history, the majority of people with diabetes didn't survive to the stage at which they reproduced successfully. Therefore, the gene that causes diabetes was 'selected against,' that is to say, the individuals who possessed the diabetes gene to the extent that they manifested diabetes had a slim chance of surviving to the reproductive stage.

"The ensuing discovery of insulin treatment greatly increased the survivability of diabetics. It has permitted diabetics to lead relatively normal lives, which includes reproducing successfully. And, the diabetic's offspring may very well inherit the abnormal diabetes gene which was in the genetic makeup of the parent. The net result is that, since the discovery of insulin, the proportion of diabetes genes in the human population has undoubtedly been increasing.

"There are many other disabilities, illnesses, and diseases that are caused by so-called 'defective' genes. It is also true that, as with diabetes, many of those conditions are now being ameliorated successfully through medical treatment. And, as with diabetes, it is plausible to contend that the medical treatment is increasing the probability that the sufferers of those conditions will reproduce successfully. Thus, their causative genes are also likely to increase in proportion in the human gene pool.

"If you believe my hypothesis that the proportion of defective genes in the human gene pool is increasing, you might tend to ask what can be done to reverse that trend. One answer would be to deny medical treatment to those who exhibit the manifestations of the defective genes. Their type would soon die out of the population. Another answer would be to require reproductive sterilization of all people who possess the defective genes. Both of those answers suggest a Hitler-like approach to the problem. I have never met a single human being who accepted those ideas. A more humane approach might be to mandate birth control for all persons until they could pass genetic screening for defective genes, a process which is just now becoming possible with new technology.

"In regard to Item 1-g on your ballot, I would like to say that we should be providing every citizen with a guaranteed minimum standard of living! There is adequate technology and sufficient wealth in the world to permit us to make that an inalienable benefit. I'm talking here about only the very basic necessities and comforts of life, things that just about everyone, including the most dyed-in-the-wool conservatives, would agree upon. I mean

2, 4, 8...(Destiny of the Human Species)

things like three well balanced meals a day; a warm, dry place with a comfortable bed to sleep at night; perhaps even the opportunity to take a shower once a day.

"I must say that I am troubled to find that even some of my most charitable friends are reluctant to hand out anything free to the unfortunate. They feel that handouts create a chronic welfare group. But, I don't think that their feeling applies to the basic minimums that I have in mind. I can't believe that a significant percentage of people would be satisfied to live permanently with the kind of standard of living that I am suggesting, if they had the ability to better their lot by getting a paying job. The minimum offering that I envision would be set up much like a prison, and would be run in military style, with sufficiently austere accommodations and sufficiently strict rules to discourage anyone from wanting to reside in those accommodations any longer than the minimum time it would take to get back on their feet financially. However, the main difference between the proposed facility and a prison would be that the residents would be free to come and go as they wished. Currently up-to-date prison-types of facilities, with a few minor modifications, would seem to be suitable for the accommodations that I have in mind. We would want them to be fairly indestructible (as most prison accommodations are), and sufficiently secure to prevent residents from harming other residents or their property.

"The statistics on the homeless and poverty-stricken indicate that our society has a definite need for the kind of safety net that I advocate here, in order to help those people who are temporarily down and out.

"One of my more charitable, yet ideologically resistant friends made a useful suggestion that he said would make the general idea acceptable to him. He proposed

2, 4, 8...(Destiny of the Human Species)

that the free room and board be coordinated with requirements for some type of minimum constructive activity on the part of able-bodied residents. That could include, among other things, job training or public service. Of course, those who had disabling problems could be at least partially exempted from such requirements.

"If you are resistant to this idea of providing a minimum standard of living for everyone, imagine for a moment that all of your net worth has just been wiped out by some physical or financial disaster. Under those circumstances, even you might think that the offering of a free minimum standard of living was a pretty good idea!

"Now let me speak to Item 1-d on the ballot. One of the characteristics that sets apart the human species from all other living species is the possession of advanced capabilities for applying logic and reasoning. Some people prefer to refer to those applications as 'thinking skills.' And, whereas other forms of life have to rely on physically oriented tropisms or instincts as their major pathways to assuring the perpetuation of their species, humans have the potential for these unusual mental abilities to help in that process. However, our having the potential doesn't mean that every human individual develops those skills to the maximum possible extent.

"I recently found what I consider to be a very practical definition of thinking skills. 'Thinking skills are those skills which are involved in the analysis of information and the formation of ideas based upon that analysis'. It has been demonstrated that formal instruction in thinking skills can not only hasten development of those skills, but can also increase the total degree to which they are developed. That being the case, it is disheartening to note that, in our schools, very little emphasis is placed upon instruction in the thinking skills.

2, 4, 8...(Destiny of the Human Species)

Unfortunately, the overwhelming bulk of educational instruction is devoted to the acquisition of information, while very little emphasis is given to the analysis of information, with consequent development of ideas. The paucity of thinking-skills instruction is not due to a complete lack of thinking-skills goals among school districts, however. I have examined the lists of broad goals of many school districts, and have found that almost all of those lists include a goal pertaining to the need for instruction in thinking skills. However, when one examines what is actually happening in the classrooms of those school districts, it can be found that very little instruction in thinking skills is occurring. One exception to that general observation is that of gifted-child programs, which are often accomplished through arrangements involving separate school buildings or classrooms for gifted students, and which are devoted to distinctive instruction for those "special" students.

"The scarcity of thinking-skills instruction is revealed in many ways. One is the absence of those skills as a curricular subject on report cards. Another is the failure of schools to designate specific amounts or blocks of time for such instruction. A third is the lack of routine testing of overall student populations for their level of such skills. Actually, if any school district accomplished any of those three, I would consider it to be serious about teaching thinking skills, but without any of the three, dedication to improving thinking skills would appear to be lacking.

"If we are going to nurture a future population of people who can make decisions about population and the environment without being unduly influenced by emotions, it is imperative that we promote the idea of more thinking skills instruction in our schools.

2, 4, 8...(Destiny of the Human Species)

"Finally, let me say a few words about our environment, that entity upon which we are so totally dependent. Almost every day we see, in the news media, reports of damage to our environment. In almost all of the cases, the environmental damage is caused by human activities. Environmentalists work constantly to develop ways to modify human activities so that those activities do less harm to the environment. One example of how they have succeeded is the limiting or prohibiting of woodburning stoves and outdoor burning in order to lower the introduction of smoke into the air. Another is the practice of requiring settling basins for the run-off from all construction projects where the surface of the earth is disturbed. That helps to prevent siltation of fish-spawning streams, among other things. There are many other notable examples of successes by environmentalists in regard to altering the results of human activities so that the effects on the environment are minimized.

"There are, however, some human activities that can never be eliminated entirely, and which are destined to forever have some negative effects on the environment. They include, among others, the need for obtaining food, the need for shelter, and the elimination of human waste products. Each of those activities had relatively insignificant negative effects on the environment during the period of human existence when the population was small, but now that the human population has increased tremendously, they all have very noticeable negative effects. All three of those activities have significant effects upon either the quality of the atmosphere or the quality of our bodies of water. Some of the effects upon the atmosphere have been fairly obvious, such as the highly polluted air in the major urban areas of the world. One of the noticeable effects on our bodies of water has been widespread deaths of aquatic animal life.

"Many scientists have been warning us about what could happen if we continue to pollute the air and the water in the way that we have been doing, but up to this point, I am not aware that any scientist has suggested that we may have already damaged those parts of the environment to a point that the damage is irreversible, and to the point that it could result in destruction of human life, either directly or indirectly. Who is to say that we haven't already damaged the atmosphere to the point where plant life will eventually die out? Of course, without plant life we can't survive, because we need the oxygen that the plant life produces. And, who is to say that we haven't already damaged the oceans to the extent that aquatic life will eventually die out, and thus our major source of protein will be eliminated.

"Let's hope that our concern about the environment hasn't arrived too late! Thank you for your kind attention."

With that, the entire audience arose in a tremendous standing ovation. Lisa was overwhelmed by their show of support for her ideas.

Chapter 43

(The next day)
Saturday, April 14, 1990

"Good morning, sunshine!" the cheery voice on the phone proclaimed.

"Is that you, John?" Lisa said sleepily. She yawned, then sat upright in bed.

"You were brilliant last night!" he exclaimed. "I talked to a great number of people who agreed with that. I wanted to tell you about it after the speech, but you were surrounded by reporters and admirers for so long, that, as I motioned to you, I finally came back to my room. I was so tired from the flight and the activities of Thursday, that I just went to bed before you got back."

"The response that I got to the speech was thrilling. I stayed around and answered questions until after 10 o'clock."

"Well, I thought that I'd better call and let you know that we have only an hour-and-a-half before the first round of concurrent sessions begins," John responded. "I've already had breakfast. Do you want me to order something for you from Room Service?"

"That would be great. Just some toast, jelly, and coffee, if you don't mind."

2, 4, 8...(Destiny of the Human Species)

"I'll call right now. It should be at your door shortly," John promised. Then he hung up.

John was presiding over a session on Genetic Screening today. He was no expert on the subject, but had recruited three medical researchers to serve on a panel during the session. They all were currently doing work in the field of genetic screening.

This year, Lisa didn't have the responsibility of presiding over any concurrent sessions. So, since her keynote speech was out of the way, she could relax and just attend some of the interesting sessions that others were conducting. She called John when she was ready to leave the hotel. They took a cab together to the Convention Center, and then went their separate ways to follow their individual schedules of sessions for the day.

As they parted, John said, "I'll meet you at the hotel about 6 p.m. Do you want to have dinner together?"

"Sounds like fun," Lisa replied, and dashed off to her first session.

About five minutes after six, John knocked on Lisa's room door. She opened it after fumbling with the safety lock, and invited him in.

"I just got back about ten minutes ago," she said. "Have you made dinner reservations yet?"

"Not yet. I thought I'd see what your status was before I called.

"Can you give me about 30 minutes?" she requested. "I want to freshen up and change into something different."

"That's fine with me. I'll call for reservations for 7:00. A couple of people that I met at one of my concurrent sessions told me about a lounge-restaurant only about a

2, 4, 8...(Destiny of the Human Species)

block from here. They have a nice combo that plays our kind of music."

"Do we have 'our kind of music,' John?" she asked quizzically. They hadn't listened to any music together for a long time.

"You know, the kind of music that the combo was playing at the convention last year in Dallas."

The thought of last year piqued her interest. "That sounds great," she said. "I'll be ready in just a little while."

In the lounge of the restaurant that John had selected, sure enough the combo was playing some of the old standards of the 1940's and 1950's when they arrived. The food was elegant, but a little pricey. But that was all right, considering that for the price of the meal they got some really good music.

After they had both finished their food, John asked, "Want to dance?"

Lisa recalled what a good dancer John had turned out to be last year. She also remembered that he had turned surprisingly romantic then. With a smile that indicated her pleasure about the invitation, she said, "Love to."

The dance floor was almost tiny, typical of those that one finds in lounges. But there was hardly anyone else who wanted to dance, so it was just fine.

Just as had happened in Dallas, John pulled her close, and they proceeded to dance cheek-to-cheek after a couple of numbers. *"Interesting,"* Lisa thought to herself, *"how he never makes any show of romantic inclinations in Seattle, but on these trips he blossoms."* She didn't mind it at all.

They must have danced for at least a couple of hours, except for about a fifteen minute break that the combo took. John held her tightly, but comfortably. She found herself putting her hand around the back of his neck. It was a sweet sensation for both of them.

Eventually Lisa said, "Maybe we ought to get back to our rooms. The first session tomorrow morning is going to come pretty early."

"That's o.k. with me," John replied, and he escorted Lisa out of the lounge and into the elevator.

When it reached the twelfth floor, they exited, and walked to Lisa's door. She unlocked it, and opened it.

To her surprise, she found herself saying, "Want to come in for a minute before you retire for the night?" She had never, ever invited a man into either her apartment or a hotel room.

"Sure, just for a little while," John responded. "Maybe we can find something in the mini-bar to refresh us."

He opened up the door of the minibar, and surveyed its contents: various kinds of nuts, soda pop, candy bars, beer, and even a couple of pre-mixed drinks.

"Hey, they've got a pre-mixed Vodka Collins here, the only drink I've ever seen you order. Do you want to try it?"

"Are you going to have anything?"

"There's also a martini. I can try that," he replied.

"O.k., open the Vodka Collins for me."

John proceeded to open the two drinks, place them in glasses, and add a little ice. He handed Lisa hers. They sat down on the love seat that was in the room.

As they sipped their drinks, John said, "I want to tell you, again, how brilliant your speech was last night. I didn't know that you had such a variety of deep intellectual thoughts in your mind. You must have done a lot of reading in order to gain the background for that speech."

Lisa said, "I've been thinking about some of those

2, 4, 8...(Destiny of the Human Species)

topics for years. But I don't usually bring them up in casual conversations, or at the office, for fear someone would think that I was radical."

She began to feel a little giddy from the effects of the drink. So did John. Neither one of them drank alcoholic beverages very much, and hadn't built up any kind of resistance. Actually, the giddiness made Lisa feel more romantic than usual, and she edged close to John. He immediately put his arm around her and kissed her softly on the cheek. She looked him directly in the eyes, then their lips met. It was a soft kiss.

That kiss was followed by one that was more passionate and firmer. John cupped her head in both of his hands, and kissed her again. Excitement raced through her entire body. She rubbed his back as he kissed her again and again. She could detect that his breathing was deeper and quicker. So was hers.

The ardor of her kisses stimulated John to do something that he had never before done: he groped somewhat awkwardly around the area of her breasts. Lisa unbuttoned her blouse, and almost immediately, John's hand slipped inside. He gently squeezed first one breast, then the other. That titillated Lisa. She reached behind her and unsnapped her bra. John quickly took the cue, and his hand slipped under the bra and made contact with her warm flesh.

The suppleness of her breasts aroused John's inherent dormant passions. He put his hand on her knee, then in a massaging motion, gradually moved it up her thigh.

For the first time in her life, Lisa didn't resist. Instead, she said something that she later thought back on with astonishment: "Do you want to go to bed with me, John?"

2, 4, 8...(Destiny of the Human Species)

John, the ordinarily shy guy, was so flush with fervor that he readily acceded.

He removed his clothing and laid it over an overstuffed chair. She removed hers, laid it on a straight chair beside her side of the bed, and flipped back the covers on the bed. They both climbed in between the soft sheets. She snuggled close to him, and he put his arm around her. He fondled her breasts and kissed her passionately over and over. Then he lay on top of her, much the way he had fantasized several times in the past.

"I just finished my period yesterday, so I should be safe."

She felt the warmth of his flesh as it entered her body. This was a sensation that she had only fantasized about up until now.

John marveled at the satisfaction it brought to him. Although this was his first time, he seemed to be doing things properly.

The tensions built up in both of their bodies as they felt the sensuousness of contact of lubricous flesh on flesh. Then John felt a sudden release, and his body pulsated as he underwent a pleasure of supreme heights. Lisa's body responded almost immediately to the warmth of his release. She experienced a corresponding release and pulsation, and she, too experienced supreme pleasure.

They locked in an embrace, and lay that way for several minutes. John dozed off in that position, and after a few more minutes, Lisa dozed off too, exhausted.

The light was shining through the curtains when John awoke with a start. He looked at the clock: 7:35. He looked over at Lisa, who was slumbering blissfully. He shook her gently.

2, 4, 8...(Destiny of the Human Species)

"Hey, dearest one, we only have an hour and twenty-five minutes to get to our first session."

Lisa opened her eyes, and said, "Let's skip the first session. I don't want to hurry."

By that time, they were both fully awake. John said, "Was that your first time, Lisa?"

"Believe it or not, yes?" she replied.

"Mine, too," John said.

She moved over against his body and put her arm around him. "We must be the only twenty-eight-year-old couple in the world that waited that long. Was it worth the wait?"

"Most definitely," he said, and he kissed her softly.

"John, you've surprised me. You never seemed to show any romantic inclinations at work or on our brief dates. Why haven't you ever made any advances toward me before now?"

"Well, we've been best friends for a long time, now, and I was afraid that if I got too familiar with you, it would ruin our friendship. You are my best friend, you know."

He kissed her again, this time more passionately. "I've fantasized about this situation many times. I've even dreamed about marrying you."

Lisa was stunned by the mention of the word.

"Would you ever consider marrying me?" he asked. "We have a lot in common. We can carry on a comfortable conversation on just about any topic. You don't have any characteristics that bother me in any way, and I hope that you feel that way about me, too."

Lisa brushed back the hair from his eyes, and said, "I don't know, John. This is all so sudden. If that's a proposal, I'll have to think about it for a few days, at least. I've never really thought about being married to you, although I have fantasized about having sex with you a time or two. Is that a proposal?"

"It sure is," John replied.

"Would you be agreeable to not having any children if we got married?"

"Why do you ask?" he said.

"I'm not sure I want any. The world is so overpopulated already, and I don't feel that a person has to have children to experience a fulfilled life."

"I think that I could live with that.

"What will the people at the office say when they hear that we might get engaged?" she said.

"Better not say anything to them until you've thought the whole idea over thoroughly and given me a definite answer."

"Let's set a deadline to make a final decision," she said. "How about a month from today?"

"Well, that's a pretty long time to wait," said John, "but I can manage it. That would be Monday, May 14th. Let's plan to have dinner at Bush Garden that evening. We can request our own little two-person private dining area. If your decision is 'no,' no one will see my disappointment, and we can still have an evening of quiet conversation. If your decision is 'yes,' we can celebrate, just the two of us, and we can plan our engagement announcement."

Chapter 44

(During the next few weeks)
April 16th to May 10th, 1990

Following their tryst in Kansas City, John and Lisa made a point of seeing each other more often - both at the office and outside the office.

However, Lisa was reluctant to engage in sex again, until she had given John her answer.

They went to several movies, attended a couple of Mariners games, and did a lot of bicycling. It was difficult to not let the office personnel catch on to their new feelings for each other. Angie, who saw everyone who went into Lisa's office, might have noticed that John was showing up a lot more frequently than previously.

As the days sped by, Lisa kept searching for reasons why she shouldn't marry John. She couldn't come up with any. It was easy to think of reasons why she *should*. There was his charm, his sincerity, his honesty. And, of course, his good looks. Any of the unmarried women her age that she knew would give anything to have a guy like John. Then, too, there was the fact that they had been best friends for such a long time. She wondered whether the friendship could survive marriage, and concluded that it should, knowing John.

2, 4, 8...(Destiny of the Human Species)

As the 14th of May, and their critical dinner date at Bush Garden approached, she convinced herself that marriage to John was the right thing. She knew that he would be pleased with her answer. They could spend the evening planning how to spring the surprise engagement announcement on their friends and co-workers!

(The next day)
Friday, May 11, 1990

"You called for me, Lisa?" John said as he stuck his head in her doorway.

"Come in. Close the door behind you." Her face had an ashen appearance.

"Is anything wrong?" he asked.

"I've missed my period so far this month. I've never been more than a day late before, and already it's been three days."

"What does that mean?" he said naively.

"It means that I might not have been as safe as I thought I was on the Saturday night at the convention. I might be pregnant."

John was stunned momentarily. But he recovered his composure, and said, "Well, we were thinking about getting married anyway. Couldn't we just announce a brief engagement, then a wedding date soon thereafter?"

"It's not that simple, John. Here I've been preaching premarital abstinence and, on top of that, I've been managing an organization that touts various methods of birth control, and *I'm* the one that's pregnant."

"You're not absolutely sure yet, are you?" he queried.

"Almost."

"John thought a moment, then suggested, "Why don't

2, 4, 8...(Destiny of the Human Species)

you wait a few more days. Then, if you still haven't had your period, you can get one of those home-pregnancy-test kits." Then he added, "Do you still want to go through with our dinner date on the 14th?"

"I don't think so. This confuses things terribly for me. Let's just find out something definite about whether I'm pregnant before we make any decisions along those lines."

"O.k.." he said, "keep me posted."

(6 days later)
Wednesday, May 17, 1990

Lisa walked into John's office, and shut the door behind her. John looked up quizzically.

"My home test came up positive. I'm pregnant!"

She began to cry softly.

"Here's a tissue. We can't let the others see that you've been crying.

"I don't think that the situation is all that bad," he said. "Unless you don't want to marry me."

"But I do want to marry you," she responded. "I love you very much, John."

"Then let's announce our engagement right away!" he replied. "We could surprise everyone Friday morning by coming in and decorating the office. I could order a decorated cake with our announcement on it, and everyone could find out as they arrived."

Lisa felt better about the whole situation as John thought aloud about the plans.

"We can have just a short engagement period, and then get married right away," he said. "Pregnancy before marriage isn't frowned on by most of the people in our field, you know, as long as the couple get married before the birth and raise the child properly."

2, 4, 8...(Destiny of the Human Species)

Lisa thought that the course that John described would work out without too many hassles. She agreed to coming in early on Friday, and decorating the office. In fact, she was even a little excited by the idea.

Chapter 45

(3 weeks later)
Wednesday, June 13, 1990

Lisa's wedding day was fast approaching. The date was Saturday, June 30th. She was ecstatic. A June wedding! The kind every girl dreams about. The engagement announcement had gone very smoothly. No one in the office seemed surprised by the announcement. Apparently John and Lisa had not disguised their feelings about each other very well. Everyone seemed not to question their hurry-up wedding date. Both of them explained that since they had been best friends for so many years, there was no reason to delay the wedding.

Lisa's mom, Cheryl, was pleased as punch, too. She helped Lisa make many of the decisions about things like the cake, napkins, refreshments, and so forth. John and Lisa had decided to just have a reception at the church, rather than to have anything fancy and expensive at another location.

All of the women at the office commented frequently on how radiant the prospective bride looked.

(The next day)
Thursday, June 14, 1990

Lisa began her work day with thoughts about CP

projects, mixed in with those about the wedding plans. Shortly after work began, John entered her office and closed the door. He looked quite solemn.

"What's the matter?" Lisa asked.

John stammered a little, which was unusual for him. "I found out that I'm HIV positive," he blurted out.

The statement hit Lisa like a bolt of lightning.

"Are you absolutely sure?" she asked.

"Positive," John replied. "I've been feeling unusually tired lately, so about two weeks ago, I consulted my doctor. He recommended several blood tests, and just happened to include the test for HIV. It turned out positive. But, I didn't want to alarm you without getting a second opinion, so I went to another clinic for another HIV test. They just informed me this morning that their test was positive, too!"

Lisa looked in a state of shock. Here she was, on the brink of the happiest event in her life, and now there was this news.

"This really complicates things for us, John."

John nodded in agreement.

(The next day)
Friday, June 15, 1990

Lisa entered the examination room at the clinic. Her regular doctor, Dr. Sharp, followed her into the room.

"What is it you wanted to see me about, Miss Billings? I received your message from my secretary, requesting an emergency consultation."

"My fiance has just found out that he is HIV positive, Dr. Sharp. I'd like to be tested for HIV, and I'd also like to ask you a few questions about HIV and AIDS."

"I'll give you a request form for a blood test for HIV.

2, 4, 8...(Destiny of the Human Species)

You can take it right over to our lab, and have the blood sample drawn as soon as you leave here. What are your questions?"

"First," said Lisa, "can a woman who is HIV positive pass the virus to her fetus?"

"Yes, that is definitely a possibility," the doctor replied. "It happens quite often."

"Do women or babies that are HIV positive *always* get AIDS?

The doctor looked stern. "About half of them get AIDS," he replied. "Of those who do get AIDS, though, close to 100 percent die from it."

Lisa was totally crushed by his answers.

"How long does it take for the AIDS symptoms to develop in an HIV-positive person?" she asked.

"It varies tremendously. Sometimes just a few weeks, sometimes several years, and sometimes the person never exhibits the symptoms."

"Well, those are all of the questions that I have now," Lisa said. "I'll go to the lab now, and have them take the blood sample. How long will it take to get the results back?"

"It takes about a week, under normal conditions, unless we put a 'rush' label on it."

"Could you do that for me? I'm planning to get married on the 30th, and it's really important for me to know about this."

"All right, I'll do it. We should notify you of the results in just three or four days."

(4 days later)
Tuesday, June 19, 1990

The phone rang, and Lisa lifted it before the second

ring. She had been on pins and needles, waiting for a call from the medical lab.

"It's Dr. Sharp's office, Miss Billings." Angie announced.

"Miss Billings," the voice on the other end said. "This is Dr. Sharp's nurse. Your blood test results just came back, and the doctor wants to see you as soon as possible."

Lisa was scheduled for a 10:45 consultation with Dr. Sharp. As she drove toward his office, her heart pounded in anticipation of bad news.

When she arrived, the receptionist promptly ushered her into Dr. Sharp's office.

"Your HIV test is positive, Lisa."

He said more, but Lisa didn't hear it. She just slumped in her chair. *"How could this have happened? I've got to talk to John."*

John looked up with concern on his face as she walked into his office and shut the door.

"My HIV test is positive, too." she said. "How could this have happened. It's so unfair. I've only had intercourse once in my entire life, and I get the HIV. How could I have gotten it from *you?* You said that time in Kansas City was your first."

"It was, Lisa. And this whole situation seems improbable to me, too. I asked my doctor about it, and he told me that I could have gotten it from an unsterilized needle. I got a flu shot about three months ago, right before our Kansas City trip."

(The next 4 days)
Wednesday, June 20 through Sunday, June 24, 1990

Lisa was devastated. She couldn't concentrate on work. She couldn't sleep at night. She was exhausted even before the work day began, just from all of the worrying. Could she go through with the wedding? Would it be right to give birth to a baby that had a high probability of dying a slow, painful death? She mulled those questions over in her mind time and time again over the next few days. The weekend was particularly stressful. She isolated herself in her apartment, and wouldn't even say more than a few words on the phone when John called, except to report that she was doing a lot of thinking.

Finally, by Sunday evening, she knew what she had to do. She had read about it in a book that one of the office's depressed clients had lent to her.

(The next day)
Monday, June 25, 1990

As soon as Dr. Sharp's office opened in the morning, Lisa called and requested some sleeping pillls.

She lied when she told the nurse, "I've been taking over-the-counter sleeping remedies, but they just don't do the job. I'm exhausted from a lack of sleep. Can Dr. Sharp prescribe something stronger?"

"I'll talk to the doctor right after he's finished with his current patient, Miss Billings. I'll call you as soon as I can to let you know what he says."

"Thank you. I'm here at my office. You have the number," said Lisa.

Several minutes later, Angie announced that Dr. Sharp's office was on the phone. Lisa shut her door, then picked up the phone.

"This is Dr. Sharp's nurse, again, Miss Billings. The doctor said he's willing to prescribe only one week's worth of a relatively strong sleeping pill. He wants you to ration them carefully, only one before bedtime each night. You may pick up the prescription any time after noon today."

"Thank you, so much," Lisa responded, and she hung up the phone.

Lisa organized her desk carefully. Then she thought, *"If I want to have a worthwhile impact, I should leave a note of the right type."*

She immediately began typing on her computer.

"To all of you who are so dear to me, let me say that I have given up all hope that the overpopulation of the earth is anything but a certainty. I can foresee only dire consequences of the failure of human beings to recognize the fact that a finite environment cannot support an infinite population. In order for the extinction of the human race to be averted, it is going to take radical changes in the attitudes of people everywhere. Perhaps this action which I am taking will place sufficient attention on the problems that loom in the future, so that my fellow humans will make the changes in societal attitudes that are essential to the prevention of the self-extinction of the human race.

"I love you all, especially you, John."

She signed the note, then placed it in a blank envelope, and wrote the one name, "John," on the envelope. She then placed the envelope on top of her desk.

After leaving work, she stopped by the pharmacy to pick up the prescription that Dr. Sharp had ordered for her. She then went home and changed clothes. She put on

2, 4, 8...(Destiny of the Human Species)

her nicest jogging outfit. On the side table alongside her bed, she placed the vial of sleeping pills, a glass of water, and the plastic shopping bag that she had selected specifically for the task at hand.

She sat on the edge of the bed and, one-by-one, she downed the seven sleeping pills, each with a swallow of water. Then she lay down on the bed, with the plastic bag within easy reach, and reviewed the major events in her life: the idyllic days of childhood, living under the tender care of 'mom,'' her exciting college days, meeting John for the first time, and learning about numerous aspects of life from her many college courses; the gratifying experiences she had as a member and officer of The Humanitarians and the Humanitarian Party; her rewarding work with Careful Procreation.

Gradually she felt more and more drowsy. Thoughts about the good times in her life came with more difficulty. When she felt that she was barely able to lift her arms, she picked up the plastic shopping bag, slipped it over her head, and pulled the drawstring until it was snug.

Breathing became deeper and quicker. Her involuntary physiological responses caused her to try to pull the bag off her head, but it was too late. Her breathing finally began to subside, and she slipped through the final exit.

(2 days later)
Wednesday, June 27, 1990

News Item:

Has history repeated itself? Some
of our older readers might think so.

2, 4, 8...(Destiny of the Human Species)

Yesterday morning, the body of Lisa Billings was found in her apartment by her fiance, John Spencer. Lisa was the biological daughter of Robert Welton, a well-known political radical on the University of Washington Campus in the early 1950's. Welton later went on to found The Humanitarian Party. It withered away from a lack of credibility because of some of the extreme beliefs that it espoused in regard to the environment and overpopulation. Welton committed suicide in 1962, along with his wife Susan. Susan was almost nine months pregnant at the time, and her baby was saved despite Susan's death. That baby was later adopted, and became known as Lisa Billings.

Miss Billings had an even more extensive history with environmentally-oriented groups than Robert Welton did. She helped to rekindle interest in The Humanitarians at the U. of W., then, like Welton, went on to be active in the Humanitarian Party, and eventually became the Chairwoman of the state organization. Her professional career centered around the Careful Procreation organization.

Billings left a suicide note indicating that she was despondent over failure of the human race to recog-

2, 4, 8...(Destiny of the Human Species)

nize its relentless course toward over-population, with resultant extinction of the race.

It seems almost like history has repeated itself, but Billings' situation was much different from that of Welton. Whereas Welton met with great ridicule and failed policies, Billings was riding a wave of success in her work with both Careful Procreation and The Humanitarian Party.

Part 3

DECLINIUM

FACTS OF LIFE!

News Item, October 10, 1993
Kutayfa, Jordan

Beyond all the hopeful talk of peace in the Middle East, a battle is shaping over an issue as powerful as land, as basic as oil: the region is running out of water, and no one, Israeli or Arab, is prepared to do with less so others can have more.

"If there's no agreement on water, there'll be no peace settlement," said a hydrologist in Amman. "Unless we come to terms on the redistribution of water, nothing will happen."

The reasons for worry are clear. The Israeli and Arab populations have expanded, but water resources have not.

News Item, January 16, 1994
Washington

Slowed growth in world food supplies provides real evidence that the planet's biological limits may have been reached, an environmental group says.

"As a result of our population size, consumption patterns, and technological choices, we have surpassed the planet's carrying capacity," Worldwatch said in its 11th annual "State of the World" report on global environmental and social conditions.

For more than two decades, scientists have been saying that the world can produce enough food to feed all its inhabitants, that hunger problems can be solved by increasing yields and improving distribution. But this new report says family planners, not farmers or scientists, hold the key to future food supplies.

News Item, February 5, 1994

By creating what they call the first precise image of the Earth "breathing" — removing and releasing carbon dioxide into the atmosphere — environmental scientists have placed a new emphasis on the importance of northern forests in keeping the atmosphere balanced. Their model gives them a monthly image of where the planet is taking in or releasing carbon dioxide. It is tuned acutely to the living cycle. Plants take in carbon dioxide when alive; it is released when they die. The model shows areas of high carbon dioxide release, such as in the tropics, where there is a great deal of rotting vegetation. By contrast, the cooler northern forests, where decay is slower, become a key point of return for the gas. One scientist says that if tropical deforestation continues, there could be one last giant gasp of carbon dioxide.

News Item, February 22, 1994
San Francisco

Earth's land, water, and cropland are disappearing so rapidly that the world population must be slashed to 2 billion or less by 2100 to provide prosperity for all in that year, says a study released Monday. The alternative, if current trends continue, is a population of 12 billion to 15 billion people and an apocalyptic worldwide scene of absolute misery, poverty, disease and starvation. In the United States, the population would climb to 500 million and the standard of living would decline to slightly better than in present-day China. The study points out that even now, the world population of nearly 6 billion is at least three times what the Earth's battered reserves would be able to comfortably support in 2100. "Comfortable support" was defined as something close to the current American standard of living.

News Item, March 7, 1994

Government officials say most of the major commercial fishing areas in the United States, outside of Alaska, are in trouble, and worldwide, 13 of 17 principal fishing zones are depleted or in steep decline.

"You can boil it down to the fact that there are far too many fishermen and not enough fish," said one fisheries expert.

Worldwide, fish provide more than half of all the animal protein consumed by people. As the global population has exploded, fishing has tried to keep up with the demand. But the oceans, which cover 70 per cent of the earth's surface, may have reached the limit of what they can produce.

News Item, March 3, 1995
Washington

Warming temperatures and the disappearance of a critical link in the food chain are turning the once-teeming ocean waters near San Diego into a dead zone, John

2, 4, 8...(The Destiny of the Human Species)

McGowan of the Scripps Institute of Oceanography says.

Dick Veit, a University of Washington zoologist said that the findings are consistent with other studies that have shown stunning losses of fish and seabird populations along the U.S. Pacific coast.

According to some theories, the burning of fossil fuels is increasing carbon dioxide in the atmosphere to the point that the Earth is getting hotter, a phenomenon called the greenhouse effect.

"If we can pin this warming of the ocean down to the greenhouse effect, then we've really got something to worry about," McGowan said.

Chapter 46

(6 ½ years later)
Friday, November 7, 1997

"Mr. Kimura, Mr. Spencer can see you now. His office is the second door on your right," said John's secretary, Jenny Wyman.

As Kyle Kimura entered John Spencer's office, John reacted with an expression of delight, and quickly arose to give Kyle a hefty hug.

"It's great to see you, again, Kyle," John said.

"You're lookin' fine, yourself, John," Kyle replied.

"What are you doing in Seattle? I thought you were pretty well tied down to your job in Atlanta."

Kyle laughed. "I'm here for the U. of W. Homecoming Weekend. I'm gonna tour the Greek district tonight, and then see the game with U.S.C. tomorrow. Want to come along?"

"I haven't attended any U-Dub activities for several years," John responded. "I couldn't get into the game, because I don't have a ticket. I hear the game's sold out. But it might be fun to see the festivities tonight. Actually, I'm free, too. Let's do it! I'll treat you to dinner, first. Let's eat at our old hang-out, The Pup House. As you probably remember, they don't have anything fancy, but it's good, and we can join the frat group that usually congregates there on Friday nights."

"That'll be fun, too," Kyle replied.

"I don't have time to talk very long, right now," John noted. "I have a visiting researcher from Brazil coming in in just fifteen minutes, and I have to get my notes for the meeting with him reviewed."

"I'm stayin' in Room 735 of the Meany Hotel — you know, the old Husky Alumni hangout. Why don't you meet me there about 6:30; then we can just walk over to the Pup House."

"Great! I'll look forward to it. We can catch up on each other's activities over dinner."

The crowd at the Pup House was already quite raucous when Kyle and John arrived. They asked for a booth in the side room, where they could converse without having to compete with the noise of the fraternity bunch. They ordered, then explored each other's recent past.

Kyle opened with "What caused you to leave your job with Careful Procreation?"

"Well, I took over the directorship after Lisa's death. I stayed with it for almost two years, but the place wasn't the same without Lisa. Then I got this offer from Enviro Inc., and decided to take it. It was a wise move for me."

"How is Enviro Inc. doin', now that you're the President?" asked Kyle.

"Really well," John replied. "Did you know that Lisa's father was the president of this same company back in the '50's?"

"No!. Wonder why I hadn't heard that before."

"Yes, he originally started out with them in 1951. It struggled along for a few years, and he finally took over in 1956. Things went well for the company for the first

2, 4, 8...(Destiny of the Human Species)

couple of years, but their business gradually declined, and in 1962, they had to declare Chapter 11. He was depressed about the status of the company, and that, combined with ridicule that he was experiencing because of his activities with the original Humanitarian Party, caused him to commit suicide."

"What happened to the company and the party after that?" Kyle asked.

"The company was reorganized under Chapter 11, and barely got enough work to survive for several years. Environmental work wasn't as plentiful then as it is now, you know."

"And the Humanitarian Party that he founded?"

"Well, it died out completely. The party that Lisa was involved with was a totally new organization that arose primarily out of the activities of Lisa and her fellow members of The Humanitarians at the U-Dub. As you may know, I'm still active in the party. I'm currently the Vice-president of our Washington State chapter."

Kyle pursued the topic further. "What about the Humanitarian Church that I've been reading about? What's its relationship to the Party? Are you involved with it?"

John's brow furrowed with serious thought for a moment. Then he replied, "Not actively. A few members of the party felt that Robert Welton's principles were important enough that they could form the basis of a new church. Those people were dissatisfied with the religious teachings of all of the existing denominations that they studied, so they started a new church right here in Seattle. Eventually, branches sprouted up in several other locations around the country. It's a growing phenomenon. Many people have left their conventional churches and have joined the Humanitarian Church. One branch in Washington, D.C. has even taken it quite a ways further.

2, 4, 8...(Destiny of the Human Species)

They're called the Humanitarian Church Reformed. They actually worship Robert Welton."

Kyle changed the subject. "What about your HIV infection? The last time I talked to you, you were afraid that you'd develop full-blown AIDS. Obviously, that didn't happen."

John heaved a sigh of apparent relief. "I'm one of the rare cases of an HIV-positive person who has never developed the symptoms of AIDS. I feel no ill effects whatsoever from the infection. But, I'm still a carrier, so I have to be careful to avoid transmitting it through a body fluid. I can't give blood anymore. And my sex life has been nil as a result of the infection. But, enough about me. What have you been up to since the last time I saw you?"

Kyle smiled broadly, and said, "As ya know, there's been no shortage of environmental problems to work on lately. My company restricts its activities pretty much to the southeastern region. We're still workin' on the problems of solid waste disposal and carbon dioxide emissions from the industrial plants in our area — nothin' exceptionally exciting, but nevertheless very rewarding. We're makin' significant progress along both fronts."

John considered Kyle's last comment, then said, "It's interesting to hear that you've been working on carbon dioxide emissions. Our worldwide data network has found indications that the carbon dioxide concentration in the atmosphere is rising significantly. For years, it was about 300 parts per million. Then, two years ago, we discovered that it had risen to over 1000 parts per million in certain areas of the world that were more or less sheltered from atmospheric circulation. That's approaching a harmful level, causing many people to experience discomfort and drowsiness. Carbon dioxide has proved to be a significant health problem above about 3000 ppm., and it has been found to be lethal to humans at about the 50,000 ppm. level. We're keeping our eyes on the data, and collect figures from a widespread network of analysis stations. By the way, do you still work out on weights every day, like you used to?"

"Sure thing; never miss a day."

By this time, they had finished their dinner. They left the Pup House, and walked toward Greek Row. It was now 7:40, and the onlookers had begun to show in large numbers to tour the homecoming displays set up by the different fraternities and sororities. Because the Huskies were playing U.S.C. the following day, the theme of the displays was "beating the Trojans." There were some about Trojan horses, Trojan warriors, Trojan battles — even one clever, but not-too-tasteful one about Trojan condoms. By 9:30, the displays began to close down, and the annual rally alongside 45th street had ended. John and Kyle decided to call it a night, and walked back to Kyle's hotel.

"Look me up, again, the next time you're in this area, Kyle. And, if I ever get to Atlanta, I'll look *you* up."

"Great," Kyle responded. "Maybe we can share ideas on some of our environmental projects."

Chapter 47

(Two months later)
Wednesday, January 14, 1998

"I have Mr. Kimura on the phone, Mr. Spencer."

"Thank you, Jenny," John said to his secretary. "Kyle? This is John Spencer. How is the weather in Atlanta? I heard that you're having some chilly weather that's damaging a lot of the fruit crops down your way."

"Yes, we're havin' one of our atypical freezing spells. Fruit's bein' damaged heavily right on the trees," Kyle Kimura replied.

"Actually, our weather is better than yours. We're having one of our atypical winters, too. The weather for the past few weeks has been not only unusually dry, but also relatively warm — up in the 60's on several days. That's really unusual for the Seattle area."

Then John got down to the serious business that he wanted to talk to Kyle about. "You mentioned when you were here in November that you've been doing some work on carbon dioxide emissions and atmospheric concentrations. Our global atmospheric analysis network has detected a significant rise in carbon dioxide concentrations in several areas of the world. Enviro, Inc. feels that this is important enough of a problem to set up a

2, 4, 8...(Destiny of the Human Species)

special research team to work on it, and your name is the first one that came to mind to head that team."

"I'm flattered, John, but not sure that I have the expertise that the project directorship would require," Kyle replied.

"I don't share that doubt, Kyle. I know for sure that you have the smarts to handle any job of this magnitude, and besides that, you have undoubtedly accumulated more experience with atmospheric carbon dioxide problems than anyone else with the qualifications. What do you say?"

Kyle remained silent for several seconds.

"Kyle, are you there?" John asked.

"Yes. I'm thinkin'," Kyle responded. "It's true that I'm pretty much of a flunky in my present position. It's not that I don't have enough challenge, but the company doesn't involve me in any major decisions, even though I think that I could contribute a lot. My gut-level inclination is to say 'Yes,' but I think that I'd better think it over tonight, and call you in the mornin'. O.K.?"

"That'll be fine, Kyle. I'll look forward to your call tomorrow. Keep in mind that Enviro, Inc. will pay for your move, and also will help you to find living accomodations here. In addition, we'll pay you a salary at least 10 per cent above your present one."

"It sounds like an offer I can't refuse," Kyle responded, "but give me the night to think it over."

"O.K., Kyle, I'll talk to you in the morning."

(The next day)
Thursday, January 15, 1998

"Mr. Spencer, Mr. Kimura from Atlanta is on line 2," Jenny announced on the comm-line.

2, 4, 8...(Destiny of the Human Species)

"Thanks, Jenny. Kyle, you're right on the dot, as usual. Are you going to join us?" John queried.

"It wasn't a very difficult decision, John. Yes, I'll take your offer. I know you to be both fair and a mover in the research field, so I've decided to come up to Seattle."

"Great," John responded, with excitement. "It'll be fun to work with my old roommate. I'm going to turn the phone over to Jenny, my secretary. She'll work out all the details of the move with you. We'd like to have you start tomorrow, need to have you by the end of the month, but are willing to wait into February if we have to."

"I see no problem with that," said Kyle.

John transferred the phone call to Jenny.

Chapter 48

Kyle Kimura entered John Spencer's office excitedly. He had been on the staff of Enviro, Inc. for only three weeks, but had accomplished a lot in that time. His research team that was set up to study the problem of atmospheric carbon dioxide had been dubbed simply 'CO2.'

"John, I think that there's a problem that definitely justifies your havin' set up 'CO$_2$.' During the three weeks that I've been the director, we've examined carbon dioxide concentrations on the basis of data gathered by a number of different organizations over the past fifty years at various locations on the globe. The most reliable appear to be those accumulated by Charles Keeling on Mauna Loa in Hawaii. The overall averages for each year since he began his records in 1958 indicate a gradual upward trend in atmospheric carbon dioxide. It was 315 parts per million in 1958, but gradually increased, so that it was 356 ppm. in 1992. But, the rate of increase rose during a portion of that time, from about .7 ppm. per year in the 1960's to about 1.4 ppm. per year in the 1980's. However, there was an abrupt shift in this trend in 1992, to .5 ppm. The current theory to explain this is that it was due to the eruption of Mt. Pinatubo. But, after a respite of three or four years, the rate began to climb again. This graph of the annual averages illustrates what I'm saying, but also notice how much more the slope of the line increased during only the last *four* years."

He handed John a standard sheet of computer paper containing a graph.

John scanned the graph, then looked up expectantly.

Kyle continued, "Now, the really significant part of our analysis is that which zeroed in on just the past five years."

He handed John another sheet of computer paper, this one containing the results of statistical analyses. "Notice that *every one* of the year-by-year comparisons was significant at the 1% statistical level. We first just made a comparison of the 1994 data with those of 1998, and, of course, found statistical significance. We were totally surprised when a rerun, comparin' each year with its successor, also showed significance in *every case*. Do you realize what that could mean?"

John thought for a minute, then replied, "It could mean that our initial concern about carbon dioxide levels was justified. Moreover, it could mean that this is just the beginning of a long-term trend, possibly even an irreversible one. If the predictions that some scientists in the past made about the dangers of global warming were accurate, the earth could be in for not only some dramatic climatic changes, but also widespread deterioration of many areas that currently are densely populated."

"Exactly," Kyle responded. "It looks like 'CO_2' has its work cut out."

"I think that we'd better budget to expand your team size, in order to give more intensive coverage on this problem," John said. "Please keep me posted on the summaries of any new data that you collect."

"Will do," Kyle replied.

They gave each other a high-five as they parted. They both knew that this might be the beginning of the most important project they had ever tackled.

Chapter 49

(8 days later)
Tuesday, February 23, 1998

John perused the report that Kyle had placed on his desk.

Progress Report Of Project CO$_2$
February 23, 1998

During the week of 2/15/98 to 2/22/98, my staff learned that not all scientists agree that global warming is certain to result from increased carbon dioxide in the atmosphere. The greenhouse effect was first described in 1861 by John Tyndall. In 1896, Svante Arrhenius postulated the relationship between increasing temperatures at the earth's surface and production of carbon dioxide produced by combustion of fossil fuels. He calculated that a doubling of carbon dioxide concentration would raise the average temperature by about 9 degrees F. That rise would be due to an increase of carbon dioxide in the atmosphere, which amplifies its ability to counter-radiate much more infrared radiation back to the surface of the earth. During the early 1990's, an increasing number of scientists rallied behind Arrhenius's figures, and warned that such a rise in temperature could cause the polar ice caps and mountain glaciers to melt at a much faster rate, and could thus result in appreciably higher coastal waters. They also warned that the rise in global temperatures could produce new patterns and extremes of drought and rainfall, seriously disrupting food production in certain regions.

However, I should point out that a significant number of scientists think that the above is an exaggerated view of the situation, and that the climatic changes due to increased carbon dioxide would be negligible.

Another interesting set of information that we obtained causes me to think that climatic changes aren't the only problem that we should be concerned about. According to our sources, carbon dioxide concentrations of 3000 ppm. can cause significant health problems in people, and the harmful effects worsen as the concentration climbs above that. We also learned that a concentration of 50,000 ppm. is lethal to most vertebrates.

Now, looking at our concentration figures from the studies of the previous three weeks, it seems clear to me that human health problems worldwide from carbon dioxide in the atmosphere are very likely to occur within five to ten years. Our data showed the average concentrations as follows:

1994:367 ppm.
1995:376 ppm.
1996:388 ppm.
1997:403 ppm.
1998:418 ppm.

That is more than just a linear increase; it is *curvilinear* ! The *rate* of increase has risen steadily! Extrapolating from the existing curve indicates a projected concentration of 1000 ppm. within only a few years!

As an environmental organization, we have the obligation to warn humanity of the potential consequences of the carbon dioxide increase. It is possible that the trend is an *irreversible* one. The human race may have already set into action a series of policies and practices that make the rise of carbon dioxide to toxic levels unavoidable in the future. I feel that our safest approach is to think in terms of creating an artificial environment for humans to live in, just in case the projections are realized. I'm thinking, for example, of something like the environment created during the Biosphere 2 project in Arizona. I suggest that we study that project's data, and proceed to undertake construction of a model somewhat like it. We could call it 'The Envirodome.'

2, 4, 8...(Destiny of the Human Species)

John was deeply concerned about the things that Kyle had to say in his report. He glanced at his watch: 5:30, too late to catch Kyle at work now. He would talk to him first thing in the morning.

(The next day)
Wednesday, February 24, 1998

Kyle's face was filled with expectation as he entered John's office and sat down. "What did you think of the report?"

"I was both impressed and concerned. There are two primary things that I want your CO_2 team to do in the next few days. One is to examine some of the more localized carbon dioxide data, especially those from areas of high population density, low vegetative cover, and low air circulation. Let's see what the specific carbon dioxide levels are in those types of places. Also, check with health clinics and other medical facilities in those places to see whether there has been a high rate of complaints about symptoms that could be due to carbon dioxide excess. Second, and only if you find significantly high carbon dioxide levels in some places, correlated with health problems, then compose a preliminary — very preliminary — plan for constructing a model Envirodome project."

"We'd need at least two weeks to get all of that done," Kyle responded.

"O.k., but get it done as soon as possible. This looks like a problem that we can't afford to delay working on in earnest."

Kyle hurried out of John's office, obviously intending to get the team in high gear.

Chapter 50

(2 weeks later)
Wednesday, March 10, 1998

"Here it is boss!" Kyle said, laying a copy of the CO_2 team's latest report on the desk, in front of John.

"Right on the dot, as usual," replied John. He picked up the report and hastily scanned it. "Were you able to get to both of the tasks that I assigned?"

"It was close, but we made it. I hope you're satisfied with it."

"I'll look it over in detail this afternoon. Right now, I have to leave for an appointment with Derek Siegal of Water Quality Corp. They're doing some consulting work for us on our Puget Sound Pollution Project."

"O.k., let me know what you think of the report as soon as you have time." Kyle then left John's office in his usual hurried manner, obviously eager to get to his next task. He was proving to be an invaluable employee of Enviro, Inc.

At about 1:30 p.m., John finally got around to examining Kyle's report.

2, 4, 8...(Destiny of the Human Species)

Report Of The CO_2 Team
3/10/98

Task #1: Summarize data from areas of the world especially inclined toward carbon dioxide excesses.

In accordance with the assignment, an attempt was made to identify areas of the world where carbon dioxide levels might tend to be highest because of high population density, low vegetative coverage, and low atmospheric circulation. We selected Los Angeles, New York, London, and Mexico City.

The 1998 levels of carbon dioxide in those cities were as follows:

Los Angeles: 694 ppm.
New York: 603 ppm.
London: 656 ppm.
Mexico City: 1014 ppm.

As you can see from the above data, Mexico City is far and away in the worst environmental condition, from the standpoint of carbon dioxide concentrations, not to mention levels of several other atmospheric pollutants. It's not difficult to understand why. Mexico City is almost entirely surrounded by mountains. It has the largest population density of all the cities in the world, not to mention the fact that the area has practically been denuded of vegetation. And, the city relies heavily upon the combustion of fossil fuels for its energy, both residential and industrial.

In regard to health problems, all of these cities reported an above average level of respiratory diseases, emergency treatment for breathing difficulties, and dizziness and general debilitation due to 'unknown causes'.

In the case of Mexico City, the death rate from respiratory difficulties and related complications is seven times that of Seattle, which had a concentration of only 516 ppm. In the Seattle area, the existence of persistent prevailing winds from the west and the Pacific Ocean keeps the carbon dioxide level from building up. Correlated with that, Seattle has approximately only one third the respiratory disease rate of Mexico City.

Task #2: Compose a preliminary plan for the construction of a model "Envirodome" project.

In the time available, we were not able to compose an actual 'plan' for a model Envirodome project, but we feel that you will be satisfied with what we did do. One of the actions that we took was to examine the characteristics of the Biosphere 2 project in Arizona. That, alone, gave us about as much information as we could cope with in this report. We will study that project further, and will incorporate more detail about it in future reports if Enviro, Inc. decides to pursue the Envirodome project as a major undertaking. We also examined technical reports from the literature on artificial environments, as well as that on life-support requirements. On the basis of our studies, we have assembled the following 'list' of major characteristics/requirements of such a project.

Requirements/Characteristics of Envirodome Project

Goals to be achieved by the project:
1. Successful operation of an environment which is completely independent of the earth's natural environment, and which will support a diversity of living things, including human beings.
   a. For the purpose, first and foremost, of dealing with the growing threat of carbon dioxide buildup in the atmosphere, and secondly, with other potential threats to the life-sustaining qualities of the atmosphere.
   b. For the purpose of providing knowledge that can be used in exploration and colonization of space.
   c. For the purpose of conducting basic ecological research.

Containment structure (housing):
1. Size and complexity limited by financial constraints.

2, 4, 8...(Destiny of the Human Species)

    2. Must be built to last at least 100 years without external repairs.
    3. Must be totally sealed off from external environment.

Life support requirements:
    1. Oxygen/air source for air-breathing inhabitants.
    2. System for eliminating/converting human waste products.
      a. Carbon dioxide.
      b. Urine.
      c. Fecal matter.
      d. Other solid wastes.
    3. Water for plant and animal inhabitants.
    4. Food for animal species.
    5. Nutrients for plant species.

Human habitat considerations:
    1. Psychologically tolerable, even pleasant.
    2. Healthy.

Technological systems:
    1. Power supply for electronic and mechanical equipment.
    2. Pumps for gases and liquids in the enclosed environment.
    3. Communications
      a. Internal
      b. External

Energy source for technological systems.

Selection of the human inhabitants.

2, 4, 8...(Destiny of the Human Species)

1. Intelligence.
2. Knowledge.
3. Physical health.
4. Inter-compatibility with each other.
5. Genetic purity.
6. Genetic diversity.

Funding:
1. Containment structure.
2. Contents of enclosure:
   a. Living species and sub-environments.
   b. Non-living aspects.
      1. Equipment.
      2. Internal sub-structures.
      3. Selection, training, and ongoing support for human inhabitants.

   4. Operations.

(The next day)
Thursday, March 11, 1998

Memorandum:
To: Kyle Kimura, Director of Project CO_2

From: John Spencer, President, Enviro, Inc.

Congratulations on an excellent report. On the basis of that report, I have decided to pursue in more detail, the Envirodome Project. In that regard, I hereby transfer you to the position of Director, Envirodome Project. CO_2 will remain under your supervision, but Craig Goodloe will assume primary responsibility for any further work on that project. As you undoubtedly realize, the problem of carbon dioxide in the atmosphere is the primary driving force behind the Envirodome Project's being established, and I see no reason to dissociate your responsibilities from that work. However, the assignment of Craig as main overseer of that sub-project will give you more time to spend on the multiple facets that must be studied as the Envirodome Project unfolds.

Please proceed at once to develop a more detailed plan for designing the details of the Envirodome Project. I have instructed Josie McClellan, our chief congressional lobbyist, to work closely with you in regard to the funding options for the project. With a project of the magnitude that I foresee, we will probably have to request federal participation in the funding. I believe that such funding can be justified because of the national and international implications of the carbon dioxide threat.

Please keep me advised of any progress that you make in the design and funding of the project.

Chapter 51

(6 days later)
Wednesday, March 17, 1998

Kyle entered John's office at the appointed time. He had two other Enviro, Inc. staff members with him. "Thanks for giving us this appointment on such short notice, John. I think you already know Josie McClellan."

Josie extended her hand. For some time John had been acutely aware of Josie's presence on the staff. A statuesque blonde, she seemed to be the antithesis of the stereotype of either a scientist or a lobbyist. She was, of course, both. In college, she had pursued a triple major — biochemistry, finance, and political science. Although her first love was biochemistry, her impressive appearance led her to gradually increasing success in the field of lobbying, where she had no difficulty getting the attention of just about any male politician with whom she wanted to get acquainted. The same couldn't exactly be said of female politicians, who unwarrantedly viewed her as a "sleep-around" social climber. In reality, Josie was a firm believer in abstinence, much to the chagrin of many of the aforesaid male politicians.

Kyle continued: "I think you also know Kurt Kleider. Kurt's our energy supply expert."

2, 4, 8...(Destiny of the Human Species)

John nodded, and extended his hand to Kurt. "Sit down, please."

"I thought that the three of us should have an informal meeting with you before I sent you any more memos," Kyle said. "There are some general concepts that we should discuss before we get into the details of funding and design. Josie, you start."

"We know that the Biosphere 2 project facility alone cost in excess of $150 million. That's not counting the operations costs. If we throw in those, we are probably looking at $250 to $300 million for start-up costs and the first two years of operation. However, there are two major factors that could significantly alter the costs of the Envirodome Project. One could reduce our outlay; the other could increase it, but not necessarily. The structure which housed Biosphere 2 was built from the ground up, and was constructed so that sunlight could penetrate the majority of the roof sections. That was for the purpose of allowing the sunlight to be received by the plants that balanced the ecological system inside. Biosphere 2 also relied upon external sources to supply its total needs for electrical energy, a process which seriously damaged the intended image of the project as being one involving an environment that was completely independent of the outside.

"Now, another factor that should be tossed into the discussion at this point is the fact that 'Fuse-Gen,' the newly developed fusion reactor now available from Fusion Tech., Inc., has the potential for drastically affecting our approach to the process of constructing and maintaining an isolated, balanced environment. I'll let Kurt say more about that, but an extremely important aspect in this regard is that an Envirodome powered by fusion wouldn't need to have a transparent roof. That fact,

2, 4, 8...(Destiny of the Human Species)

alone, makes it conceivable that our project could be housed in an existing structure like the Kingdome. Because it was mothballed after the players' strikes and the downturn in the economy, it might be available at a fairly low price."

"Interesting conjecture," was all that John could say in response to Josie's comments.

Josie continued, "I think that you should hear what Kurt has to say about the general implications of fusion-based energy for the Envirodome."

Kurt attempted to smooth back his slightly rumpled, very curly hair. "We're fortunate, in a way, that this new fusion reactor has just come on the market. It changes significantly our outlook on energy supply. Josie is right: the use of this reactor could eliminate any need for transparent roof panels. But, there are some other factors that make the use of a fusion system even more attractive. The Biosphere 2 project not only relied on solar illumination for its plant life, but also assumed that solar energy would always be available on the normal diurnal basis. But, there are a couple of scenarios that could make it wise not to operate on that assumption. As long as we're recommending this kind of monetary investment in the project, we might as well design it to provide a friendly environment for the inhabitants even if all sunlight were blocked out — as could be the case in a nuclear winter resulting from another war, or in a situation resulting from the collision of a large asteroid with earth. You probably know about the hypothesis that almost all living things were wiped out millions of years ago by such a collision. If it were to occur again, it might take several decades for the opaque dust cover to settle out of the atmosphere. Meanwhile, a dome run on fusion energy could continue to function."

2, 4, 8...(Destiny of the Human Species)

John nodded approvingly, and said, "I can't disagree with anything you've said here. Kyle, why don't you summarize these concepts in an official memo to me, so that we'll have it for our records. Josie and Kurt, I'm going to leave to Kyle the major decisions on how to proceed with the design and planning. But you both have my endorsement of your ideas, and I want Kyle to give you all of the support that he can provide from our various resources in the company. Josie, I think that you should work closely with me on our lobbying efforts. I don't want them to get ahead of our technological capabilities. In addition, I think that we can get some help in our lobbying effort from the Humanitarian Party. They're concerned about preserving the human species and about the environmental threat to its survival. I'll talk to the national board of directors to see what kind of help that they can give us. Thank you to all three of you."

Chapter 52

As the occupants of Flight 742 disembarked at Washington National, John Spencer arose and retrieved his and Josie's carry-on bags from the overhead compartment. They were pressed for time, because it was only an hour and a half until their appointment with Senator Blevens and his staff. The good senator had proved to be their most favorable ally in the senate, where they hoped to see the companion to House Bill 1046 passed. The House of Representatives had confirmed that bill by a narrow margin, and John and Josie, and the rest of the Enviro, Inc. staff were hopeful that it would also receive approval in the senate. If that happened, Enviro, Inc. could proceed with more detailed plans for the Envirodome Project. The bill would fund the project in increments, contingent upon progress in each preceding phase. Kyle Kimura's team had decided to request funding initially for support of the 'resident identification' phase - that of selecting the people who would inhabit the Envirodome, and who would carry out all of the essential processes within it. It was a relatively inexpensive, but vital phase. After their selection, they would assume the major burden of responsibility for the planning of the structural and operational details. Funding for the planning phase would therefore have to follow the selection of those people. And, subsequently, the funding for actual construction, and then the ongoing operation of the Envirodome would have to be approved in stages.

At 3:10, John approached the door lettered with the words *Senator Howard Blevens.* He pulled it open, and motioned for Josie to step inside the reception room. He approached the receptionist and announced, "I'm John Spencer. This is my associate, Josie McClellan. We have a 3:15 appointment with Senator Blevens."

"Please have a seat. I'll tell the Senator that you're here," she said curtly.

It was about ten minutes before she indicated that they could see Senator Blevens. She led them to a private office down a short corridor.

"Welcome to Washington," the senator greeted them. "Have you had an opportunity to rest up from your flight from Seattle?"

"It wasn't all that bad. Actually, Senator, we were able to nap on the plane, so we feel quite refreshed," John replied.

"Excellent. May I assume that you're ready to discuss the details of our strategy for getting this bill through the senate?"

"Yes, sir," John responded.

"Well, as you know, the vote in the House was close. I have sent out feelers to the members of the Senate, and it appears that we need two more votes to get this thing through. As I indicated in my fax to you last week, two senators who are on the fence are Morten Johnson of Kansas and Ryan Hartzig of Indiana. It's going to be up

2, 4, 8...(Destiny of the Human Species)

to you to help convince them that there is an urgency to the Envirodome Project. If after meeting with them tomorrow, you and your lovely associate would host a dinner for them, it might help. Josie can certainly turn a man's head, and maybe even his vote."

John had to agree. Josie was very alluring as lobbyists go. Their appointments for an afternoon meeting and a dinner engagement with the two senators could be a key factor in swinging their votes.

Senator Blevens then launched into a detailed explanation of his plans for shepherding the bill through the Senate.

After the meeting with the Senator, John and Josie ate dinner at the restaurant in their hotel.

During the meal, John advised, "We have to make sure that there aren't any flaws in our presentation tomorrow. Also, we want to meet with Representative Borders before we return to Seattle, and thank him for guiding the bill through the House. It might be helpful to point out to Johnson and Hartzig that we've raised $30,000 for Borders' campaign fund, and that the same kind of effort for their campaigns is a distinct possibility." Then, as an apparent afterthought, John said, "Would you be interested in visiting the Humanitarian Church Reformed while we're in town? I'd like to see what type of service they have. They meet on Saturday mornings. We could drop in for the service before we have to leave for the airport."

Josie responded with, "Sure, why not. It might give you something significant to report back to the Party Directors."

As they ate, John and Josie reviewed the various sections of the funding bill. They also looked over the notes that they took while meeting with Senator Blevens. It was 9:30 p.m. before they realized it.

"Time for me to hit the hay," Josie announced. "Besides that, I have unpacking to do, and a few notes to look over yet tonight."

"Me, too, I guess," John confirmed.

They left the restaurant, and took the elevator to the fourth floor. John accompanied Josie to her room, where she took out her key and unlocked the door.

"I'll see you in the restaurant at 7:30 in the morning for breakfast," she said. "Whoever arrives first can get a table."

"I'll see you then," John said. He took one last look at her as she turned to go inside her room. She looked very seductive in her V-necked blouse, with tailored jacket and above-the-knee skirt. *"Too bad I'm HIV positive and she doesn't believe in sex before marriage. This would be a good opportunity to make beautiful music together."*

The door closed behind her, and he went to his room.

(The next evening)
Friday, May 21, 1998

Josie stood up in front of her place at the table. Even before she spoke, all eyes of the diners at the table were on her. She had purposely worn one of her sexiest dresses. "I would like to thank you, Senator Johnson and Senator Hartzig and you, their staff members, for rearranging your schedules in order to meet with us this afternoon, and in order to have dinner with us this evening. As we pointed out this afternoon, the Envirodome Project could represent a critical form of experimentation to design measures for adapting to significant changes in the environment. One of the most important of those changes is

2, 4, 8...(Destiny of the Human Species)

the rise in carbon dioxide concentrations in the atmosphere. Besides that, there are, of course, other key scientific questions that can be answered by pursuing this project. I would like to offer a toast to the two Senators for assigning enough credibility to the project that they were willing to give us their time."

With that, she took her seat. The rest of the evening was taken up almost exclusively by the exchange of pleasantries.

(The next day)
Saturday, May 22, 1998

John and Josie's taxi pulled up to the curb in front of the Humanitarian Church Reformed at the corner of Dexter and 32nd Street. It looked much like any Christian church from the outside. Apparently, after it had been vacated by the Presbyterian church, the Humanitarians had done nothing to change the exterior appearance. As they entered the front door, however, they were struck by the presence of a large photograph of a man on the wall behind the altar. John whispered to Josie, "That's Robert Welton in his earlier years." It looked like it could be his college graduation photo.

They took a seat, and John noticed a book in the rack on the back of the pew in front of him. It was entitled *The Book of Humanitarianism.* It wasn't very thick, and as he thumbed through it, he noticed that it was organized along the lines of Robert Welton's goals.

They were just in time to witness the beginning of the service. The minister said, "Let us all pray. Oh Supreme Power that governs the universe, we gather here today to show our respect for your Son, Robert Welton, and all that he stood for."

2, 4, 8...(Destiny of the Human Species)

Then, the minister continued, "Please open your worship books to Article 2 of the Weltonian Principles, and follow along as I read."

He then proceeded to read verbatim from Article 2. "Whereas we believe in the maximization of quality of life for all human beings, and whereas the life of those afflicted with genetic defects is usually below the level that is desirable, we hereby vow to promote the policy that all fertilization of human eggs be accomplished by *in vitro* fertilization, and that genetic screening of all gametes prior to that in vitro fertilization take place."

That statement was a mild shock to John, who had privately adhered to the idea of genetic screening, but who had never heard it stated in this way.

The minister proceeded to elaborate on the statement, offering additional justification that was not contained in Article 2. After the sermon, the entire congregation of about 35 people joined in song, singing some of the happy philosophical songs that had been written in the 1950's and 1960's, the later years of Robert Welton's life. They included "On A Clear Day," "What The World Needs Now Is Love," "You've Gotta Have Heart," and "Pick Yourself Up."

John and Josie had to leave for the airport, and consequently couldn't stay and talk with any of the members of the congregation. They barely made it to the airport in time for their flight.

(Two weeks later)
Wednesday, June 9, 1998

Josie's intercom buzzed. It was John's secretary, Jenny. "Senator Blevens is on Line 2, Miss McClellan."

2, 4, 8...(Destiny of the Human Species)

"Thank you, Jenny." Then, "Good morning Senator Blevens. I'm surprised to hear from you!"

"I wanted to be the first to tell you that your funding bill passed the Senate late last evening. Congratulations!"

"You're the one who deserves the congratulations, Senator," Josie responded. At the same time she was wondering why the senator had called her instead of calling John. "*I must have left an impression on him,*" she thought to herself. "I'll let John know right away. When can we expect release of the funds for the first phase?"

"The first increment of $210,000 for selecting the dome residents will be available July 1st. After that, your project will be audited and evaluated before the next increment will become available. Please let me know when you're ready for the auditing and evaluation to occur."

"I'll certainly do that, Senator, and thank you, again, for all of your efforts on behalf of the bill."

"It was a pleasure working with someone as delightful as you, Josie. Let me know if I can help you out in any other way."

Chapter 53

(Two weeks later)
Tuesday, June 22, 1998

John Spencer was sitting in on the meeting of the Envirodome Project team. Addressing the team, Kyle announced, "The funds to support our selection process will be available on July 1st. Before then, we have to make a determination about the required characteristics of the selectees, as well as the number of selectees. That can't be done without first arrivin' at an estimate of the amount of space needed for various functions that'll be accomplished within the dome. These aspects of the project are inextricably intertwined. Let's begin with a brainstormin' session on the size of dome that would be advisable for the project."

Enrico Alleo, structural specialist began. "There are several factors that should guide our considerations of dome size. One is the size of various existing structures that are currently available. Another is their price. A third is the fact that we might be well advised to plan something close to the size of Biosphere 2, since we'll be using a lot of the data from that project as a basis for much of our other planning. We might as well build on the results of that project as much as possible, rather than

2, 4, 8...(Destiny of the Human Species)

assembling a project from the ground up. Anyway, the funds that have been built into the congressional legislation for this project pretty well limit us to something close to that size. The funding that we requested to be included in the bill was aligned with the assumption that an existing dome would be used to house the project."

"Good points, Enrico," said Kyle. "Anyone else?"

Allyson Loucks, agronomy specialist, nodded. "The Bios experiments that were carried out in the Soviet Union in the 1960's and 1970's indicated that about 230 square feet of growing area were needed to support one person's oxygen and food requirements. Of course, those experiments were conducted on a very limited scale. Then, there was the work by Salisbury that showed that a growing area about the size of a football field could support about 100 peoples' needs. Those two figures average out to about 150 people to be supported by a growing area of that size. Biosphere 2 involved only eight people, and actually enclosed an area about three times the size of a football field."

Ruth Trumball fidgeted in her seat before finally speaking up. "But, don't forget, we're talking, now, only about the growing area that's needed. There are a lot of other areas that have to be included in the dome. For example, there's the waste recycling system, the living quarters, the communications room, the reactor space, the medical lab, analytical labs, and possibly several others."

"You're right about that, Ruth," said Kyle, nodding.

Josh Albright brought up another point. "We shouldn't establish the number of envirodome residents anywhere near the upper level of supportability for the space within the enclosure. If we want this project to succeed, it'd be wise to avoid any risks like that. Let's leave a comfortable

2, 4, 8...(Destiny of the Human Species)

cushion between the maximum that the enclosure would support and the number that we decide on."

Enrico Alleo offered more. "The Kingdome right here in Seattle should definitely receive consideration. After all, it was remodeled only a short time ago, and should easily last through the required 100-year time period. It's as well built as any dome in the country - all concrete, you know. And besides that, it's available for only $25 million. It originally cost about $65 million, and that was years ago. It's size approximates that of Biosphere 2 closely enough to permit fairly easy utilization of data from that project. Then, too, another factor that could be important to us is that the Kingdome is right here in our own region, easily accessible from our head-quarters."

Allyson spoke up again. "If we're going to think in terms of a structure the size of the Kingdome, and if we're also going to work in the realm of parameters of Biosphere 2, we should probably plan to house between ten and fifteen residents. No more than fifteen would give the cushion that Josh suggested."

Kyle immediately responded. "Didn't Biosphere 2 have only eight occupants?"

Allyson replied, "We'll have more growing area for crops to support the human population because we aren't planning to create a miniature mock-up of the earth. Biosphere 2 had several biomes that we probably won't include — like an ocean, for instance, and a desert.

Enrico interjected, "Let's not forget that hypotheti-cally, we could be selecting the last survivors of the human race!"

"What do you mean?" asked Ruth.

"Well," Enrico continued, "aren't we planning a structure that would allow people to survive a dramatic change in

2, 4, 8...(Destiny of the Human Species)

the environment? Isn't it possible that eventually the environment could become so hostile that the only people that could survive would be those in the Envirodome?"

Ruth mulled that over, then said, "I hadn't really thought of this project in those terms, but you could *hypothetically* be right."

"Well, then," said Enrico, "shouldn't that possibility have an influence on our decision about who these ten or fifteen people will be? Let's face the facts. If these residents of the Envirodome were to be the last survivors of the human race, wouldn't we want them to be the best of the best?"

"Best in what way?" Allyson questioned.

"Best in *all* ways," Enrico retorted.

"You mean all Italians, like you?" Josh joked.

"Don't be ridiculous, Josh," Enrico replied. "I mean best in terms of physical condition, intelligence, mental stability, knowledge, genetic heritage, and a lot of other things."

Ruth's brow wrinkled, and she asked, "What do you mean by genetic heritage?"

"I mean, for example, wouldn't we want to assure both genetic diversity *and* genetic purity? Wouldn't we want to include as diverse as possible a gene pool in this dome population? Who's to say that one race is superior to all others on earth? We might be well advised to include genetically pure specimens of several different races."

"How many different races are there?" asked Kyle.

Enrico was quick to reply. "Officially there are four different major races: Caucasians, Mongolians, Ethiopians, and Native Americans. But, there are anywhere from a dozen to twenty sub-races, depending on how you

2, 4, 8...(Destiny of the Human Species)

categorize them. If we were going to go with fourteen residents, they could be from seven different sub-races."

"Why seven?" queried Allyson.

"Two each — a male and a female — of each of seven makes fourteen," Enrico replied.

Allyson rolled her eyes. "Are you suggesting a *breeding* experiment here, Enrico?"

"Call it what you want," answered Enrico, "but we could be selecting the progenitors of our species. You don't think these people are going to exist for years, even decades, without sex, do you?"

Allyson blushed, then said, "I suppose not."

At that point, John broke into the discussion. "It's obvious that the Envirodome is going to house a unique set of individuals, who will be living under extraordinary circumstances. Hadn't you better set some guidelines for social behavior and ethical standards for the group?"

"Give us an example," Ruth replied.

"The only example that I have in mind is something like the set of goals that were adopted by the old Humanitarian Party — the ones that were originally composed by Robert Welton."

"Who's Robert Welton?" Josh asked. Being as young as he was, he probably had never read or heard anything about Robert Welton.

"He was the founder of the original Humanitarian Party," John answered.

Kyle interrupted, "We're short on time, John, so we'll have to cut off this discussion. But, I'll go over Welton's list with the team, and we'll see if we can't come up with somethin' like you're suggestin'."

Then, turning to the members of the team, he said, "This has been an illuminatin' discussion. I'll send you a memo summarizin' what's been said in this meetin', and then I would like to ask you to put some thought into these topics before we have another meetin' a week from today to formulate a list of required characteristics for those people who'll be selected to serve as the residents of the Envirodome. We'll also discuss the Weltonian Principles."

Chapter 54

John Spencer picked up the report that Kyle Kimura had given to him earlier in the morning. The cover note read:

> John: Here is the final draft of our suggested bulletin to go to all news media worldwide. Please let me know as soon as possible whether you want to make any changes in it.
>
> Kyle

NEWS RELEASE
June 30, 1998

Enviro, Inc., headquartered in Seattle, Washington, U.S.A., announces a search for exceptionally qualified people of the following native sub-populations to serve as residents/scientists in the Envirodome Project.

Norwegian
Russian

2, 4, 8...(Destiny of the Human Species)

Slovakian
French
German
Italian
Hungarian
Egyptian
Iranian
North Chinese
Japanese
Vietnamese
Mongolian
North American Indian
South American Indian
West African
East African
East Indian
Sri Lankan
Hawaiian

Requirements:
1. Must speak fluent English.
2. Must be genetically pure descendants of at least five generations of their native stock (genealogy required), and must be unmarried and romantically unattached.
3. Must be in the top 1 percent of their native population in respect to:
     a. physical strength and endurance.
     b. intelligence.
     c. mental stability.
     d. knowledge.
     e. typical appearance.

2, 4, 8...(Destiny of the Human Species)

4. Must be sexually fertile. Men, ages 30 to 39; women, ages 25 to 34.
5. Must have a functional knowledge in all of the following scientific and technical fields:
     a. Ecology
     b. Chemistry
     c. Physics
     d. Mathematics, through calculus
     e. Computer technology
     f. Agronomy
     g. Research methodology
     h. Mechanical repair
6. Must agree to the implantation of a permanent birth control capsule in the body.
7. Must agree to spend at least five years inside the Envirodome after it begins operations in the year 2001, performing assigned tasks and living in harmony with thirteen others of seven different sub-populations. Prior to that time, they will assist with planning the structure, arrangement and operations of the Envirodome. Selectees will be paired with the opposite sex of their own sub-population.

Qualified persons who are interested in obtaining more information on this project should send inquiries to: Envirodome Project, Enviro, Inc., 534 Eason St., Seattle, WA, 98109. Formal applications must be received by August 1, 1998.

2, 4, 8...(Destiny of the Human Species)

John buzzed Kyle on the intercom.

"This is Kyle," the familiar voice announced.

"Kyle, this is John. I just finished reading over your proposed news release. I noticed that you listed twenty different sub-populations. I thought that you were seeking seven.

"That's because this is only a preliminary identification effort. We assume that there'll be some sub-populations for which there won't be a pair of qualified candidates, and we want to give ourselves a cushion. There won't be any difficulty in narrowing the field down to seven eventually."

John continued, "I can accept that. Then, I also noticed that you had different ages listed for the men and women. Why is that?"

"Well, we have to compromise on ages, between the ages of sexual viability and ages of high knowledge attainment. We want to select people who are at an age of maximum fertility, but who also are old enough that they have had time to acquire significant knowledge and experience. We know that the fertility of women drops off fairly significantly after age 34, so we set that age as the maximum for women. In men, fertility continues well beyond 34."

"That sounds logical," John replied. "By the way, you should mention that the salary will be equal to the median salary of medical doctors in the U.S."

"That'll be easy to add," Kyle responded.

John went on. "The release of this bulletin is bound to set off accusations of violations of ethical and moral standards. You know — things like 'Why these specific sub-populations and no others?', or 'Why are men and women being paired? Is this a human breeding project?,' or 'Are you trying to create a super-race?'"

"We've already anticipated questions like those, boss, and are confident that we can defend all of our decisions. Anyway, few people will tend to look upon this project as the determiner of the last survivors of the human species. Hardly anyone views the potential deterioration of the environment with the concern that we do."

"You're probably right. All right, then, with the addition that I suggested, you have my permission to circulate this news release."

John thought for a minute, then continued, "Kyle, have you considered applying for selection as one of the residents of the Envirodome?

"No, the thought never occurred to me."

"You should think about it," John suggested. "It looks to me like you're definitely qualified. I examined every requirement, and you fit all of them as far as I can tell."

"It'd be a tremendous opportunity to put my ecological expertise into practice," Kyle responded. "I'll think it over and let you know."

Chapter 55

(5 weeks later)
Wednesday, August 4, 1998

The Envirodome team was assembled in the small-group conference room. Kyle began the meeting. "As you know, the deadline for Envirodome applications was the 1st. I think that it's now safe to start the screenin' process. We want to eventually narrow the field down to two men and two women from each of seven sub-populations. Before we reach that point, I think that it would be wise to have a preliminary screenin' in order to narrow the field down to *four men* and *four* women from each sub-population. We can do that fairly easily by applyin' some of the criteria that are less difficult to administer. One of those is 'typical appearance.' We can do that by comparin' their photographs with photographs that we've obtained of typical members of the various sub-populations. Another is the administration of I.Q. tests and tests of both general knowledge and specific knowledge. Those tests can be administered in their own countries by certified testers that we hire. Then we can bring the semifinalists here to Seattle, and subject them to examinations of fluency in English, mental stability, physical strength and endurance, and DNA tests for defective genes."

2, 4, 8...(Destiny of the Human Species)

Josh looked puzzled. "Why are you talking in terms of eventually narrowing the applicants down to two men and two women of each sub-population. I thought we were going for *one* of each, so that by having one male and one female from each of seven sub-populations, we would end up with fourteen."

Kyle answered, "We want to narrow the field down to two men and two women, because then we'll put all four of them on the payroll somewhat permanently. All four will work on the plannin' phase, and durin' that period, we can assess the compatibility of the alternative pairin's. We won't tell *them* about this, of course, but that process will enable us to determine the most compatible couple of the four possible pairin's. We want the male and female of each sub-population to be highly attracted to each other, since they'll be livin' together in the closed environment for a long period of time."

Allyson spoke up immediately. "I *still* think you're planning a human breeding experiment!"

"Let's avoid giving it that label," Kyle cautioned. "It's true that, hypothetically, these seven pairs of residents could eventually end up producing offspring, but that would be at least several years down the road."

Allyson mumbled, but the others nodded agreement.

"Did we even *get* applications from at least *four* men and *four* women from every one of the twenty sub-populations that were listed in the bulletin?" Ruth asked.

"Only ten of them," Kyle replied. "There weren't enough from the Russian, Slovakian, Egyptian, South American Indian, Sri Lankan, Hungarian, Italian, Vietnamese, Mongolian, or Hawaiian sub-populations. Therefore, those sub-populations will be eliminated from further consideration." Then he added, "I should probably tell you that I'm one of the Japanese applicants."

2, 4, 8...(Destiny of the Human Species)

A surprised Josh immediately queried, "Does your genealogy go back through *at least five* generations of pure Japanese? I thought your parents were born in this country."

"They were," answered Kyle, "but none of my ancestors from over ten generations back ever married a non-Japanese."

Ruth then spoke up. "Don't you think that you'd better distance yourself from the screening of the members of the Japanese sub-population, since there's a potential conflict of interest here?"

"I was just goin' to suggest that," said Kyle. "That'll be easy to arrange."

Then Josh asked, "Do you really have a desire to possibly spend the rest of your life in the Envirodome?"

"It could be excitin'," Kyle responded. "Livin' with thirteen of the worlds finest human specimens, especially when one of them is the Japanese woman that I could be paired with. I've never really pursued women. Not that I haven't had the urge. Just never had the nerve."

Chapter 56

(Five weeks later)
Tuesday, September 7, 1998

The Envirodome team was assembled once again for the purpose of discussing the selection of residents or "domies" as they had come to call them.

John Spencer began by saying, "As you know, the results that were returned to us by the deadline for the preliminary screenings have enabled us to narrow down the field of potential selectees to eight for each of the following sub-populations: Norwegian, Russian, French, German, Hungarian, Iranian, North Chinese, Japanese, North American Indian, West African, East African, and East Indian. We can now bring these 'semifinalists' here to Seattle, and subject them to the remaining criteria. I've asked my secretary to make all of the travel and housing arrangements. The rest of the screening procedures will be applied at the University of Washington by professional staff that we have hired there. Any questions?"

No one was inclined to say anything.

"O.k., then, we'll proceed as outlined."

2, 4, 8...(Destiny of the Human Species)

(Three weeks later)
Monday, September 27, 1998

John stepped to the podium in the Enviro, Inc. auditorium. The entire staff was on hand for the introduction of the twenty-eight finalists for selection as "domies."

"Welcome to you all. This is a notable occasion, indeed. The twenty-eight people who will plan what could be the beginning of extraterrestrial colonization by humans from the earth are going to be introduced. Each will stand as I read his or her name.

"First, the East African group: Jomo Lule, Yosufa Kenyatta, Ruby Nyerere, and Kikuya Amin.

"The East Indian group: Savitri Kamar, Krishna Hademani, Rajiv Chandre, and Indira Shingi.

"Next, the German Group: Ernst Borgmann, Anna Roeder, Friedrich Hallberg, and Greta Himmler.

"The Iranian group: Ghulaun Pahlavi, Muhammad Kashani, Suyyida Azhari, and Shaula Bahonar.

"The Japanese group: Yoko Tamachi, Ariyoshi Nakamura, Fumi Miyamoto, and Kyle Kimura."

Although there had been polite applause for each group up to this point, the applause was deafening when Kyle's name was announced. He was extremely popular with the staff members of Enviro, Inc.

"Next, the North Chinese group: Hsu Zujang, Deng Yaobang, Zhao Ling, and Margaret Chang.

2, 4, 8...(Destiny of the Human Species)

"And finally, the Norwegian group: Svein Torberg, Magna Gerhardsen, Inge Iversen, and Karen Jorgensen."

John continued. "Would all of you finalists please stand again?

"Let's give the entire group an expression of our appreciation for their courage and dedication in volunteering for this unique and universally important experiment."

The audience arose in unison, and gave a resounding round of applause.

Then John said, "These people will be on the payroll of Enviro, Inc. from now on, and will be busy full time in planning the structural, compositional, and operational aspects of the Envirodome. Please make them feel welcome to our staff."

Then he went on, saying, "If we maintain our present schedule, the Envirodome should be operational by about two years from now. At that time, the final seven pairs of selectees, or 'domies,' will be designated, and they will subsequently enter the dome permanently. That concludes this assembly. Thank you, everyone, for your participation."

(The next day)
Wednesday, October 8, 1998

Kyle had assembled the finalists in the large conference room for orientation purposes. He began by saying, "As you should know from our previous bulletins that were sent to you, from now on, you will lead gradually more and more restricted lives. Next week we'll start you on the conversion diet, which will be phased in over the next two years, so that your digestive systems can adjust to the ovo-lacto-vegetarian diet that will be adhered to in the Envirodome."

Rajiv Chandre raised his hand. In his pronounced East Indian accent, he asked, "Does that mean that we will be *required* to abstain from eating all other foods except those that you prepare for us?"

"Yes," replied Kyle. "It's essential that your bodies be adjusted to the permanent diet by the time the 'domies' are sealed in the dome."

Then he continued, "Tomorrow you will all receive your Concap birth control capsule implantations. That will prevent pregnancies until such a time that the birth of babies can be permitted in the dome. If that time ever arrives, there is an antidote that can be administered for the purpose of allowin' pregnancy to occur. Those who aren't selected as domies will automatically receive the antidote if they wish.

Magna Gerhardsen fidgeted, then asked, "What is your policy on sex by members of this group?"

A chuckle arose among the group.

"We aren't either encouragin' sex or discouragin' it. However, please keep in mind that we want sex not to be outside sub-population boundaries at this point. Eventually, two finalists — a male and a female — will be selected from each sub-population group, and those two will be paired for the life of the project."

Kyle then went on to explain housing assignments, work assignments, and work schedules, before dismissing the group.

Chapter 57

Josie approached John's secretary, Jenny, about five minutes before her scheduled 10:15 appointment with him. "I'm here for my appointment," she announced.

Jenny buzzed John on the intercom. "Miss McClellan is here, Mr. Spencer"

"Send her right in," was the reply.

Josie entered John's office, sat down in the overstuffed chair facing his desk. She crossed her legs, displaying a tantalizing portion of thigh above the knee, as was her custom, much to both the delight and the frustration of her male friends and co-workers. John tried not to be too obvious in glancing quickly at her legs, then looked her in the eye and said, "Thanks for meeting with me, Josie. I want to talk with you about the next step in our lobbying effort. Now that we have essentially completed the finalist-identification phase of the project, it's time to request the funds for the next phase — the two-year planning phase."

"I'm glad you called me in," Josie replied. "I, too, think that we're about there. I think that I'd better fly to Washington, and schedule meetings with Representative

2, 4, 8...(Destiny of the Human Species)

Borders and Senator Blevens, since they're birddogging our funding measures. Do you want to come along?"

John thought for a minute. *"I'm tempted to say 'Yes,' it would give me an opportunity to get to know Josie better. On the other hand, that could be dangerous, and we might end up getting sidetracked from our lobbying."* Then he said, "I'd better not, Josie. I'm pretty tied down with work to be caught up on. You can do a good job of getting what we want by yourself."

"I'm confident that I'll be able to do that, but I was thinking that we could have some fun together while we were in D.C."

John was surprised at the latter comment. What did she mean by *fun*? He realized that she was known to resist sex, but he felt slightly sorry that he had turned down her suggestion.

The intercom buzzed. Jenny announced, "Mr. Kimura is here to see you. Should I tell him to wait?"

"No, we're just finishing up. Send him in."

Then he turned to Josie, "Kyle's coming in. Let me know how things went in D.C. as soon as you get back."

She passed Kyle in the short corridor outside John's office.

"Kyle!" John said, eager to hear how things were going in the finalist group.

"'We've given out work assignments, and everyone seems content with what they've received. They're workin' in four seven-person teams. One team has been assigned to plannin' for the ecological systems; another is workin' on energy supply and management; the third is workin' on livin' quarters and habitat-friendliness; and the fourth is plannin' the details of the structural characteristics —

both the enclosure itself and the internal partitionin'. Every Friday, representatives from all four teams meet to coordinate their efforts."

"Sounds great," John exhorted. "How are the social relationships in the group turning out?"

"Better than expected, especially in my Japanese sub-population. I can't help but admit that I'm somewhat excited, both intellectually and emotionally, by the two Japanese women. They're both very attractive *and* intelligent. I must say that my libido is up. Fumi Miyamoto especially appeals to me."

John smiled, and cautioned, "Be sure that you don't let your *libido* blind you to objectivity in running this project."

Chapter 58

(Three weeks later)
Friday, October 22, 1998

It was obvious that it was Friday afternoon. Most of the Enviro, Inc. employees were getting psychologically ready for the end of the work day, and the weekend ahead. But John still had late afternoon appointments with Josie; with Craig Goodloe, Manager of the CO_2 Project; and with Kyle.

Josie arrived at his office at 2 p.m. sharp. She was as appealing as ever, in her customary tailored type of jacket and low-cut blouse, short skirt, and high heels.

"I hope you have good news for us," John opened.

"For sure, John. I received warm welcomes from both Representative Borders and Senator Blevens. We talked about the details of the funding of the second phase, and they both agreed to apply pressure in the right places to get the funds released within two weeks. They practically fell all over themselves to be accommodating. The good Senator even suggested that I might want to spend a weekend at his Catskill retreat sometime. I didn't give him a definite answer."

"What will your answer be when he presses you for one?" John asked.

2, 4, 8...(Destiny of the Human Species)

"I'll think of some way to avoid the issue if it comes up again."

Josie handed John a detailed report of the funding procedures and then asked, "Are you free tomorrow night, by any chance?"

John's heart skipped a couple of beats. "I don't have any definite plans at this point. Why?"

"I was given two tickets to the performance of La Boheme today by a friend who had to give them up because of an emergency trip out of town. I would enjoy having a male escort, especially you."

"This sounds like a date to me. Are you sure you want to do this?" He was sounding out her intentions.

"No reason why co-workers can't socialize off the job is there?"

"We don't have any company policy preventing it. Give me your phone number. I'll call you tomorrow morning in order to make the arrangements to pick you up."

"623-4534," Josie said.

"All right, then, I'll call you. Right now, I have to see Craig Goodloe."

Josie smiled invitingly, and left the office.

"Jenny, send Mr. Goodloe in, will you?"

Craig Goodloe was dressed quite casually, but then that was more or less typical of the environmental types on the staff. He offered his hand, and said, "I thought that you should hear what we've discovered about the trend in the carbon dioxide concentrations in the atmosphere in the last few months. In March, the concentration at Mauna Loa was 435 ppm. In July, it was up to 463, and just this week we got the report for October, which showed it to be 475. The rate of increase is rising at an alarming rate."

2, 4, 8...(Destiny of the Human Species)

"It's a good thing we're making good progress on our Envirodome project," John responded. At this rate of carbon dioxide increase, the health of people everywhere might be threatened. Thanks for the report, Craig. Keep me posted on any significant changes."

Craig turned and went out the office door.

"Jenny, is Kyle there yet?"

"Yes, he's waiting, Mr. Spencer."

"Send him in," John instructed.

Kyle entered, smiling confidently as usual.

"What do you have for me this afternoon?" John asked.

"Just a short report on some of our major dome activities. The Ecological Systems team has decided on the primary food supply system. In accordance with your desire to adhere to Robert Welton's principles, they've definitely decided not to include the chickens and goats that were originally included on the list. The chickens were for egg production, not meat production, and the goats were for the production of milk, not meat. Besides that, the original thought was that the chickens and goats would help in the recyclin' process, because they'll eat just about anythin'. However, the team came to the realization that aged animals would either suffer a slow death or they would be butchered for food, and we didn't want either to happen. So, a strictly vegetarian diet has been decided upon."

"Can they get all of the essential nutrients from a strict vegetarian diet?" John asked.

"That's no problem," Kyle responded. "They've identified the main food plants that'll be grown in the dome. They include peas, lima beans, and soybeans to provide many of the essential amino acids, especially lysine. Then there'll

325

2, 4, 8...(Destiny of the Human Species)

be corn and wheat to provide other amino acids, especially methionine. So the protein in the diet will be adequate. Most of the essential vitamins and minerals will come from carrots, broccoli, potatoes, radishes, lettuce, and tomatoes - all easy to grow. Sweet treats will come from grapes, dwarf apples, squash, sweet potatoes, and strawberries. Fat will come primarily from peanuts. And, of course, carbohydrates will come from many of the plants already mentioned. For seasoning, there'll be onions, garlic, basil, thyme, oregano, and peppers. One vitamin that's ordinarily lackin' in vegetarian diets is B-12, but they can derive that by fermentin' soybeans. We're gonna include one colony of honeybees. That's not so much for the honey that they'll provide as it is for their pollination function."

John looked pensive. "Will there be enough growing area to support all of those plants?" he asked.

"Definitely, since we're not plannin' to incorporate any biomes of marginal use, like a desert or an ocean. The team also has designed partitioned-off sections for temperature controls on some of the plants. Many plants won't complete their growin' and reproduction cycle without sub-freezing temperatures, you know."

"I was wondering how you would deal with that problem. It sounds good to me."

"The team that's workin' on habitat and livin' quarters has adopted much of the schematics from the Biosphere 2 project. They were pretty happy with what the biospherians had worked out. The structural team is findin' the characteristics of the Kingdome to be very easy to adapt to for our purposes. They want to spray a coating of epoxy resin over the entire interior of the dome walls and ceilin' to insure a complete seal from the outside environment. Double air locks will be installed at the

2, 4, 8...(Destiny of the Human Species)

entrances on two opposite sides of the dome. All other entrances will be sealed off permanently. The team had no problem in adaptin' the needs of the other teams to the basic structural characteristics of the Kingdome."

Kyle paused, and waited for John to respond.

"Is that it for today?" John asked.

"That's it."

"Keep me up to date, especially if any unexpected problems arise," John advised.

They parted company. John turned off his office lights, walked to the front reception room, and locked the front door as he left the office complex.

(The next day)
Saturday, October 23, 1998

John arrived at Josie's condo just a few minutes before 7 p.m. He climbed the short stairway to her front door, and rang the doorbell. When the door opened, there stood Josie, more stunning than ever. John thought she had worn her sexiest dress to the reception for the senators in D.C., but this one beat it by a long ways.

On the way to the theater, Josie avoided any talk about work topics. Instead, she mentioned her love for travelling, especially to visit foreign cultures. She had actually been on quite a few trips, apparently always with some female friend or other. She was well acquainted with Mexico City, as well as Tokyo, Oslo, and even Katmandu. She knew a lot about many of the sites and sights in France.

"I've never had the privilege of travelling to foreign places with a male escort, but it would be fun," she mused. "Do you have any desire for that kind of travel, John?"

327

2, 4, 8...(Destiny of the Human Species)

"I've always been so tied down to my work, that I haven't given it much thought," John answered."

"You ought to think about it."

"Was that an invitation?" he thought.

La Boheme was entertaining, although opera was not John's first choice for an evening's activity. But, being with Josie made it even delightful.

Once they got back to her condo, she unlocked the door and stepped inside. "Want to come in for a coffee or hot chocolate?" she invited.

"I'd better not," John replied. "Lots of work to catch up on at the office tomorrow." Actually, he was afraid of what might happen if he accepted her suggestion.

With that, she stepped forward, put her arms around his neck, and kissed him full on the lips - not just a kiss between casual acquaintances either. It was a tender, moist kiss. John held the kiss for a moment, then tactfully withdrew and said, "It was a very enjoyable evening. Thanks for the invitation. I'll see you at the office on Monday."

"She's certainly very friendly for someone who doesn't want any romantic relationships," he thought to himself.

Chapter 59

(Two and a half months later)
Monday, January 3, 1999

Kyle entered John's office and sat down. He looked well-rested and full of energy, as usual.

"What did you do for New Year's Eve?" John queried.

"I showed the other members of the Japanese team the kind of thing we typically do here in the U.S.," was his reply. "I'm really gettin' to like all three of them, so I invited them to come to my home for a party, along with some other members of the Seattle Japanese community. We played a few party games, watched the countdown on Channel 5, and then had a post-midnight buffet. It turned out very well. What did you do?"

"Josie invited me to a party that she was hosting for a group of friends, none of them company employees."

"You're spendin' quite a bit of time with Josie, aren't you?" Kyle suggested.

"We do something together every week or two."

"Is it gettin' serious?"

"It probably could, if I'd let it," was John's reply. "She's very amenable to the idea of spending more time together, but I'm afraid that if she found out that I'm HIV positive, it might turn her off. I'd just like to keep our relationship the way it is — a casual date every now and then. We both seem comfortable with that."

Then Kyle shifted the topic. "We just received the compilation of data from our carbon dioxide reporting stations. Craig Goodloe summarized it for me. I thought that you might like to hear the summary first hand."

"Definitely."

"The concentrations have continued to rise at the accelerated rate that I reported last March. The current readin's are: Mauna Loa, 516 ppm.; Los Angeles, 732 ppm.; New York, 678 ppm.; London, 734 ppm.; Mexico City, 1123 ppm.; and Seattle, 567 ppm."

"How do these figures compare with those of March?" John asked.

"They're up an average of about 12 per cent, with not very much deviation from that in any individual case. Mexico City, of course, continues to have the worst problem of all. And, they still have the highest incidence of respiratory diseases and resultant deaths."

"Are the authorities in Mexico City doing anything to reverse the trend?"

"They've tried, but no segment of the population is willin' to give up anythin', even outright luxurious conveniences, in order to reduce the carbon dioxide output. No one wants to give up their car, or their fireplace fire. None of the industries is willin' to curtail use of fossil fuels, because they contend that they would lose money otherwise. It's a situation that's typical in other countries, too."

John nodded as if in agreement, then changed the subject. "Are the Envirodome hopefuls all getting along well?"

"There's a little friction between some of them now

and then, but nothing major. Our psychological team counsels the combative parties whenever a problem seems to be loomin'. Sociologically, things are going pretty much as we had hoped."

"And what about the progress of your planning teams? Are they able to coordinate their plans successfully?"

Kyle smiled, implying that progress was satisfactory. "We shouldn't have any difficulty in havin' the Envirodome ready for full-time residents by our projected deadline of October, 2000 — maybe even before that. The contractors are just about finished workin' on the remodeling of the internal structure to fit our needs. The fusion reactor set-up is about 50 percent complete. After it's ready, we can install the lightin' systems and temperature control systems. Once that's completed, we'll be able to begin movin' in our plant species."

John assimilated that information, then said, "Are you and Fumi Miyamoto still getting along famously?"

"Definitely. She's not only intelligent and attractive, but extremely personable, too. Just the kind I'd like to spend the rest of my life with."

"Well," John offered, "you may just get the opportunity to do that."

Chapter 60

(Eight months later)
Sunday, August 13, 1999

The Envirodome hopefuls, all twenty-eight of them, filed off the bus that had been hired by Enviro, Inc. to take them to the reviewing stand at the Seafair races. This was a special treat cooked up by John and Kyle. Most of them had never seen anything quite like the hydroplane races. They were eagerly anticipating the excitement that was ahead.

John accompanied them. John said to Kyle, "Have you gathered any data on the inter-compatibility of the various sub-populations groups?"

"We're just about ready to make our final selection of the domies, based on our observations. You'll notice this afternoon that certain pairs of individuals appear to be obviously attracted to each other, while others are fairly aloof. There's a promisin' pairing in every one of the seven sub-populations. By next week, we should have identified the final selections for permanent residence in the dome."

"What about yourself?" John asked. "Are you still in the running?"

"Of course I'm biased," Kyle replied, "but I person-

2, 4, 8...(Destiny of the Human Species)

ally feel that Fumi and I should be among the domies. We've discussed the possibility of bein' paired for the life of the dome project, and we both feel comfortable with that idea."

The sudden roar of hydroplane engines startled both John and Kyle. The first heat of the races was about to begin, so they turned their attention to the boats and the race course.

(Six days later)
Friday, August 18, 1999

The assemblage in the Enviro, Inc. auditorium included only the twenty-eight hopefuls for domie status, plus the four original members of the Envirodome Project team: Josh, Ruth, Allyson and Enrico.

Ruth, who was chairing the assembly, announced, "As you all know, we're going to reveal our selections for residency in the Envirodome this morning. Before I do that, though, I want to point out that those who aren't selected will, nevertheless, be offered positions on the Enviro, Inc. staff at full pay. They will play a very active role in the operation of the Envirodome, working as outside facilitators and evaluators."

Then she took out her list of selectees, and read the pairs of names, one by one.

"First, from the East African group, Kihuya Amin and Jomo Lule"

An enthusiastic round of applause arose, as the two took their places in two of the fourteen seats on the stage.

"Next, from the East Indian group, Savitri Kamar and Krishna Hademani."

More applause.

2, 4, 8...(Destiny of the Human Species)

"And from the German group, Friedrich Halberg and Greta Himmler."

Friedrich and Greta walked to the stage, hand in hand.

"Next, from the Iranian group, Suyyida Azhari and Muhammad Kashani."

Applause.

"From the Japanese group, Fumi Miyamoto and Kyle Kimura."

A cheer arose, in addition to the applause. All of the other envirodome applicants had come to be very fond of Kyle, and had hoped that he would be selected. This meant that he could continue to coordinate the Envirodome activities, even from inside.

"From the North Chinese group, Margaret Chang and Hsu Zujang." Both took their seats on the stage.

"And finally, from the Norwegian group, Svein Torberg and Inge Iversen."

With the announcement of the last pair, several seconds of clapping in unison broke out, then quieted when Ruth began speaking again. "Congratulations to the final selectees. You have an extremely important task ahead. No less important will be the support activities that the rest of you will perform."

Then she concluded with, "The meeting is now over. All of you have your work cut out for you."

Then Ruth confided in Josh, "I think we made all the right choices. Did you notice that every couple that was selected spontaneously held hands as they came to the stage. I'm sure that there's more than just an intellectual attraction involved in these pairs."

Chapter 61

(5 months later)
Monday, January 22, 2000

Excitement was in the air as John faced the fourteen domies who had gathered in the company conference room. They knew that he was probably going to announce the date for them to begin moving their belongings into the Envirodome. He began with a terse statement.

"As you know, the preparation of the Envirodome for your residency is ahead of schedule. As it looks at this time, you'll probably begin to occupy your living quarters in the dome about February 1st."

A murmur of approval arose from the group, then rousing applause. They were clearly eager to set up 'housekeeping' in the dome. John wasn't sure whether it was the thought of the potential for their being the survivors of the human race or the prospects of being paired permanently that appealed to them the most.

Then he said, "I'll now turn the meeting over to Kyle Kimura. He'll explain some of the tasks that have to be accomplished before the final move."

Kyle was greeted with cheers. "I know that you're all as excited as I am to begin this unique experiment. But,

2, 4, 8...(Destiny of the Human Species)

we're gonna approach it gradually. We'll actually begin movin' some of our belongin's into our quarters next week. At that time we'll only take a few essentials. There'll be a transition period of about five months, durin' which we'll be permitted to come and go to and from the dome at will. However, durin' that period, the stabilization of the interior atmosphere will take place, so we'll be enterin' and leavin' through the airlocks. We'll eat most of our meals on the outside; they'll be prepared by the cafeteria staff, as usual. We won't actually occupy the dome permanently until July 1st. At that time, we'll take with us a one-year food supply, which will give us one year to manage our food crops to the point that they'll support us on a permanent, un-supplemented basis."

Svein Torberg raised his hand.

"Svein?"

"Do you mean to say, then, that by July 1st of 2001 we'll be permanently dependent on the crops in the dome for food?"

"That's what's intended, Svein." Then Kyle continued, "Between now and next July 1st, you should accomplish any tasks that have to be done by you in person outside the dome. After that, you'll only be able to communicate electronically with the outside."

Fumi raised her hand.

"Fumi."

She said in a very confident voice, "We all know that the original, primary reason why this envirodome project was initiated was the threat of carbon dioxide buildup in the atmosphere. Is that threat continuing to increase as it was projected to do?"

Kyle responded, "Yes. In fact, the increase in the *rate* of buildup is even greater than what had been extrapolated from our previous data."

2, 4, 8...(Destiny of the Human Species)

Fumi looked concerned. "Does that mean that there is a possibility that we'll eventually be the last survivors of the human race?"

"In a worst case scenario, that could happen," Kyle replied. "Any other questions?"

No questions from the group.

"I have one more item to announce. Tomorrow, we'll all get our first injection of 'Thymone.' That's a very rare and costly hormone that's extracted from the thymus glands of fresh human cadavers. Only the glands of humans between 17 and 20 years of age can be used, and the hormone has to be extracted within 24 hours of death. That's why it's so rare and expensive. It will permanently keep us at biologically the same age as we are now. A new injection is needed every year, but we're hopin' that by this time next year, we'll be able to produce it in our own Envirodome lab by genetic engineerin'."

When Kyle had finished this last announcement, there was a lot of excited whispering among the members of the audience. "Any more questions?"

They were apparently in too much a state of surprise from the last announcement to think of any questions.

"Well, then, let's all get back to our work stations, and resume our progress toward our goal of July 1st."

(The next day)
Tuesday, January 23, 2000

John Spencer had called Craig Goodloe to his office. Although Craig's primary responsibility was that of manager of the CO_2 Team, John wanted to talk to him about a report that was sent in by the branch office of Enviro, Inc. in San Antonio, Texas.

"Good morning, John," Craig said.

2, 4, 8...(Destiny of the Human Species)

"Good morning, Craig. I just wanted to tell you briefly about an environmental problem that's been reported near the small south Texas town of Alice. We've been requested to investigate it. The field investigations will be conducted out of the San Antonio office, but I'd like you to contact Gary Jameson, the field unit supervisor there, and keep me updated on what they find."

"What kind of a problem is it?" Craig asked.

"They don't know, yet. All they do know is that the birds, rats, and other vertebrates in the vicinity of the nearby landfill are dying in droves. What's more, some of the personnel who dump garbage at the landfill are suffering from frequent dizziness and nausea."

Craig thought for a moment, then asked, "Do you think it's from an excess of carbon dioxide?"

"Could be," John answered. "We do know that carbon dioxide can cause dizziness and nausea. But, the air circulation in that area is almost too good to allow an unhealthful buildup of carbon dioxide. They have almost constant winds off the Gulf of Mexico."

"I'll contact Gary, and keep you informed," Craig said, as he got up from his chair and left the office.

Chapter 62

(Six days later)
Monday, January 29, 2000

"I talked with Gary Jameson in San Antonio this morning," Craig Goodloe announced to John Spencer. Craig had requested a brief emergency meeting with John about two hours ago. "Since I talked with you last week, a garbage hauler at the Alice landfill has died. He was about the only one who spent an extended time at the landfill, because his truck broke down while it was dumping garbage. When his body was examined by the coroner, it was discovered that his lips, ears, and nose had all turned a slight bluish color. Combined with dizziness and nausea of other workers, do you know what that indicates?"

"I don't have the slightest idea," John said.

"Those are all the signs of cyanide poisoning!" Craig exclaimed.

"Is that what caused the death of all the birds and rats, too?

"It could be," Craig answered. "The field unit is doing autopsies on some of the birds and rats in order to find out for sure."

2, 4, 8...(Destiny of the Human Species)

(Two days later)
Wednesday, January 31, 2000

"Craig, this is Gary Jameson!" The voice on the phone sounded excited.

"We've finished the autopsies on some of the birds and rats. Sure enough, they contain a lethal concentration of cyanide!"

"Do you have any idea where the cyanide came from?" Craig queried.

"Not yet. We've quarantined all of the area within a mile of the landfill. We're going to send in a couple of our biochemists in moonsuits to gather samples for lab testing."

"Please let me know right away what you find," Craig requested. Then he hurried down the hall to tell John what he had been told.

(One week later)
Wednesday, February 7, 2000

"Gary, this is Craig Goodloe. My secretary said that you called while I was out. What did you want to talk to me about?"

Gary Jameson could barely contain his concern. "Craig, you're not going to believe this. The same situation that we had at the Alice landfill has broken out in another landfill about forty miles north, near the town of Three Rivers."

"Did you find indications of cyanide poisoning there, too?"

"Yep!" was the terse reply.

"Have you found out where the cyanide is coming from?"

2, 4, 8...(Destiny of the Human Species)

"Not yet," Gary replied. "But if we do find out, I'll call you right away."

Craig hung up the phone, then lifted it again, and dialed John's desk.

"John Spencer," was the familiar greeting.

"John, I just talked to Gary Jameson in San Antonio. There's another occurrence of cyanide poisoning at a landfill about forty miles from the first one, in south Texas. As Enviro, Inc.'s chief specialist in atmospheric gases, should I fly down there and try to help them find out where the cyanide's coming from?"

"Sure thing, Craig. We want to nip this problem in the bud before it springs up anywhere else. You don't have any problem with going to Texas, do you? I mean, you being African-American and Texas still having subtle vestiges of racism."

"No problem, boss."

(Two days later)
Friday, February 9, 2000

After Craig's flight landed at the San Antonio airport, Gary picked him up and drove him to the company's San Antonio office.

On the way, Gary announced, "We're not sure where the cyanide's coming from yet, but our field personnel discovered an unusual abundance of some species of *Clostridium* bacteria in both of the affected landfills. There's not much of that strain in any other landfills that we examined. I'll have you talk to our chief bacteriologist, Janet Branson when we get to the lab."

Janet was an intense, anorexic-looking brunette. "Glad to meet you, Mr. Goodloe," she said.

2, 4, 8...(Destiny of the Human Species)

Craig surveyed her lean framework, then said, "I'd like to hear what you've found that you think might be the source of the cyanide coming from those two land-fills."

"The guys in the moonsuits brought back a lot of samples," she began. "Dead birds and rats. Various samples of garbage of all types. The macro-biologists couldn't find anything that they thought was the source, so they asked me to run microbiological tests on the stuff. I compared the materials from the affected landfills with those from several other landfills. The only basic difference that I could find was the presence of a fairly uncommon strain of bacterium in the samples from the affected landfills. *Clostridium pastorianum*, to be exact. Now, that bacterium is found in *small* numbers in just about any kind of fertile soil."

"How do you know it's that specific bacterium?" Craig questioned.

"Well, we can never be 100 per cent certain in any test for bacteria, but it has all the characteristics of *pastorianum*, and no combination of characteristics that would suggest any other bacterium. It's gram positive, is easily decolorized, has idiophilic granules. It ferments glucose, galactose, fructose, sucrose and dextrin, but won't ferment glycerol, starch, lactose or Calcium lactate. I thought at first that it might be *Clostridium butyricum*, but I changed my mind when I discovered that it had *triangular* spore envelopes."

Craig tried to assimilate that information. Then he asked, "Do you have any idea what the connection might be between this bacterium and the strong presence of cyanide?"

"Not for sure, but I do know that *Clostridium pastorianum* is able to fix atmospheric nitrogen. As you probably know, the cyanide ion has one atom of nitrogen affixed to an atom of carbon. Perhaps this strain is able to take nitrogen from its environment and attach it to carbon from the environment. We'll have to study our samples further before we can come up with anything definite."

"Thanks for the review," Craig said. Then he turned to Gary and asked, "Would you mind driving me over to those two landfills tomorrow? I'd like to see the sites for myself."

Chapter 63

(Two weeks later)
Thursday, February 22, 2000

Janet Branson entered Gary Jameson's office, accompanied by her main assistant, Hal Kantor. Hal, just out of college, had a bachelor's degree in microbiology.

Janet had a demeanor that radiated self-assurance. She began her meeting with Gary by saying, "I've found a *very* interesting set of organisms and materials during my investigation of the samples from the landfills. I have a hypothesis about where the cyanide is coming from. All of the data support it."

"What kind of hypothesis?" Gary asked.

"Well, it's a pretty complicated set of factors, but I'll try to piece them together for you. The main sites of the *Clostridium pastorianum* concentrations in the samples were, believe it or not, disposable diapers. Both of the affected landfills have a high percentage of disposable diapers among the garbage. I know that this bacterium is an anaerobic nitrogen-fixer, but I couldn't make a connection between it and the disposable diapers. But Hal did some checking in the literature on cyanide, and discovered what that connection might be. It seems that there is a possibility that the urea in the diapers is con-

344

verted to cyanide by *Clostridium pastorianum*. Although this conversion hasn't been reported in the available literature, we do know that ammonium cyanate can be converted to urea by the application of heat. That was demonstrated by Friedrich Wohler way back in 1928. We're hypothesizing that a mutated *Clostridium pastorianum* gained the ability to bring about a more or less reverse reaction. We're not sure, yet, how to explain the conversion of cyanate to cyanide, but it's not a very big jump in the scheme of things. Normally, this bacterium doesn't flourish without the presence of pyruvic acid, but Hal has an idea to explain that."

Hal jumped at the opportunity to join the discussion. "We know that pyruvic acid is an intermediate compound in the formation of amino acids — you know, the building blocks of proteins. What I hypothesize is that the breakdown of the proteins that are abundant in the garbage results in the creation of enough pyruvic acid to support the needs of this bacterium."

Then Janet continued, "If our hypothesis is valid, this cyanide-production phenomenon could theoretically spread to any garbage dump that contains an abundance of disposable diapers."

Craig mulled over the statements that Janet had made. "If this bacterium could cause this reaction in garbage dumps under the presence of the urea in diapers, why couldn't it do the same thing in sewage treatment plants?"

Janet explained, "It isn't likely to happen in sewage treatment plants, because the sewage is aerated there, and Clostridium pastorianum is anaerobic. It only lives in the absence of oxygen, in places like landfills where the garbage is covered with soil daily."

Janet paused.

"Anything more to tell me at this point?" Gary asked.

2, 4, 8...(Destiny of the Human Species)

"Not yet," Janet replied, "but as soon as we get anything definitive, I'll let you know."

(Eight days later)
Friday, March 2, 2000

Kyle Kimura was beaming as he handed his progress report to John. "We're still ahead of schedule. I think you'll like what you read in here."

"Are you smiling because you think I'll like the report, or because of your relationship with Fumi?" John asked.

"A little of both. All in all, my future looks very bright and pleasant. By the way, the latest reports on carbon dioxide concentration indicate a continuin' increase in carbon dioxide levels. The concentration at all of our monitorin' stations went up an average of 18 per cent over a year ago. It's a good thing we're constructin' the Envirodome."

"That may not be the only reason for constructing it," John responded. "Have you heard about the cyanide problem in Texas?"

"No, what problem?" Kyle asked.

"It seems that a mutant bacterium is causing the production of lethal concentrations of cyanide around some landfills in southern Texas. It started in just one, then spread to two more within a couple of weeks. Now, I just got a call today from Craig Goodloe. He's learned that the problem has spread to three more landfills. The spread appears to be in a northerly direction. They think that it's related to the presence of disposable diapers in the landfills. If that's true, then this could escalate into a much more widespread problem. Most of the currently

346

active landfills in the world contain disposable diapers, you know."

"Wow, boss. That has the potential for making the carbon dioxide problem seem pretty minor by comparison."

"I know, Kyle. That's why I've asked Craig and the San Antonio office to let me know immediately if there's any more spread of the problem."

(One week later)
Friday, March 9, 2000

Janet held the culture plate up to the light. "There's no doubt about it, this culture of *Clostridium pastorianum* was able to metabolize the urea that we injected into the medium along with it, and it produced a small quantity of cyanide."

Hal Kantor and Gary Jameson were standing beside her in the lab.

Gary pointed out that the cyanide problem had emerged in yet another two landfills — both north of the previous ones. The last one was near Pleasanton, Texas.

Hal pondered. "Why do you suppose this thing is spreading northward, and not to the east or west?"

"Good question, Hal," Gary responded, "but I don't think that anyone knows the answer at this point."

"Well," Janet speculated, "all of the affected landfills have been quarantined. No humans are able to get in, so it's not likely that it's being transmitted by people. No vehicles are going in or out either."

"Could it be airborne?" Gary wondered.

"That's not likely," Hal interjected. "The prevailing winds are from west to east in these more northerly regions of Texas. If it were in the air, you'd expect the spread to be more from west to east."

"What kind of potential vector would go only from south to north?" Janet mused.

"The most abundant inhabitants of all at these land-fills were the crows," Gary pointed out. "They're found just about everywhere in the states, you know. Maybe they're carrying the bacteria on their feet."

"I thought all of the birds around these landfills got killed by the cyanide," Hal offered.

"We don't know that for a fact," Gary said. "We know that large numbers of crows were killed, but that doesn't mean that some didn't survive the cyanide."

"But why would they only spread it northward?" Hal asked.

"Maybe it's because their migrations in late winter and early spring normally are in a northerly direction," Gary explained.

"Sounds logical," Janet agreed.

Later that day, Gary called Craig Goodloe to tell him about their discussion.

Craig retorted with, "If what you're suggesting is true — that is, if it's this bacterium that's causing the problem, and if it's getting its nourishment from the urea in diapers, and if the crows are spreading it — then we could have a major problem on our hands. The crow is found in most parts of the world except for the frigid zones, and so are landfills containing disposable diapers!"

"You got it!" Gary responded.

Chapter 64

(Four days later)
Tuesday, March 13, 2000

By now, the domies had been occupying their living quarters in the dome for almost six weeks, but they were permitted to leave whenever they wished. They were gradually working into the routine of dealing with the responsibilities that their respective special assignments required, as well as their shared responsibilities of cooking and working with the food crops. Those assignments were as follows:

Overall Coordination:	Kyle Kimura
Medical lab.:	Sayyida Azhari
Fusion reactor specialist:	Friedrich Hallberg
Waste disposal systems manager:	Margaret Chang
Atmospheric monitoring:	Kyle Kimura
Horticulture specialist:	Hsu Zujang

2, 4, 8...(Destiny of the Human Species)

Water recycling:	Kihuya Amin
Communications:	Greta Himmler
Electrical systems:	Svein Torberg
Plumbing/Pumping systems:	Krishna Hadamani
Analytical lab:	Savitri Kamar
Nutritionist:	Joma Lule
Computer programming/ Data processing:	Muhammad Kashani
Historian:	Fumi Miyamoto
Temperature controls:	Inge Iversen

In most cases, their overall duties overlapped. Each person had at least one secondary area of responsibility, in which he or she acted as an assistant.

One responsibility which they all shared was the management of the foodcrops, under the direction of Hsu Zujang. The plants needed daily attention and monitoring for signs of insect pests or diseases. Up until July 1st, they were going to be allowed to use insecticides and fungicides to eliminate those kinds of problem organisms. After that, the complete isolation of the dome atmosphere would not permit those types of chemicals to be released inside the dome.

Their living quarters were comfortable, but not spacious. They had a studio-apartment arrangement; all of the facilities were more or less in one room, except for the bathroom. There was a small kitchen, bed, writing desk with chair, and clothes closet. A lot like a small cabin on a cruise ship. The members of each sub-population pair had adjoining rooms, which could permit interior entry from one to the other if they wished. Within a few days of the original move into the dome, some of the pairs had set up conjugal housekeeping.

The domies were so intent on their work, that most of them seldom left the dome to engage in any kinds of activities on the outside, even though they could theoretically come and go as they wished. The excitement of participating in this unique experiment, plus the challenges that it presented, were enough to keep them occupied both mentally and physically.. If they desired exercise, they could work out in the weight room, or jog on the track that had been set up in the concourse that ran around the full interior circumference of the dome, at the 200 level.

The support crew on the outside — those finalists who hadn't become domies — were kept busy, too, helping to develop solutions to minor problems as the domies encountered them. Numerous unanticipated difficulties came up, but, as Kyle had pointed out before their entry into the dome, they were to "expect the unexpected." Hopefully, before the scheduled July 1st sealing-off of the dome, all problems that required entry or exit of materials and people could be solved.

The normal annual and diurnal light patterns of the outside world were duplicated inside the dome. The temperature and light sequences of the seasons, as well as those of day and night were followed in order to keep the organisms inside on their regular physiological schedules. The area where the apples and grapes were grown would have to experience alternate six-month periods of warm temperatures and cold temperatures in order to stimulate fruit production . All of the other plants could be grown under more consistent temperature conditions, although the seeds of those plants which were propagated by seed culture would also have to be refrigerated for at least two months in order to germinate successfully.

Chapter 65

(One week later)
Tuesday, March 20, 2000

Gary Jameson dialed the phone number of Enviro Inc. in Seattle. When the receptionist answered, he said, "This is Gary Jameson at the San Antonio office. Could I speak to Craig Goodloe, please?"

"Mr. Goodloe is in his office. I'll connect you."

"This is Craig Goodloe."

"Hi Craig, this is Gary. We have some more troubling news for you. The cyanide problem has broken out at several more landfills, all somewhat to the north of the other sites, but also somewhat to both the northeast and the northwest. We have reports from Cuero, Stockdale, Devine, and Uvalde. It's interesting to note that all of the landfills where the problems are occurring have been open in recent years. Landfills that closed before 1981 aren't reporting any problems. Do you know the significance of the year 1981?"

"Nothing comes to mind," Craig responded.

"Well, that's the year that the disposable diaper first appeared on the market in the U.S. Since then, sales increased to the point that 17 billion were sold in the U.S.

alone in 1990, and almost all of them ended up in land-fills."

"Amazing connection," was all that Craig could say.

Gary continued, "The cyanide levels at all of the reported sites are above 200 parts per million. Research of the literature on cyanide poisoning tells us that as little as 30 minutes of exposure to concentrations in that range can be fatal to humans. We're advising all Public Works officials in south Texas to immediately close off any landfill where numerous bird deaths are noticed. At the original site, near Alice, the cyanide concentration has risen to over 500 parts per million as far away as two miles from the landfill. We're projecting that a similar phenomenon is likely to occur at the other affected land-fills. If that happens, the whole of south Texas is in danger of having vertebrate life wiped out."

Craig thought a minute, then asked, "Why do you specifically say *vertebrate*?"

"Because the cyanide poisoning is caused by a reac-tion of the cyanide gas with the hemoglobin in the blood. All vertebrates have hemoglobin in their blood."

Craig was beginning to feel a bit panicky. "I'll get this information to John Spencer right away. He might want to contact the White House about the potential threat nationwide."

(3 days later)
Friday, March 23, 2000

Craig answered his phone. It was Gary again.

"Craig, our worst fears are being realized. We now have some problems in landfills on the outskirts of San Antonio. What's more, this situation has spread to land-fills as far east as Huntsville, and as far west as San

2, 4, 8...(Destiny of the Human Species)

Angelo. In addition, we have an unconfirmed report of a problem near Monterrey, Mexico. Numerous deaths of people in the affected region of south Texas have been attributed to cyanide poisoning. A panic is developing. People are packing their belongings in every available vehicle, and are rapidly moving to areas outside the perimeter of the affected zone. Actually, I see no reason why this thing couldn't spread throughout the United States, and even into other countries — wherever there are crows and landfills containing disposable diapers."

Craig gasped at the thought, then said, "I talked to John Spencer a couple of days ago. He has contacted the White House, and they've sent out an alert. This whole situation is now dominating the national newscasts, you know. A feeling of panic is gripping the entire country. The government is relying on our monitoring network for data on the cyanide concentrations in the atmosphere. We've notified all twenty-six of our stations to monitor cyanide as well as carbon dioxide, which continues to rise, also. Mauna Loa just last week reported a carbon dioxide concentration of 612 ppm."

"Don't you think that you and I should meet with John and Kyle Kimura as soon as possible?" Gary asked.

"Why Kyle?" Craig responded.

"Because the Envirodome might suddenly turn out to be a necessity rather than just a scientific experiment if this cyanide problem continues to spread at its present rate."

"I think you're right," Craig answered.

(Two days later)
Thursday, March 25, 2000

John, Kyle, Craig, Gary, and Josie were gathered in

2, 4, 8...(Destiny of the Human Species)

John's office. Gary had flown in from San Antonio earlier in the day.

John began, "Gentlemen, and Josie, I don't think I have to remind you of the urgency of this meeting. Our Envirodome Project has recently taken on a new significance. As you know, the original reason for undertaking it was to scientifically experiment with it as one way to deal with the slowly increasing carbon dioxide concentrations in the atmosphere. However, recently the cyanide problem in Texas has increased the possibility that an isolated environment like the Envirodome might become a necessity for the survival of human life long before we had envisioned it to be so."

Kyle Kimura's face showed concern. "What do you want me to do in response to this new threat, John?"

"I think that you had better alert your staff to the need for moving up the schedule for complete isolation in the dome. That should happen as soon as you can arrange it, Kyle. And Josie, you should keep our contacts with the White House open at all times, so that we can notify them of any spread of the cyanide problem to any new areas, and can keep them apprised of our progress on the dome project. Craig, you keep in touch with Josie, and be sure to let her know anytime a new outbreak occurs."

With that, John dismissed the meeting.

(Four days later)
Monday, March 29, 2000

Kyle faced the audience of domies in the meeting room of the dome. There were expectant looks on their faces.

He said, "As most of you know, a problem with

2, 4, 8...(Destiny of the Human Species)

cyanide gas in the atmosphere has occurred in Texas, and it appears that it could spread to most parts of the country, and perhaps to most parts of the world eventually. We have no idea how long it will take the problem to crop up right here in the Seattle area, but we have to expedite our preparations for final isolation from the outside atmosphere. Under the circumstances, I don't think that it's unreasonable to expect all of you to cut at least ten percent off your time line. By the day after tomorrow, I would like for you to submit to me your abbreviated schedules, aimed at the goal of final isolation of the dome on June 1st rather than July 1st."

Chapter 66

(Two weeks later)
Monday, April 9, 2000

John Spencer picked up his phone in answer to the ring. It was Gary Goodloe.

"John, I'm calling to let you know the latest word on the spread of the cyanide problem, although I suppose that you've heard it on the news. The area that's affected has spread out in a fan-shaped pattern from the original site in Alice, Texas. The most distant sites, from west to east are Springerville, Arizona; Greeley, Colorado; Ames, Iowa; Terra Haute, Indiana; Knoxville, Tennessee; Macon, Georgia; and Tallahassee, Florida. We have no way of stopping it. It looks like it will overtake the entire country within a few weeks. What's more, it has now been confirmed in Mexico, as far south as Aguascalientes."

"Do you think it'll reach Seattle?"

"It's just a matter of time," Gary responded. "I'd say no more than four to five weeks. We've moved all of the staff out of our San Antonio office, and they're now here in Seattle. The deadly zone — the one inside which the atmospheric concentration has exceeded 200 ppm. — now reaches out in a circle about 600 miles from Alice."

2, 4, 8...Destiny of the Human Species)

(That evening)
Monday, April 9, 2000

The evening news broadcast told of the panic that was building in the path of the disaster:

"Most human life in south Texas has either been extinguished or the people have left the area. In addition, almost all vertebrate animals have died from cyanide poisoning. Every vehicle that was available has been packed with belongings, and the residents of most of south Texas have migrated out of the danger zone, spilling into towns outside the edge of the spreading plague. Those towns are being overwhelmed with panic-stricken refugees. A mass migration northward, eastward, and westward continues.

"Scientists state that it is only a matter of time before the problem spreads over the entire country. Those residents who can manage it are advised to travel northward toward the colder climatic zone in Canada, where it is speculated that the problem may not reach because of a lower abundance of diaper-filled landfills, and lower temperatures that may not permit the causative bacterium to multiply."

(Two days later)
Wednesday, April 11, 2000

Kyle Kimura had assembled the domies for an emergency meeting. He began with, "As you might have heard, the cyanide problem that began in Texas is rapidly moving northward, and it's predicted to reach our area within just a few weeks. It's imperative that we have the dome prepared for permanent sealing-off from the outside environment by then. That might be even before the

2, 4, 8...(Destiny of the Human Species)

June 1st deadline that was established earlier. I need to know whether any of you will have difficulty in meeting an earlier deadline, and if so, what we can do to help you meet that deadline. Please raise your hand if you think that you need help."

Only four people raised their hands: Margaret Chang, Kihuya Amin, Krishna Hadamani and Friedrich Hallberg.

Kyle called first on Margaret Chang. "I think that we'll be ready in time, but Kihuya, Krishna and I have to work on some minor details for coordinating the waste disposal systems, the pumping systems, and the water recycling systems. Perhaps you could import a team of about five plumbing/electrical/pumping specialists to help us work out the minor bugs that still exist."

"O.k., consider it done," Kyle responded. Kihuya and Krishna put their hands down.

"Friedrich, what problems do you still have to overcome? Your systems are the key to the success of the entire project, you know. Without the operation of the fusion reactor, we're going to get nowhere."

Friedrich responded with a slight smile. "With a little outside help, I see no reason why the reactor can't be operating smoothly in time. About all the help that I need is a fusion reactor specialist from the Department of Energy to help me work out a couple of fairly minor problems."

"I'll get someone immediately," Kyle said. "Anyone else?"

No hands. "Well, then, I'll let you get back to work. We have no time to lose."

Chapter 67

(Two weeks later)
Thursday, April 26, 2000

Josie sat down in the chair in front of John's desk. "You wanted to talk to me?" she asked.

"Did you hear the latest? The cyanide problem has cropped up in a landfill in Battleground, Washington, — only about 200 miles from here?"

"No, I hadn't heard specifically that, but I did know that it was projected to arrive in this state soon."

"What is the thinking at the White House about this mess?" John queried.

"Essentially, there is no 'White House' staff as such any longer. The cyanide concentration in the Washington, D.C. area reached 200 ppm. last week. There's no sign of human life around there any more," Josie replied.

"Has the government completely given up any hope of counteracting the problem?"

"It appears so," Josie answered resignedly.

At that point, John's phone rang. "I told my secretary not to disturb us," he said, agitated.

"Mr. Spencer, it's Mr. Goodloe on Line 2. He says it's urgent."

"Put him on," said John.

2, 4, 8...(Destiny of the Human Species)

"John, this is Craig. I never thought I'd see it happen, but it has. The outbreak has spread across both the Atlantic and Pacific. There's a site of cyanide poisoning at a landfill on the coast of China, and another on the coast of France. We have no idea how it was transmitted, but it might have been by rats from freighters. If the problem spreads as fast on those continents as it did here, all vertebrate life may be endangered in the tropical, subtropical, and temperate zones of the world. We think that the concentrations of cyanide might not reach dangerous levels beyond about the 60th parallels, north and south, though. I thought that I'd better tell you right away."

"Thanks, Craig." John set the phone down, his face exhibiting concern. "It has spread to Asia and Europe. Craig thinks that the only areas of the world where the cyanide might not reach toxic levels is beyond the 60th parallels, north and south."

"Does that mean that we may die soon?" Josie asked with a tremulous voice.

"Not necessarily. I have a plan that you might be interested in. I have a 32-foot Winnebago motorhome, you know."

"What about it?"

"How would you like to set up housekeeping in the motorhome with me for the rest of our lives, however long that may be? We could stock it with supplies and drive northward, and try to keep ahead of the cyanide. If the predictions are correct, we could survive for a long time, maybe for years, by living north of the 60th parallel."

"Could you tolerate such a life with *me* ?" Josie queried, highly hopeful about what his reply would be.

"Not only tolerate it, Josie. I would *love* it. Life north

2, 4, 8...(Destiny of the Human Species)

of the 60th parallel could be harsh, but I've often fantasized about living with you. It's a tantalizing idea."

"To tell you the truth, John, I've fantasized about life with you, too. I think that we could lead a lovely existence together, even under such harsh conditions." They were holding hands across John's desk now. He got up, walked around the side, and embraced her. "Let's do it!" he exclaimed.

(The next day)
Friday, April 27, 2000

John ran off a copy of his final modification of Robert Welton's goals. He wanted to give it to Kyle before he and Josie left for the trip north. He felt that if the domies survived to repopulate a reconditioned earth some day, the Goals could provide valuable guidelines for the new society, in order to help them avoid getting into the mess that the current human society had led itself into. He scanned the finished copy, which was updated to reflect recent technological advances.

The Weltonian Goals

A. To promote a decrease in the human birth rate.

    1. through government dispersal of free birth control information and devices to all who want them.

    2. through government sponsored school birth control counselling programs every year for all girls who have reached puberty.

       3. through government tax disincentives for having large families.

  B. To promote the principle of genetic screening of all aspiring parents for genetic defects, and to promote the principle of mandatory birth control through the implantation of ConCaps for all persons until they have passed genetic screening, and until they have passed the governmental parenting test.

  C. To promote the principle of gamete screening, with subsequent limitation of human fertilization to in vitro fertilization.

  D. To promote the idea of mandatory government-supported Parent Education Classes for all pregnant women and their spouses.

  E. To promote the idea of requiring classes in thinking skills for all students, so as to maximize the probability that life decisions will be made on a rational basis rather than an emotional basis.

(The next day)
Saturday, April 28, 2000

Pandemonium reigned over the city of Seattle. Interstate 5, the main route northward, was packed with people fleeing in every type of vehicle imaginable. John's loaded and fully supplied motorhome stood just outside

2, 4, 8...(Destiny of the Human Species)

the entrance to the Envirodome. He and Josie were saying their final goodbyes to Kyle and Fumi.

"Well, old college buddy," John began, "we've had a wonderful friendship for these many years. It's too bad that the world had to come to this. We could have had some great times together in the future, otherwise."

A very uncharacteristic tear flowed down Kyle's cheek. "We're really goin' our separate ways now, aren't we? Who knows which one of us will survive the longest."

John handed Kyle the copy of The Weltonian Goals. "Here," he said, "if you and your fellow domies ever survive to repopulate the earth, these goals might provide some guidelines to help you to avoid the pitfalls that led the world to the sad state that it's in."

Kyle thanked him one last time. They exchanged hugs all around. Then Kyle and Fumi entered the airlock of the Envirodome, waved their last goodbyes, and closed the door behind them for the last time. John and Josie climbed into the motorhome, then slowly maneuvered their way through a maze of stalled vehicles, and toward the jam-packed on-ramp to I-5 North, on their way to a highly uncertain future.